SNOW BLIND

The Big Sky Series Book 2

KWEN D. GRIFFETH

ISBN -13: 978-1688379855

INTRODUCTION

A horror exists across this great country and it infects Canada as well. Girls and young women are disappearing. Some are runaways, some are taken and some just vanish. Exact numbers of the missing are difficult to determine due to the conflicting jurisdictions, legal boundaries, and human biases. By best estimates, in the state of Montana, native females make up 30% of the missing. Native females are 3% of the general population.

CHAPTER 1

Robert "Bad Bobby" Trent, Jr, sat in the almost deserted diner and sipped his coffee. Anyone who didn't know him would take him to be an unemployed cowboy. His white, long-sleeved, western cut shirt was clean but worn. At both the collar and the cuffs, the material was thin, the wear noticeable. His jeans were faded, his boots scuffed and unpolished.

It was mid-morning, and he sat alone, while most everyone else in Wapiti, Montana, was at work. He had chosen a booth in the front of the place, next to the big window. That window allowed him to watch the street before him.

The road was mostly deserted, as only necessary travel is attempted during winter. Tall mounds of snow had been plowed and stood guard over the narrowed streets as they demanded their space. The usual four lanes of travel during summer, was reduced by half most of the distance of the street. As his dark green eyes watched, only a few brave souls, bundled against the cold hunched against the wind, trudged the street,their efforts marked by the breaths of vapor that trailed them.

A pickup truck rounded the corner just up the block and slid sideways. The reflected light bounced off the windshield and stabbed Bobby's eyes. Reflexively he closed them, and the dancing dots before him indicated temporary blindness. The winter sun of Montana can be almost cruel in the tricks it plays. He gently rubbed the tears from his closed eyes, then fingered his curly brown hair back and away from his face.

As he blinked the return of his sight, he scanned the diner and its subdued lighting when compared to wintertime sun. It was typical in that while the one wall held a row of windows, the other three were solid. A few prints of western paintings hung on the walls, intermixed with mounted deer heads and one elk. On the back wall, reproductions of Native American art hung. The diner had a counter with swivel stools attached to the floor. People on the stools sat with their backs to the bank of windows while those who sat in the booths could watch the people passing. The row of booths and the counter served a second purpose; together they formed a path that led to a dozen tables in the place's rear. Leaning on the backside of the counter, doing the crossword in the Billings newspaper, was Lilly.

Lilly was, as the saying goes, the chief cook and bottle washer. As the owner, she was also the waitress. She was a big woman, tall and square, blonde and proud of her Nordic ancestors. In earlier times, she would have been a Viking shield maiden, and a mean one. Usually friendly, but reserved, Bobby had seen her escort more than one unruly customer from her place. Lilly didn't serve alcohol, but at times, the overly enthusiastic debating of University of Montana football, or politics, became loud or crude. Her rule was simple: get loud, get kicked out. And she enforced the rule herself.

She must have felt him looking at her as she lifted her eyes and by gesture, asked if he needed a refill.

He held up his cup and nodded.

Lilly missed little, so as she approached the booth, she noticed the dark brown felt cowboy hat sitting on the table, crown down. She saw the denim jacket with the fleece lining on the seat beside Bobby, but what focused her attention was the six-point star that spun on the table before the man. The star was the badge of office for the Lodge Pole County

Sheriff.

As the spinning slowed, and she poured the refill, she watched as he gave the piece of metal another spin using his thumb and forefinger.

"Badge a little heavy this morning?" she asked, and he looked up at her.

Twenty years or so, earlier, Bobby had been the Mr. Everything in high school. Handsome, his dark eyes helped welcome many girls into young womanhood by giving them someone to dream about. Easy going, other students were drawn to him. He was popular and athletic though he never claimed to be intelligent. At times, he went out of his way to prove that. He was tough, determined and one of the best rodeo cowboys in the area.

His father, Robert Trent, Sr., had been the sheriff for many years, and a good one. The man had been murdered some five months earlier, and the county commissioners, as a show of respect for the elder Trent, asked Bobby to complete his father's term in office. With the same motivation in mind, Bobby accepted. Now, in over his head, Bobby realized Lilly was correct. The badge was, indeed, heavy.

"Still not sure if it belongs hanging on my shirt," he admitted.

"You are doing a fine job," she countered. "Don't be so hard on yourself."

He smiled a "thank you," and she nodded as she left to pour coffee elsewhere.

The diner, in downtown Wapiti, was not far from the Sheriff's Office. Bobby frequented the place to get a better cup of coffee than what Deputy "Bud" King could make.

King should have been retired, but his father, out of some unknown sense of loyalty or sympathy, kept Bud on after the man's wife died. His father also kept the man on after medical problems slowed him down. King was permanently assigned to the office and no longer worked patrol. He was in charge of all reports, evidence security and the running of the place. He took his job seriously, and the others called the man "his Highness." Bobby thought the man couldn't make a decent cup of coffee to save a life.

The booth in which he sat was not only next to the big front window, it was also next to the main doorway. From time to time, a patron would enter and a little bell above the door announced their arrival. Within seconds, as their eyes adjusted, they would see him.

"Good morning, Sheriff," they greeted.

He'd smile, nod and respond.

Others walked past him to exit. Again, there was the muttered, "Take it easy, Sheriff," or "Be careful."

Again, Bobby nodded, smiled, and exchanged pleasantries, as the tinkle of the bell told all of the departures.

Mostly though, he sat, drank coffee, and spun his badge.

Being it was mid-morning, Bobby knew he had another hour or so before the lunch crowd rush would invade the place. He planned to be gone before then. He had no particular reason or claim for sitting in that specific booth, other than it was a glorious Montana morning and the location allowed him to see the sky and watch the passing of marshmallow clouds. He was proud the people of Montana declared the sky as theirs, what with the "big sky" country being their claim to fame. The sun was bright and approaching midday height, but it reflected wickedly off the snow. Bobby, even after five months as sheriff, was still caught off guard when recognized as such. Most of the time, he merely tried to not make a fool of himself and stay out of the way.

"Mind if I join you?"

The voice both startled him and brought a smile. The mere sound of her voice caused a spike in his pulse, and it had been like that since sophomore year in high school. The woman owned him, and she knew it.

He shifted his gaze from the bright outside and looked at the figure standing next to the booth. He could only see silhouette until his eyes adjusted to the darker interior, but he recognized the voice. It belonged to KC Simms, the one that got away, and he looked up to see her smiling at him.

She was bundled in a thick woolen coat closed tight

around her neck. The coat was a dark blue, and it intensified the beauty of her dark eyes. On top of her head, she wore a thick knitted white cap, and only the dark hair that escaped out from under it was visible. He struggled to ensure his expression hid the excitement her smile ignited in him.

"Well, are you going to let me sit down?"

Her voice was deep for a woman, husky, and her tone carried a mix of chastisement and tease. She stood over the man and would have even if he was standing. KC stood right at six feet, without heels and while Bobby told everyone, he was five foot ten inches, he had to stretch to get there. The truth was, he was five foot nine. Athletically built, with a thick chest and strong arms, he carried grace and balance about him that most men didn't have, or didn't dare show. Tough and hard-headed, he had been born to be a rough stock rider until an injury sidelined him.

"Good morning, KC," he said, as neutral as he could make his voice sound, and he slid aside the cowboy hat that was on the table, "of course you can sit down."

She lowered herself onto the bench seat across from him and removed the gloves on her hands. He raised an arm and motioned for Lilly.

"No point in having her come all the way over here, just to send her back," he commented. "I already know you'll want something hot."

KC had removed her scarf, undone the top couple of buttons on her coat, and removed her cap when she turned her head and looked at Lilly, some twenty feet distant.

"Yeah, it would be a shame if she had to walk a few extra steps; maybe get a cardio workout," she said.

Lilly, who had been named for her grandmother, Evangeline, was almost as tall as KC. She too stood within a whisper of six feet, though she was twice as wide and thick. Her hair was turning grey, and her expression was gruff. She looked older than her fifty-odd years.

"Give her a break, KC," Bobby said. "She can't help what her genetics are."

"You mean she's part Hereford?"

Bobby looked at the woman across from him as Lilly

arrived, placed and poured a cup for KC, and then refilled his own.

"Is there anything else you would like?" Lilly asked. "I can heat some apple pie."

"No, thank you," Bobby shook his head, and answered for both, "Not right now, at least."

"Just let me know," the woman nodded.

"You're in fine form this morning," he said as he refocused on the woman across from him, "was the milk on your cereal sour?"

KC huffed as she emptied a packet of sugar substitute into her cup and stirred it.

"I guess I did sound a little snarky."

"A little," Bobby agreed, "what's going on?"

KC sipped her coffee and studied the man she had, at one time, planned to marry. They had dated through most of high school and left for college together. She was going to study law, and he intended to become a veterinarian. Rodeo got in the way. Rodeo, too many available women, and a nickname of "Bad Bobby." Eventually, she gave back the ring, kicked him out, and sent him on his way. She became a lawyer, and he dropped out of school. She took a job in Denver; he returned home still a rodeo hero to many. She married, divorced, and returned to Wapiti to lick her wounds, regroup, and now, have coffee with the man who started the ride. She decided to share her frustrations with him.

"Two months ago, I applied for a position in the DA's office in Lancaster County and this morning I learned I wasn't accepted."

Bobby managed to maintain a calm expression, as he said, "Well, it's their loss."

"That may be," she wasn't consoled, "but, I'm still here."

"Where is Lancaster County, anyway?" he asked.

"Lincoln, Nebraska. It's the county Lincoln, Nebraska is in."

"Nebraska? Why would you want to move to Nebraska? They did you a big favor. I've been to Nebraska once and I won't go back. Living there is like living on a pool table."

She glared at him, "It's the capital of the state. It would have been a great job with several possibilities to advance. Maybe even move laterally into politics."

Bobby gave a quick shake of his head.

"Politics and flat land? They really did you a favor." He faked a shudder.

"I could get used to it," she responded bluntly.

Bobby shook his head, "No, it would never work out between the two of you."

He pointed a finger at her, and said, "You told me, recently, that you were tired of making mistakes like your ex-husband and me."

"My personal life has nothing to do with this, and certainly nothing to do with you."

"But that's where you're wrong," he teased. "A career, job, profession, whatever you want to call it is the same thing as a husband or a wife."

She rolled her eyes and said, "Bad Bobby Trent, the great philosopher."

He laughed, but said, "Hear me out. A career, just like a spouse, demands you be loyal and forsake all others. Does it not?"

She looked at him.

"You're only allowed one, no professional polygamy."

She sipped her coffee and rolled her eyes a second time, but a small smile crept onto her face. Bobby could always make her smile.

"Oh," he continued, "some careers will let you have jobs on the side, but you know as well as I do, those are just short-lived flings that don't, in the long run, mean anything."

"How recently has anyone called you an idiot?" she asked as the smile grew against her wishes. "You're overdue."

He grinned the grin he made famous while in high school, and she wagged her finger to block the effect.

"I'm immune to that, Bobby. You wore it out on me."

"Don't be mean," he said. "I'm not sure I could go on in life if I truly thought you were immune to my charms."

"You still have charms?" she asked, underneath an arched eyebrow.

"Look," he said, "this isn't about me, it's about you, and you're a U of M Grizzly. There ain't no way you could get along with a bunch of Corn Huskers."

She looked at him as if he was a child and she had to explain Santa Claus.

"Bobby, you know that doesn't even make sense. College mascots are just..."

He motioned her silent with a wag of his finger.

"Don't say that. That's not true. You are what you graduate. The way I see it, you're lucky they turned you down. You'd be miserable there. You dodged a bullet. On top of the job not being right for you, you'd wind up marrying some overfed grain farmer and popping out eight, maybe ten, kids. All of them would be bucktoothed and have big old Hereford ears, and every one of them will grow up and want to show pigs at the annual fair."

She shook her head, "Bobby, are you as simple as you put on?"

His grin remained, "I think it would be in your best interest if you run by me any job you are thinking about applying to. It's obvious you're not thinking through all the ramifications of such a move."

She grinned, "You're going to appoint yourself my career counselor?"

"Just trying to help," he said, and she noticed the star on the table between them.

"What's with that?" she asked and pointed to the star with her chin. "Uncomfortable this morning, is it? Isn't that supposed to be pinned to your shirt or something?"

He followed her gaze and flicked the badge into a spin.

"Franklin Blue and I just talked about that very thing," he said, absently.

"And?" she asked. "What did our DA have to say?"

He flicked the star again, watched it spin, and as it slowed, said, "We don't see eye to eye on a couple of things."

"Such as?"

"My old man was Sheriff here a long time and you know as well as I the only reason I have this thing is that he got killed."

"Yes," KC nodded. "Your dad was Sheriff something like thirty years, I think?"

"Not quite that long, but close," Bobby nodded, "and he always wore the uniform."

"Yes," she sipped her coffee, "I remember. I thought he always looked sharp."

"So do a lot of people," Bobby sighed.

"I don't understand the issue between you and Franklin?" she asked.

"He wants me to wear the uniform. He says the county expects it. He says that's what the people are used to."

She scowled, "Bobby, I'm not following. What's the big deal? If they want you to wear the uniform, wear the uniform."

He shook his head, "It's not that easy. I don't want to wear a uniform, any uniform. My dad was into that sort of thing, but not me."

"I guess I don't understand what the big deal is," she confessed. "The deputies all wear the uniform. It would seem to me it's kind of like being on a team; you know, football, baseball, whatever."

"Yeah, well, I guess I'm not much of a team player," he said.

She snorted a chuckle and then said, "Your dad wore that uniform every day for a long time. I have to think you knew that was a part of the job when Blue asked you to be the Sheriff."

Bobby spun the badge again, and then said, "When he hit me up about this, the subject of clothing never came up. But he says people are expecting me to wear the uniform; they're complaining. They want me to look like my old man."

"So wear it," she said, in a tone meant to settle the dilemma.

He shook his head, "I can't. If I dress like him, within a week, they'll expect me to be like him. I can't do that. Even if I wanted to, I couldn't be like him. Wouldn't even know where to start."

KC raised her hand, caught Lilly's attention and motioned for refills. As they waited, she mused.

"I remember being at your place a couple of times and watching him iron his uniform for the next day. It always amazed me how precise he was."

Bobby nodded, "It was just his way. He wanted to present a perfect image when he was about on county business. You know, he wouldn't even let my ma iron his uniform. It was something he saved for himself."

Lilly arrived, poured the coffee, and looked at Bobby, "Still have that pie, Sheriff. Your father loved my pies."

He snorted a quick laugh, and then smiled at the woman, "Tell you what. You set me back a slice, Dad's favorite, and I'll come back this evening and have it before I head to the house."

Lilly nodded, "That would be a good time for pie."

She turned to KC, "Ms. Simms, would you care for anything more?"

"No, thank you, Lilly," she said.

The woman turned and left the two to their discussion.

"So what are you going to do?" KC asked.

Bobby spun the badge, "Well, that was what I was contemplating while I was sitting here. Blue asked me to finish my dad's term in office, and that's roughly another eleven months. There's not much that goes on around here that amounts to more than silliness and I like the idea of finishing what Dad started. It's something I can do for him...but I won't wear that uniform."

She reached across the table and covered his hand with hers. He looked at her long fingers with the French-manicured nails. He liked it when she touched him, even in the most superficial way. He swallowed to keep his heart rate even and looked at her mouth. She was wearing the neutral gloss that highlighted her lips without painting them. He fought the urge to kiss her.

"Bobby," she was saying, "I know you, and I know you can do most anything you put your mind to. You like the idea of being the good old boy with the straw sticking out of his teeth, but that is not the real you. You're far more capable than that. You can do whatever you decide to do. You always could, when you weren't busy tripping over your own feet."

He shrugged his shoulders, "That may be, but I can't do this."

"Have you even tried?"

He showed a flash of irritation. As soon as it arrived, it left.

"Of course I've tried, and every time I put that uniform on and look in the mirror, I see a little boy playing dress up. I see me trying to be him. I can't do that. I won't do that."

She studied him for several seconds. He met her gaze, but silently kept track of the coming and going of the patrons as lunch time was arriving. By his rough count, Lilly was up by about half a dozen.

"You know," KC said, and interrupted his figuring, "for a broken-down cowboy you have a certain amount of insight."

He canted his head and narrowed his eyes, "Broken-down cowboy?"

"Yeah," she smiled, pleased she had turned the tables on him. After all, he had made fun of her not being selected to go to Lincoln. "You're a broken-down cowboy."

She leaned back against the booth, which removed her hand. He felt forgotten. She looked proud of herself as she said, "I heard about you trying to ride that bronc a month ago, and I was told he got rid of you in about three jumps."

"It was more than three," Bobby defended, as he rubbed his injured hand.

"I also heard he was only half wild and used mostly in junior rodeos."

"Now, you're just being hurtful," Bobby moaned.

He flexed his left hand, opened and closed it several times. The hand had been crushed by a horse's wayward hoof. Since the injury, he hadn't tried to ride but once, and that disaster was the attempt KC teased him about.

"Seriously, Bobby," she said, "how bad is it? Is it healing at all?"

"Oh, it's healing," he said, "but it's not ready for competition."

"Do you think it ever will be? I mean, just between you and me, will it be?"

He smiled at her insinuation that they were a couple who

shared secrets.

"Between you and me? I don't know. It's taking more time than I like. Sometimes, I'm scared it won't and that I'm done."

"There's more to life than rodeo," she offered. He smiled at her.

His smile didn't reach his eyes. "Not for me, there's not."

The little bell over the door announced customers, and he looked up and noticed several men walk in. He guessed the count to be eight, and he knew them to be men of the BNSF Railroad. The BNSF had a yard in Wapiti where the rolling stock, the train cars, were repaired and serviced. The men who worked the yard were hard men, men who lifted heavy parts of the rolling stock including axles and wheels that weighed several tons each. They were men who used chain hoists and come-a-longs to move the parts where they needed to be moved and heavy sledgehammers to beat the parts into submission. On their cleanest days, they still had the smell of heavy-duty lube oil on them. They were men who worked hard and were proud of that fact. Bobby noticed them and slipped the badge into his shirt pocket.

KC noticed his change in demeanor. She saw him pick up of the badge and she watched the men who passed them on their way to a large table in the back of the diner. Most of the men glared at Bobby. None of them spoke to him.

"What's going on?" she asked.

"Nothing," he replied. "They're just here for lunch."

"Yeah," she said, and then added, "a couple of them look like they want a piece of you."

He smiled, "They wouldn't like me. I'm tough to chew on, not much fat and I have a lot of gristle."

She nodded to his cell phone, "Why don't you call for backup. Isn't that what you police do?"

His smile grew, "I don't know, they just put me in the job. Said to learn as I go."

She shook her head, but her concern was apparent. Bobby liked that.

A large man with thick black hair and a matching beard approached the table. He wore the bib-overalls of the maintenance men. At some time that morning, he had gotten grease on his face. He had wiped it off, but the stain remained, leaving him with a two-toned look. His boots were scarred from scraping against heavy metal objects. His hands were callused and his jaw set. There was no friendship in his ice-blue eyes. He stopped at the edge of the table and looked down on Bobby.

"Trent," he said.

Bobby looked up at the man.

"Morning, Kettling," he said and smiled.

Calvin Kettling was a supervisor of a crew that replaced, repaired or maintained the bogies, axles and the wheels of the rolling stock.

"You and me got business," Kettling said as he leaned over Bobby and rested his upper body on his knuckles on the table.

Bobby sipped his coffee and nodded, "Yeah, I suppose we do. What's on your mind, as if I didn't know."

KC realized the hush in the diner.

"You got my little brother in jail," Kettling leaned lower to be closer, and more intimidating, to the Sheriff.

"I do," Bobby nodded, in agreement. "He got out of line."

The big man frowned, "He's got a job to do. Let him out."

"I'm new at this job," Bobby said, "but I'm pretty sure that's not how the system works."

"That's how the system works today."

Bobby shook his head, "No, I don't think so. I'm pretty sure my job is to lock them up, but a judge has to let them out."

He turned to KC.

"We have a lawyer right here, and most likely the smartest person in town."

He grinned at the large man, and added, "Much smarter than you and me combined."

Kettling said nothing, just glared.

"Can you help us out?" Bobby continued. "Doesn't a person have to bond out of jail? They can't just have their overbearing big brother order the Sheriff to let them out, can they?"

Kettling turned and scowled at the woman, who kept her eyes on Bobby as she said, "That is right. They have to bond out."

"See that?" Bobby said to the man, "I was right. I might be the Sheriff after all."

"But that ain't even right," Kettling moaned. "Look, Marcus got a little drunk, but it wasn't his fault he tore up the place. It was that little redhead's fault. If she hadn't teased him, he wouldn't have gotten so angry."

"Teasing men is that little redhead's job," Bobby said. "You, me, and half the men in this county, at one time or another, has gone into Stetsons to drink away a tough day. Whatever it was the day took from us, that little redhead with her smile, her flirting, her wiggle, helped us remember we're men. She helped us face our tomorrow. Your brother slapped her across the room because she's good at doing her job."

"All he wanted was a little kiss," Kettling said.

"It ain't her job to kiss big-bearded slobs. How long's it been since Marcus even trimmed that beard of his? Has to be at least a decade."

"Her givin him a little kiss wouldn't have hurt nothing."

Bobby shrugged, "Maybe. But giving men kisses isn't in her job description. If she kisses some guy, that is a gift from her. She didn't owe Marcus a kiss."

"Well, if she'd just given him a kiss, none of the rest of it would have happened."

"Unless he decided he wanted two kisses, or maybe he wanted to get a feel of her, or have a dance, or take her out to his truck. At what point is it acceptable, in your world, for her to say no?"

Kettling studied Bobby, and some of the anger left him. He shook his head and then sighed.

"Look, Sheriff," he said, "you and I both know Marcus was out of line with the redhead."

Bobby nodded, "On that we agree."

"But," Kettling continued, "that don't give your deputies the right to come out there and beat on him the way they did."

Bobby didn't try to hide the grin.

"Kettling, how big is Marcus?"

"Oh, I don't know for sure, but he's maybe six foot six or so, maybe six seven."

"And how much does he weigh?" Bobby asked.

"He's a big boy," Kettling admitted, "He'll scale out at three-fifty, maybe a bit more."

"Yeah, and the two deputies in question, Nixon and Chunk Fisher, neither one of them is in the same weight class as Marcus. Even the two of them standing on the scale together; Marcus outweighs them by a good fifty pounds."

"Yeah," Kettling agreed, "That Marcus always was a big boy."

"Yeah he was, and he is. When the redhead said no, he slapped her and sent her across the room. That wasn't good enough for him, so he went to work tearing up Stetsons. He knocked holes in walls, tore paintings down, flipped over a pool table. Do you have any idea how much one of those slate tops costs?"

Kettling shook his head.

"Of course you don't," Bobby continued, "And neither do I. But your brother wasn't satisfied. He broke chairs, pool cues and generally raised all kinds of hell. By the time the deputies got there, the place was in shambles."

"Still..." Kettling tried to interrupt.

"Still, my foot," Bobby said, "They told him he was under arrest, and he attacked them. Backhanded Nixon, sent her flying and went after Chunk."

Bobby shook his head, "He should have remembered Chunk played linebacker for the Grizzlies. I'm told old number fifty-three showed perfect form, a shoulder in the bellybutton and arms around the legs. Lift and drive the runner onto his back. Chunk drove him into the floor so hard, it knocked the wind out of Marcus."

Kettling frowned.

"Before he could catch his breath, Nixon had him flipped over facedown and handcuffed. Now, you want to tell me what my deputies did that was so out of line?"

"They could have talked him down," Kettling said, without enthusiasm.

"Talk him down?" Bobby canted his head, "Let me tell you about talking him down. Your brother is lucky two deputies showed up. At that time of night, normally only one is on duty. Nixon had the night shift, and Fisher was on his way home from the day shift. He heard the call and headed out to back Nixon up. If she had shown up alone, and Marcus would have acted like that, she'd have been within policy to shoot the big dumb ox. But for a couple of things out of the norm, your brother would have been in the morgue, not the jail."

"Well. He is in jail, and you have to let him out. He'll lose his job and not be able to pay his mortgage. The bank would like nothing more than taking his house from him."

Bobby thought for some time and then looked at Kettling.

"I'm guessing he can't make bail?"

Kettling snorted, "Are you kidding? He couldn't pay for a gallon of milk."

"Can you help him out?" Bobby asked.

Again, a snort, "No, I wish I could. Even if I had the cash, my wife wouldn't let me."

"You've given Marcus money before?" Bobby asked.

The big man shrugged and Bobby nodded.

"Look," Bobby said, "you have your lunch, relax, talk with your friends. After lunch, you can swing by my office, and we'll work through this."

"What do you plan to do?"

Bobby shook his head, "Right now, I don't have a clue. But we'll get it handled one way or another."

Kettling looked at Bobby and then said, "I didn't think you would help us out. Thank you, Sheriff."

Bobby grinned, "Don't thank me yet. Haven't done nothing, yet."

"Just the same."

Kettling stuck out his hand and Bobby took it.

"Give me a couple of hours," Bobby said. "Then stop by the office."

Kettling turned and returned to his table.

As he watched the man depart, Bobby sipped lukewarm coffee. He glanced at KC and her expression was one he had not seen in some time. She looked like she was proud of him.

"You want to tell me what you have in mind?" she asked.

Bobby shrugged, "Right now, I honestly don't know. However, I think I should get a discount from what you charge me. You know, a referral discount. I just brought you another client."

She rolled her eyes.

"What are you talking about? I'm the public defender. I have to take him and he'll cost me more money than what the county will pay."

"Not this time," Bobby said. "This time, he'll pay your full fee. It will be a part of whatever I can work out."

"Bobby, you can't do that. If a man has no money, how you gonna make him pay?"

The Sheriff shrugged and then said, "Okay counselor. Here we have a man who assaulted a person, destroyed property and frightened a room full of people. He assaulted two law enforcement officers causing one to break a tooth. If he's convicted, how many years do you think he'll get?"

She shook her head, "I don't know. It could be several."

"Yeah, it could be several and I don't even know the law. If I can figure out a way to keep Marcus Kettling from serving several years, he'll figure out a way to pay you your full fee."

"You can't do that," she argued. "The Constitution promises legal services for those who can't afford it."

"Even I know that much. But this serves a higher calling," Bobby said.

She pursed her lips, "Higher than the Constitution? And what would that be?"

"Helping me convince you to stay in Wapiti. I want to show you all the money you can make, not to mention all the people who need your services."

He grinned. She didn't.

KC stood and gathered her coat, scarf and hat.

Bobby sipped his coffee and watched her.

"You are beyond a doubt, one of the most egotistical and infuriating men I have ever met," she huffed. "You think you can bend the rules, change the Constitution, do whatever you want, when you want, to fit your needs. Just as long as Bobby

Trent gets his own way. You haven't changed a bit since you were six."

Her voice rose in volume as she finished her statement and several people turned from their meals to watch the pretty woman berate the Sheriff. When she had finished, she took a moment, looked around and then turned on her heels and left the diner. The onlookers moved their gazes to Bobby when the little bell tinkled her exit. Bobby smiled.

"She likes me," he said to the gawkers. Then he rose, left money for the tab, slipped into his coat and placed his hat on his head.

"Thank you," he called to Lilly, then he followed KC out the door.

CHAPTER 2

Bobby felt the cell phone in his pocket vibrate as he climbed into his truck. The vehicle was not his regular truck, but the county provided a Ford 4X4 with the short bed. It was the truck his father had driven: it was Unit One.

Usually the bed was empty, but during this time of the year, when snow could rise as high as a man's beltline, the bed carried an Arctic Cat SnoProZR 6000...a snowmobile with a 599cc two-stroke engine that could flat fly across snow-covered terrain. Also carried was a tri-fold ramp for the loading and unloading of the machine.

"Trent," he said into the device after he worked it out of his pocket. He rarely looked at the caller ID screen.

"Sheriff, this is Bud. You need to come by the S O as soon as you can. A man is waiting to see you."

"Bud, I'm here at Lilly's. Give me a couple of minutes."

"Will do, Bobby, I mean, Sheriff."

Bobby disconnected the call.

The Lodge Pole County Sheriff's Office was located in a strip mall. Adjacent to the main doorway, just inside, was an open area where people could wait. A few industrial chairs were there as well as a small table with magazines touting the wonders of Montana. The deputies called the place the lounge. The lounge was on the far side of the counter that ran the width of the room and separated people from the desk area the deputies used. Only after being invited back could a visitor cross the bat-wing door threshold.

Bobby walked into the department through the back door which placed the counter between him and the visitor. King, at that counter, noticed the Sheriff and pointed to the man with a nod of his head. The man was sitting, head hanging forward, his chin resting on the dun colored down-filled coat the man wore. The black wide-brimmed hat hid the features of the face. Using both hands, he held a cup of coffee. Bobby poured himself a cup, grimaced when he took a sip and moved through the passage to join the visitor. When he got close, the head raised slowly, and Bobby recognized him.

"Been a long time, Royal," Bobby said as he sat down. "How're things out your way? Bud tells me you want to see me."

Royal Durning, sixty plus years old, irritable, and heavy-set was a cattle rancher who owned some 6,000 acres northwest of the Trent place. He sat hunched over the cup he held with both hands. Bobby noticed little of the liquid had been drank. Royal Durning was one of the few men Bobby knew that tucked his pants down his boots.

"Seen a body today, Sheriff," the man said, as he removed his hat and then raised his hand to brush back the grey hair covering his eyes. He said it with the same level of excitement he might use if he had seen a turtle. He sat listing to his left side and Bobby knew the man had been thrown from a horse some years back and never entirely healed correctly.

"You saw a dead body?" Bobby asked.

"Ain't that the only kind of body there is?" Durning replied. "If'n it hadn't been dead, it would still be a person, right?"

"Yeah, I believe you're right," Bobby agreed. "Where did you see this body?"

"My boy and me were riding along Whipsaw Creek about a mile past where it bleeds into the Yellowstone. You know that area?"

The old man looked at Bobby with smoke-grey eyes hooded by brows of the same color. The man's nose and his chin were sharp, though the latter was covered with a full growth of whiskers that Durning only wore during cold months. Summer, he sported a mustache that would have made Wyatt Earp jealous.

Bobby nodded, "You know I do. You and I ran cattle off that small ridgeline up that way about five years ago. You rode that brown gelding I wanted to buy off you."

Durning grinned, "That's right. Should have sold that horse to you. Wasn't but a year later he broke a leg and I had to put him down. Hated doing that. He was a hell of a horse. If'n I'd sold him to you, he might still be around."

Bobby shook his head, "He was indeed a horse, but you made the right choice. Can't live life by what should have or could have been."

"Ain't that the truth," the old man agreed.

"So," Bobby redirected the conversation, "tell me about this body."

"Well, ain't much to tell. Samuel, my oldest, and me was riding up that way checking the snow depth, trying to figure out when we could plan on letting the stock onto the range, and we see'd it laying there in the snow. Money's getting tight this time of year. Be nice not to have to buy more hay."

Bobby nodded agreement while Durning sipped his coffee.

"Anyway, there we were, riding our machines, and we see'd it. It was just there, face down, arms out like a bird, legs straight out. Looked like a big T in the snow."

"Man or a woman?"

Durning shook his head, "Don't know. Like I said, it was face down. Not that I'm a judge of such things, but I'd guess either a large boy or a woman. It was in a parka with the hood up over the head and it had winter pants and boots. But even so, it wasn't big enough to be a full-grown man."

"So you didn't touch the body?"

"Heavens no, why would I want to do that? It was obviously dead, and it had a light coating of snow over it. It looked to be frozen."

"You're not sure?"

"No, I'm sure. Anyway, I told Samuel to stay there. Didn't want critters getting to it, not now, not after we'd spotted it. I came to town to get you."

"You're telling me the body is undamaged? No wildlife has got to it?"

"Now Sheriff, can't say for sure. But I didn't see any sign of it being tampered with. I didn't get but about four feet next to it and I didn't touch it, didn't roll it over, so what it looks like on the underneath side is anybody's guess."

Bobby checked the clock on the wall and shook his head.

"If we left right now, we'd still not get there until way after dark," he said.

Durning nodded, "Yup, figured that. Samuel and me don't get that far away from the house this time of year without our overnight packs. Never can tell when a machine will break down with you or you get held up. Have to spend the night.

"You mean, like when you find a dead body?" Bobby smiled.

"Well, this is a new one for me," Royal grinned back, "but, yeah. Anyway, I left Samuel my pack, and he has his own, so he's got two space blankets, bottled water, some freeze-dried food, coffee makings, and all the necessaries to cook it. He'll be good till morning."

Bobby thought for a few moments and then nodded his head.

"Yeah, I'm thinking that body has been there a while, and won't be going anywhere. If we run up there tonight, we'll be tromping all through the dark, and with snow as deep as it is, chances are good we'd destroy any evidence."

He turned to King and asked, "Who's on day shift tomorrow?"

Without checking the roster, the man said, "Same as today, Nixon."

"She's busy up at Cold Camp, isn't she?"

"She is," King nodded, "and most likely will be tomorrow. Several reports of livestock gone missing up that way."

Cold Camp, Montana was a town of some thousand people in the north end of the county. Wheat and sheep farms surrounded the town. There were also a few cattle ranches. The agricultural people shared the area with loggers, as harvesting timber was the principal employment. The lumber mill there trimmed and shaped logs before trucking them south to load onto the BNSF Railway in Wapiti.

Bobby nodded, "So that means Chunk is RDO and Stewart is overnight?"

"Yup," King said, "You got it. You want me to call Nixon and have her make sure her cold weather gear is ready?"

Bobby shook his head, "No, we need her to finish what she's on and also be available to answer any calls. Let's call Chunk and have him come in for part of the day."

"You'll owe him either overtime or an extra day off," King reminded the new Sheriff. "Overtime is time and a half. If he works half a day, you'll owe him a full day plus."

Bobby nodded, "Yeah and one way or the other, I'll pay him back."

"It'll have to be extra time off. The county won't go for paid overtime."

Bobby nodded again, "Ask him to come in. Tell him I'll square it one way or another."

The deputy nodded and left to use the phone. Bobby turned back to Durning.

"How early can you be ready to go tomorrow?" he asked the rancher.

Durning thought for a moment, and as he did, he stroked the full beard.

"How you planning on getting there?" he asked the Sheriff.

"Assuming Chunk will come with, I'll have him at my place long before daylight. We'll need to tow a sled behind his Arctic Cat, so that will slow us down a bit, but we can be over to your place around six, I'm thinking."

The old man nodded, "If you don't mind, let me suggest a different plan."

"Go ahead," Bobby said.

"Why don't you and your deputy leave your place, but follow the Yellowstone, and not come to my place. I know where I'm going, and the surest way for you to get there is to just follow the river."

Bobby nodded, "And you'll head back the way you came. We'll meet at the body."

Durning agreed, "You'll need to cross the river, so find you a place where you won't get wet. The body is on the north side of the Yellowstone and west of Whipsaw creek. It's maybe... fifty yards from the bank right at the foot of that rise."

"I think that'll work," Bobby nodded.

"Good. That way, I can get back to my boy sooner and while he's good for the night, I can take him some coffee and some chicken soup his ma makes. Make sure we get him warmed up."

The old man grinned.

"You could bring some of Mrs. Durning's soup for me," Bobby laughed.

"I'll see you tomorrow, Sheriff," Durning said as he replaced his hat to his head, worked it to set just right, and started for the door.

"Thank you, Mr. Durning," Bobby called to the rancher.

"Just doing my civic duty, Sheriff," Durning called back.

Bobby walked the length of the large room, past the six desks sitting two by three, with the walkway down the middle. At the end of the room, was a door with a window of frosted glass. The logo of the county was centered on that opaque glass and the words "Lodge Pole County" crested the logo. Along the bottom of the circular crest were the words "Sheriff's Office."

Bobby stopped and read the sign several times. There was a spot where his name should be stenciled onto the door, but he hesitated to make that claim. He was there only because his father had been murdered. He lost his father and was awarded the old man's job — what a twist of fate. The older Trent had been on the job a long time, and Bobby figured the county wasn't ready to call another man Sheriff. He entered the room and closed the door behind him.

The office was square, the doorway on one wall, windows

on the next and two solid walls to complete the enclosure. A desk, a few chairs, a bookcase and a shelf mounted on the wall made up the decor. The US flag and the Montana flag stood behind the desk. A map of the state was mounted on the wall between the two. If Bobby walked out of the room and never returned, there would be nothing to show he had even stopped by. He walked around the desk and sat in the chair.

"Well," he spoke aloud, "you have stepped in it this time. Middle of winter, snow up to my back pockets, a dead body, and I don't have a clue of how to proceed or what to do."

He let his head fall forward and caught it with his hands. He was sitting like that, elbows resting on the desk, when King knocked and then swung the door open with his foot. When he entered, he carried two cups of coffee. Bobby looked up.

"Coffee, Sheriff?" King said as he held out a cup.

"Thank you," Bobby said and took what was offered.

"Mind if I sit for a minute?"

"Course not."

The old deputy sat, sipped, and then looked at Bobby.

"You know; you can turn this over to the state."

"Turn what over?" Bobby asked.

"The dead body. You can turn it over to the state DOJ. That's what the office is there for. They know small counties don't have the resources to handle death investigations. As Sheriff, you can request the state handle the dead body and focus on the missing cattle."

Bobby looked at King over the top of his cup. "So, we're good enough to find lost cattle, but not much else?" he asked.

"That's not what I said," King defended. "Nobody in this department ever worked a death case. The state stepped in to investigate your dad's killing, or did you forget that? That's what the DOJ is for; to help out the smaller counties."

Bobby sipped his coffee, "And they've done such a bang-up job, they still haven't found who killed my dad."

"Well, they had some bad luck."

"How so?" Bobby asked.

"They had a suspect in the hospital in Billings and he got

away from them when the pig slop fire got started."

"Yeah," Bobby agreed, "and now you want me to turn another death case over to them."

"Just pointing out your options as Sheriff, Bobby."

"And I appreciate it, Bud. How about we check out the body first, and then decide. Might just be a lost hiker. I think we can handle that."

Bud King smiled and shook his head.

"What's that mean?" Bobby asked.

"It means, I've known you since you were a boy. No way you're turning this over to the state."

Bobby grinned, "If I didn't, what would I need to do first?"

King sipped his coffee, "Well, there're procedures to follow; secure the body and send it to Billings for a complete autopsy and lab work up. Course, you got to try to search the scene. See if there's anything that can shed light on what happened."

Bobby shook his head, "I don't see how we can do that. There's got to be three, maybe four feet of snow out there. If we tromp around, there's a better chance we'll bury something, not find it."

King smiled, "You got a lot of your old man in you, boy. Any ideas how to get around that?"

"Did Chunk call in? Is he willing to work tomorrow?" Bobby asked.

King chuckled, "Is he ever. I guess his in-laws are visiting and you calling him in has them thinking he's the most important man in the department."

"Bud, I want you to get a hold of Chunk. Tell him to gather up a dozen of those tall nylon poles, the kind the road department uses to mark the shoulder of the highway during this time of year."

King nodded.

"Also have him bring a pair of snowshoes and a couple of rolls of crime scene tape. Don't let him forget to bring a body bag."

"Okay," King said, "You think this is a crime scene?"

Bobby shrugged, "Don't have a clue, but I think there's a big maybe."

King grinned, "Share with me what's on your mind?"

"You want to see how warped my thoughts are?"

King shook his head, "No, but your dad used me as a sounding board. I'm just trying to give you what I gave him."

"Well," Bobby said, "If it's a male, I think there's a chance the death is accidental. I mean the guy could have been a hunter or a trapper. Along the Whipsaw is good trapping."

King nodded, "Could be."

"But if the body is female, I think it's more likely we have a crime of some kind."

"Women hunt, and some even trap," King reminded the Sheriff.

"Yeah, that's true, but in fewer numbers than men. As a rule, women are more careful. I can't see a woman, alone, that far out. She'd have a partner. Face it; they're smarter than we are."

King snorted a laugh that caught him mid-swallow. He spat coffee down the front of his shirt and some dribbled onto the floor.

"You want to know what bothers me about this?" Bobby asked.

"Sure, that's what I'm here for," King said.

"Okay, first: Durning said the body hadn't been touched by critters, his words."

"Yeah. What's that mean to you?"

"It has to mean the body has only been out there a short time. I can see the birds ignoring it for a few days, what with it all covered up, but wolves, coyotes, even badgers with their sense of smell, and at this time of year, they'd be all over it."

"I don't disagree with you," King said.

"So why didn't they?"

King only shrugged his shoulders.

"You always this much help?" Bobby asked.

"I only do what I can. What else bothers you?"

"Well, Durning said the body was covered with a light dusting of snow. The last snowfall we got around here was four days ago. If that body was out there, before that storm, well, I'm back to the critter question. Why haven't they bothered it?"

Bobby stood and walked to the windows. He looked out and watched the little bit of traffic that maneuvered between and around the piles of plowed snow, some ten or twelve feet high. The small mountains of snow were turning grey, subject to the exhaust of passing vehicles. But still, they were white enough to bounce sunlight into the eyes and cause temporary blindness. Bobby made a mental note not to forget his sunglasses tomorrow. Trying to figure out what happened was not the place to be snow blind. Over his shoulder, he spoke to King, who had not moved.

"How did the body get out there?"

"What do you mean?"

"Durning said nothing about tracks of any kind. It's laying on a covering of deep snow, so there should be signs of something. There should be signs of disturbance, right? How did it get to where it died? I seriously doubt it flew and then fell out of the sky."

"Maybe it didn't die there."

Bobby spun around and looked at the deputy.

"What did you say?"

"I said, maybe it didn't die there."

Bobby thought for a few moments, shook his head and said, "Oh, now you're just being mean. If the body was transported there, then every question I have is simply multiplied by a bunch. You're making this no fun at all."

King grinned.

Dusk comes early in the mountain country during winter, and Bobby saw the lights of the vehicle as it navigated the roughness of the snow-covered lane to his house. He had been in the kitchen, checking on chili he was experimenting with when the lights bounced off the walls. Bobby turned the stove down to keep the chili warm and walked into the living room as he dried his hands on the towel stuck in the waist of his pants. Wearing his customary t-shirt, and going bare foot, he stood in front of the big window and watched the vehicle approach.

Deputy Doreen Nixon braked the county-supplied SUV hard enough it slid close to ten feet before coming to a stop. Watching from the window, Bobby chuckled to himself. She was mad about something.

He watched the athletically-built woman jump from the driver's side door and slam it closed so hard, the force caused her to slip. She had to grab the mirror to keep from going to the ground. Bobby smiled again and promised himself not to tell her of his observations. The snow on the lawn hid the pavers that usually marked the path, but she followed his footprints and covered the distance as fast as she could. As she stepped onto the porch, he opened the door.

"Good evening, Deputy Nixon," he said. "What brings you out to my place on this wintery night?"

Without speaking, she stomped past him, her insulated boots leaving bits of snow and ice marking her entrance. He closed the door and turned to face her. He stood with his thumbs hooked in the top of his pants, and she pulled the fur-lined cap from her head. Her reddish-blonde hair was mussed by the removal of the head covering, but like his seeing her slipping on the frozen ground, he decided not to mention it. It was obvious she was not happy.

Her hazel eyes glared at him. "I want to know why I'm not going with you tomorrow to investigate and collect the body? I'm the one on day shift. We're assuming the investigation during the day shift and it should be me."

"I thought you were investigating the missing livestock?"

"I am, but you know murder takes precedence over any other crime."

"What makes you think it's murder?"

The cold weather had kissed her skin and her overabundance of freckles was easily seen. Now her intensity made them almost glow.

"What do you mean? 'Why do I think it's murder?' Why else would a body be out in the middle of nowhere?"

"Maybe, looking for lost sheep."

She glared and pointed a finger at him, "Don't you even start with me. You know I deserve to go with you. I'm the day shift officer. It should be my investigation."

He studied her and managed to keep the smile, which she would take as condescending, from his face. She wore a dark green oversized high-necked sweater that covered her past her hips, blue jeans and winter boots. High on her right hip, he saw the change in the sweater's flow indicating where her off-duty gun was. He wondered if he noticed it, or did he just know it was there?

"Nixon, I will not debate this with you. Chunk will go to Whipsaw creek tomorrow. I have already decided it and he has been called in. You've still got the Cold Camp situation to deal with."

"It's not right," she maintained. "I'm day shift. It should be mine."

Bobby shrugged, "Maybe so, but other plans have already been made. Can I make it up to you and offer you a bowl of the best-tasting chili you've ever had?"

She glared at him a moment longer, then challenged, "Is it really the best chili I've ever had?"

"Come on," he smiled, "you can be the judge."

She followed him into the kitchen then stopped, stunned, her mouth forgot to close.

"Bobby, what have you done?" she managed.

He turned back to her, a massive smile on his face, "I told you I would redo the kitchen."

Slowly, as she took in the counters, the appliances, the island surrounded by stools in the room's center, she repeated, "My oh my oh my."

What had been, at one time, a simple but effective country kitchen had been turned into a made-for-television cooking show monstrosity.

Bobby's excitement boiled over and he rushed to an appliance.

"Look at this," he said, as he touched the refrigerator. "This is a Sub-Zero. It's one of the best on the market."

Nixon said nothing, as she was overwhelmed.

"And this?" he asked. "Do you know what this is?"

She looked at what she took to be an oven.

"It's an oven?" she guessed, not quite sure.

"No. It's a Viking double oven with a proofing oven for bread. Look at this," he said as he pulled open a door, and pointed into the box. "This has a halogen light in there, and all the knobs are backlit, so they're easy to read."

"Bobby," she observed, "it's all silver."

"That's because everything is stainless steel," he bragged.

"It looks like it's turned into a robot."

"What?" He stopped, his smile dropped, and he was honestly let down by her comment.

Nixon shook her head.

"I'm sorry," she said, "I've seen nothing like this. I mean, on TV sure, but not in real life. You're going to have to give me a visit or two to get used to it."

Bobby recovered and laughed, "I think that can be arranged."

He moved to a square-shaped eating island in the center of the room. Gone was the old dining table of his parents. The island had two stool-style chairs on each side, and overhead, hanging upside down, was stemware.

"I've got everything I've ever dreamed of," he said, as he sat on a stool. "I've increased the size of the counters, so I have more space on which to work, and over there..." he pointed away from the kitchen, "is a wine rack." I mounted the rack over there so the heat from cooking wouldn't affect the taste."

He stood, stepped to the side of the room
 where he pulled out two standing drawers, each one six feet tall. They were vertical shelves, and each shelf was stocked with spices, oils and other sundry items a chef would need.

She couldn't help it, she laughed.

"What?" he asked. "What's so funny?"

He stepped to the double sink, one with a regular faucet and the other with a pull-down model.

"Look at this. Above the sink area, I have a rack from which to hang all my pots and pans. All of them, out here, where they're easy to get to."

Nixon took in the kitchen. Gone were the designs of chickens and roosters, put there years ago by Bobby's mother. In place of the old wallpaper, the walls had been painted a white with just a hint of blue. The logs of the house, which were darker, countered and yet balanced the new paint. The old countertops were gone and replaced with a medium tan granite that blended the entire room into one. The wooden cabinets had been sanded and refinished, and they were now the white of a country farmhouse.

Nixon chuckled. She knew she had to break the spell or fall in love with the place.

"So?" Bobby persisted. "What's so funny?"

"You are." She laughed harder and he scowled.

"I'm sorry Bobby," she tried to regain control. "Everyone thinks of you as this rough and tough rodeo cowboy, who is now the Sheriff, and you're acting like an eight-year-old girl with her first easy-bake oven."

"Call me all the names you care to Miss Nixon," Bobby grinned. "If you knew the number of nights I laid awake in some flea-bitten motel fantasizing about this kitchen, you'd be excited for me."

Nixon crossed to him and without hesitation, wrapped him in her arms.

"Oh, Bobby, I am excited for you," she said as she hugged the man.

Taken off guard, Bobby became motionless, and then he laughed and hugged her back. She raised her eyes to look at him. In her boots, and him without, they stood equal. He blinked twice and took in her fresh-faced beauty. Then, without warning, she kissed him. She kissed him on the mouth. He hesitated only a moment, then he allowed the warmth of her, the taste of her, the feel of her to overwhelm him, and he returned the affection.

As they held the kiss, he worked his arms free and drew her to him closer and tighter. The kiss was long, intense and enjoyable. Some seconds passed before he gently pushed her back far enough so he could see her.

Her face was flushed, her eyes alight with desire. Bobby was sure he looked the same, as he felt the heat of wanting her.

"I've been waiting a long time to do that," she whispered, and her tone held no apology.

He grinned, "Well if you'd told me, I'd been receptive sooner."

Her smile turned timid, and she looked away.

"I remember the kiss you gave me when I was in the hospital. I've wanted to repay it."

"Oh," he said, "That was you repaying a debt?"

She blushed, "You don't think less of me, do you?"

She backed away, and he allowed her freedom to distance herself.

"Think less of you?" he shook his head. "No, I've thought about this myself; several times."

"But, you didn't," she said.

"I wasn't sure it was right."

Her eyes grew clouded, ashamed and, shaking her head, she pushed herself further away.

"I'm sorry Bob... Sheriff, I shouldn't have done that. You're my boss. This is wrong. I'm sorry."

She turned and headed for the front door when Bobby reached out and took her by the arm.

"Wait," he said.

She allowed him to stop her, but she remained facing away.

"You can't leave like this," Bobby said. "If for no other reason than what would we say to each other next time we crossed paths?"

Slowly, she turned to face him.

"I feel like such an idiot. I feel like we're back in high school, and..."

"Quit," he said, and he pulled her close to him.

She allowed him to embrace her. Again, they were close and looking into each other's eyes.

"Nixon, I've wondered about kissing you since I woke up after you tased me. I can honestly say, no other woman affected me quite how you did."

Her face flushed as she remembered the time she arrested him. She turned her face away from him, rested her head on his shoulder.

"I am sorry about that," she murmured. "It seemed right at the time."

She felt him laugh and barely heard his chuckle.

"This, hesitation between us, is not a lack of desire. Not on my part," he continued. "It's a question of timing. Right now is not a good time for me. I'm in so far over my head with this Sheriff thing. I feel like I'm some kind of rat in a maze looking for cheese."

She lifted her head and looked at him. He softly traced the contours of her face with his fingers.

"If we threw caution to the wind and just focused on us," he said, "I'd lose my way completely. I would enjoy you as a lover, but right now, I need you as a friend and the best deputy in the office. I can't risk one at the expense of the other."

She pulled her head back so she could look into his eyes, "You think I'm the best in the office?"

He nodded, "I do, and I'd appreciate it if you didn't spread that around to the others."

"Better than Stewart?"

He laughed a quick and abrupt laugh, "Yeah, better than Stewart."

She stepped back so they no longer touched, but she held his hands in hers.

"I promise not to tell the others about me being the best, except for Stewart. Let me just tell him."

Her smile was mischievous and her eyes sparkled with tease.

He returned her smile, "It's plain to see you are trouble, Deputy Nixon. Now, come let me feed you some chili, and if you have time, I'd like to talk to you about the body."

Bobby, though it was cold, stood in his doorway, with only his t-shirt and pants on and watched Nixon drive the quarter mile back to the highway. In the best of months, that length of the driveway was rough, but when it was covered with hard-pack snow, it could just as quickly throw a vehicle off and into the deep stuff as not. He wanted to make sure she got onto the asphalt.

"Someday, I'll grade that," he promised himself, and he raised his fingers and touched where she had kissed him. He remembered the feel of her in his arms, tight against him. She had been willing as well as demanding. She had been a mixture of Dove soap; tense, but accepting lips; and the taste of peppermint.

The bouncing lights of her vehicle swung in a ninety-degree arc and then went smooth. She had reached the highway. He turned, ready to close the door, and in the shadows, saw him. He saw the wolf. As always, he was big and grey. Though he couldn't explain why, Bobby knew the animal was male: an alpha male. The animal held his gaze for several seconds. He was shivering when the wolf released his gaze and allowed him to close the door and shut out the cold.

The following morning, Bobbie rose extra early so he had time to feed and care for the horses and the cattle he had brought in the fall before. The horses were a task of personal enjoyment. He spoke to each as he fed them grass hay and a spot of grain. The mare now heavy with foal, as she was due in a couple of months, also had vitamins mixed in as supplements. He took the time to scratch their necks and finger-comb their manes. The barn, in which they lived during cold months, was inviting and he would have enjoyed spending the entire day with the horses.

If caring for the horses was a personal enjoyment, feeding the cattle was a required task. The couple of hundred head of stock he had wintered over, lived in a large fenced-in area that was wedged in between the horse barn and a small unnamed creek. Every couple of weeks on his Arctic Cat, he circled the fence line making sure the snow had not worn it down. A dozen wind breaks with overhangs were scattered through the enclosure.

Not barns, but better than nothing to break the force of the Montana winter wind. Also scattered throughout were large round frames made of metal. Using a tractor with lifting arms attached, he'd carry fresh hay to these frames as often as the cattle needed. He never stopped to talk to the cattle, other than to yell at them, as he placed the hay in the feeders. Cows exchanged no communication. Often, he debated with himself the idea of getting a dog to keep the cattle out of the way.

Now, he stood in the front yard of his house, bundled against the cold and he looked over the valley. How he loved Montana. It was rough country and it could be unforgiving. It lets a person make a mistake or two, but no more variance than that was allowed. The body waiting for him was proof of that. How it died was not the point. The wilds of Montana now claimed it.

The snowmobile was gassed and ready. He had lashed his snowshoes onto the machine and loaded a survival pack. The pack included a space blanket, an inflatable splint, two freeze-dried meals, and a small first aid kit. It also had a small tin stove that folded flat and used a jellied fuel from a small can — almost everything a person stranded in the Montana wilderness would need. Of course, he had loaded his silver-bullet style thermos and it was filled with fresh coffee. As he surveyed the snow-covered, pre-dawn Montana prairie, he sipped from a cup of coffee in hand.

He saw the wolf.--the same wolf who had visited last night, but taking into account that exception, had not been seen since last summer.

"You're back," Bobby said to the animal. "What are you getting me into?"

The size always impressed and intimidated Bobby. The wolf was grey and sitting with the backdrop of white he appeared darker than Bobby remembered from before. He was some fifty yards away, yet Bobby could see the yellow of his eyes. They seemed to pierce the shadows. Bobby was not an expert on wolves, or anything else for that matter, except riding bucking horses and bulls. Until the death of his father, that had been his occupation, and more than that, his life. Now, the county had asked him to complete his father's term of office. Had his father seen the wolf?

Now, he looked at the animal, knowing it was male, and not knowing why. Can a wolf communicate with men? Could this one communicate with him? He didn't know and when he tried to talk about it with Lucas, the man tried to teach him about Native American customs and beliefs, something he generally cared less about than the abilities of wolves. Still, seeing the wolf made Bobby think of his friend.

Lucas Black Kettle, descendant of Chief Black Kettle who had been killed by Custer's 7th Cavalry, had been friends with Bobby since boyhood. In many ways, they were opposite sides of the same coin, but that didn't stop them from cutting thumbs and becoming blood brothers at age eight. Lucas, always determined to make the lives of his people better, had gone to a white college and was then accepted into the FBI Academy, where he graduated in the top ten percent. After refusing his federal posting, he returned to Montana to become Chief of the Cheyenne Tribal Police. Intelligent, methodical, dedicated, he also believed in and respected the customs and beliefs of his people. Lucas was a complicated mix of old world and new. He had tried, with little success, to share that knowledge and faith with Bobby after the elder Trent was murdered.

A pair of headlights bounced wildly, and Bobby smiled to himself, "That'll be Chunk."

The snow-packed driveway was rough. Any vehicle that dared traverse it this time of year would rattle the driver's teeth.

"I'll bet he complains," Bobby said to the wolf when he turned back to look at him.

The wolf said nothing and had turned away. He trotted a natural gait across the snowpack, little more than a dark grey shadow on the white. Only once did he turn his head and glance back at Bobby.

Charles "Chunk" Fisher, also known as Unit Six, stopped the county-issued pickup and stepped out.

"Holy crap, Sheriff," he called as he rounded the pickup to the side where Bobby stood. "You'd think the county's top law dog could get the road department to plow his driveway."

Fisher, a square-built man, had been an All-American middle linebacker for the University of Montana Grizzlies. Two seasons he had led the conference in tackles, and all who knew him, or knew of him, assumed he was headed to the NFL. Several teams looked at him, a few gave him a tryout, but none of them signed him. It seems the NFL likes their linebackers taller than five foot eight inches, no matter how fast, tough, or determined they are. Fisher, with his criminal justice degree, applied at Lodge Pole and it was the older Trent who christened him as Chunk. As the man filled the lower two-thirds of the doorway, waiting to be invited into the office, the Sheriff had looked up and quipped, "You're a chunk of a man." The name stuck.

"That bumpy driveway is my first line of defense at keeping the riff-raff at bay," Bobby explained. "You have to know where the smooth parts are."

"I'd appreciate you letting me know, Sheriff. I'll have to have my suspension checked when I get back to town."

"Want some coffee?"

"Love some."

"Come on into the house; I've got fresh on. We'll grab a couple of to-go cups. Do you have a thermos?"

"I do. I stopped by Lilly's and had it filled. I'm good."

Bobby gave a quick shake of his head, "I don't know if she works harder than anyone else in the county, but I swear Lilly works longer hours than the rest of us."

"Yeah," Chunk nodded. "It's just her and Raul in there, yet, they're open at like four in the morning and they don't close till ten at night."

"Long days," Bobby agreed, then he changed the subject.

"Did King tell you the gear to bring?"

"He did," the deputy replied. "Mind if I ask what the long poles are for?"

Bobby sipped his coffee while Chunk unloaded the sled and then extended the ramps from his pickup bed to the ground.

"I'm looking at this as a crime scene, and there's no way we can search the area around the body with three feet of snow there. We'd bury whatever might be there even deeper. If we mark the area with the poles and string tape to corral the spot where we find her, then come next spring, after the snow's gone, we can come back and do a proper search. Anything in the snow now should be laying on the ground then."

The ramps extended from the bed of the truck to the ground and Chunk sat on the machine.

"Don't think I'm kissing up, but that sounds kind of smart,

Sheriff."

"Thanks. We'll see."

"You mind if I ask you something?"

"No, go ahead," Bobby replied.

"Why aren't we just turning this over to the state?"

"You think we should?"

"I didn't say that. I only asked why you weren't."

Bobby shrugged, "Maybe we will, but we're going to check it out first. Whatever it is, it happened in our county. I think we owe whoever it is that much, at least."

Chunk nodded.

Before Bobby could reply, the man fired up his Arctic Cat and backed it down and out of the truck.

Once on level ground, Chunk shut off the machine and then hooked the cage-like sled to the hitch. The ten-foot long fiberglass poles the Sheriff had asked for were tied down.

"Ready to go when you are," Chunk called.

Bobby nodded, threw out what was left in his cup, placed the cup on the post of the yard fence, and climbed aboard his machine.

"I'll lead," he called, "We'll follow the Yellowstone. We'll need to cross over at some point."

"How far you figure?" Chunk asked.

"Not sure. Durning and his son will be there waiting for us, but I'm guessing ten miles or so from where we are right now."

Chunk nodded, and they fired up their machines.

CHAPTER 3

John Perez became convinced--and in truth, disappointed--he wasn't dead when that damned beam of sunlight lasered through the hole in the living room curtain and forced its way under his eyelid. If it had stopped there, he would have ignored it as best he could, but it did not. Like all things that sucked in his life, that beam demanded more and kept going. It assaulted the very core of his brain, igniting a headache that could have caused his ears to bleed.

It was the thoughts of blood on the carpet that forced him to try to get up. Try being the operative word because it was then he discovered his neck was bent and he could not move his head. He couldn't move it at all. It was forced to the right and jammed against the top of his right shoulder.

He found the idea of a broken neck comforting as he was sure a major system shutdown would soon occur and it would free him from this pit called existence. He was not a religious man and whatever faith he had in his youth had been lost. He didn't wonder what was on the other side of the veil, or through the curtain of darkness, or over the River Styx. He didn't care what the poets, the writers, and the ministers called it. He would simply be happily dead. He forced a smile, closed his eyes, and silently welcomed whatever shit came next. After several minutes, he realized nothing came next. He just laid on the floor.

Frustrated, he lifted his left arm, fully aware, and in fact, hoping irreparable damage would be done. He needed to find out why his head wouldn't move. Why was it jammed against his shoulder at a right angle to the rest of my body? He still hung on to the broken neck idea. If he could just get a hand up and next to his head, maybe he could jerk his head to the side and finish the job that had been started. That would work. A quick snap of the neck, like a chicken, and he'd be free. Life had beaten him. He was done playing the game. He silently called the contest due to lack of interest on his part.

He couldn't even do that right. He snaked his hand up along his body and found the offender. It was the sofa that held his head immovable. As he touched the fabric, images of the previous night flooded his brain. Drunk, he had fallen and jammed his head between his shoulder and the sofa. Damn the luck — no broken neck.

Using elbows and arching his back, he scooted far enough away so he could flex his neck and align it with his body. He wished he hadn't. A broken neck would have released him of pain. A simple kinked neck increased it, and he closed his eyes to block the torture. After several moments, he dared open them and noticed his left leg rested atop a rust-colored ottoman that did not match the sofa. Scuffed, scarred, padding showing, it had seen better days, and he vaguely remembered getting it at a garage sale. The position of his leg perplexed him. How did it get there? And why did it not have a boot and sock on?

Slowly, carefully, he shifted his focus and became determined to locate his right leg. He moved his eyes and followed the length, starting at his hip. There it was. It was on the floor, and it was covered. There was the boot which had to mean the sock was under it, right? He wiggled his toes in an effort to feel the sock, but couldn't. Where was the missing sock? By the taste in his mouth, he wondered if he'd ate it. As if thinking of eating anything was a cue, he belched, and the taste of stale beer flooded his mouth. The odor of the drink, not the sock, filled his nasal passages. The acid in his stomach churned.

Groaning, recognizing the belch as a warning of what more was to come, he pulled and shifted himself until, while still on the floor, he leaned on the front of the sofa. His head felt like he wore an anvil for a hat. The extra weight stopped it from exploding. His eyes refused to focus and each time he blinked, small needles shot into his brain. Fearing permanent disability, he rubbed his eyes and wasn't surprised that some of what came away was crusty. He looked around the living room.

Sofa, some shade of green--someone had given it to him. The deadly ottoman dared him to pass it again. A chrome floor lamp in the corner and a patio rocker sat under it. Next to the chair, on the floor, rested a stack of horse magazines, one Playboy, and a couple of used paperbacks. The carpet was dirty and stained. Empty beer cans, with fast food wrappers, decorated the place. The place could use a woman's touch, he thought and then said, "That ain't gonna happen." Rhonda, his ex, left long ago, and she made it clear she would not be back.

He scanned the area. Dirty, ignored, stained, filled with second-hand items that no one else wanted; he accepted the clutter of his life. No wonder she left. He found his sock, and on the second attempt, managed to cover his foot with it. His boot was just out of reach, so he crawled to it. He'd learned it's not wise to stand when the head outweighed the body. Still sitting on the floor, he tugged the boot into position. There, he thought, I'm ready to face the day.

Face? He dragged his fingers across his jaw and cheeks. It's been... well, it's been a while since he'd shaved, he thought. He wondered if he'd pawned the razor, or maybe it just didn't work. Who knew? Who the hell cared? He struggled to his feet. He used the ottoman to help stand. It seemed fitting since it had been what tripped him. A wave of dizziness washed over him, and his stomach reminded him it wasn't happy. He swallowed the urge to vomit.

Listing to the left, he made his way, with unsteady steps, to the kitchen. Resembling a tight-rope walker, he used his arms the way a kid's bike uses training wheels. Then he saw her.

There she was, in a cheap plastic, eight by ten-inch frame, astride her horse. She's rounding the first barrel of the three-barrel pattern. She's headed toward number two. Her eyes were ablaze with desire and determination. A small smile on her lips framed her gritted teeth. She knows she's got a good run going, maybe a winning run. Her hat is pulled low, pinned to her black pig-tailed hair, so it won't fly off.

"You had your mother's hair," he said to the picture.

Her left hand is holding the reins, and her arm outstretched, giving her horse his head. Her right hand is on the saddle horn, her legs extended. She's bent low over the horse's neck, asking him for more.

Slowly, John Perez shook his head. That bay gelding had been one hell of a horse. Fifteen hands tall, he had been seven when the picture was taken, and he loved the girl as much as her father. John Perez was sure of that. Hard running, but easy to control, the horse did all the girl asked for and more. The photographer caught the horse with his ears laid back as her braids were flying. His nose outstretched, as her chin was tucked low, he's doing all he can to cover the distance as fast as he can. At the moment the photo was taken, his hind legs are gathered, ready to explode, building the strength not just to propel them forward, but in an attempt to fly. His front legs, while folded, are beginning to reach for a place to momentarily land and offer him another chance to gather and push himself and the girl to victory. He was beautiful. He was powerful. He was a twelve-hundred-pound dancer as all he did had grace. Between the two of them, horse and rider, they were a team that won as often as not. They had it all — beauty, strength, grace, determination, grit, courage. Both are gone.

The realization kicked him the way a horse will. His stomach cramped, not because of beer, but the unfairness of life. He gasped for air and his sight blurred. Rage fueled by helplessness overwhelmed him and he slammed a punch into the photo on the wall. His fist collapsed. Knuckles hurt. Wrist, elbow, and shoulder absorbed the impact and complained with shock and numbness. The glass shattered, cut his fingers, and the photo reverberated off the nail and dropped to the floor.

Her image shattered. She's covered, and surrounded, by broken pieces of glass and frame, as surely as her life has been destroyed. On the floor, she's small, hurt, and she looks up at him begging for help.

"No," he sobbed as he collapsed to his knees in an attempt to rescue her, but there's no saving her from the damage done. She's broken. She's damaged beyond repair. He cradled her, covered in shards of glass, surrounded by a twisted frame and he stood.

"I'm sorry. I'm sorry. Oh baby, forgive me. I'm sorry."

He begged for forgiveness.

He wiped across the photo, wanting only to clear her vision. Wanting to remove the broken pieces from her sight. The shards bite and several stab and cut his hand.

"Damn you to hell," he screamed. The pain demanded too much. He Frisbee'd the photo across the room, and as he threw it, he sliced open his thumb. One last insult before she crashed into the far wall and fell to the floor, not moving.

The tears won't stop, and they brought with them, not only snot, but the anguish of guilt that punched him as he stumbled into the kitchen. He's sick, and his vomit covered dishes that should have been washed days ago. He hung his head, rested his elbows on the edge of the sink and begged to die. He let her down. He failed her and now, she's gone. He didn't even know where she was.

It was still early on the side of mid-morning when Bobby and Chunk parked their snow machines next to the ones ridden by Royal and Samuel Durning. Not ten feet away, the two men sat next to a small fire. The older Durning called as Bobby stood and stretched, trying to work the kinks out of his back from the ride.

"Got coffee on. Was beginning to think you boys took the day off, maybe went and played golf."

Bobby grinned at the old man, "Well, you know how us public servants are. The coffee smells good."

The makeshift camp was located on the downwind side of the beginning of a small ridge. The grade was little more than a bump some twelve feet high or so at this point, but even the most prominent mountain had to start somewhere. The snow was three to four feet, depending on which side of the slope a man stood. The Durnings had tramped down the snow around the fire.

"Where's the body?" Bobby asked after he and Chunk had filled provided cups.

Samuel--who, while much thinner, still resembled his dad--looked up from where he sat and pointed with a gloved hand.

"She's about twenty yards around the slope there."

"She?" Bobby asked. "You know it's a she?"

"Oh, I don't know," Samuel replied. "I ain't been close to the body, but looking at it from a distance, I got to thinking of it as she. Sounded better in my mind, I guess."

"I can understand that," Bobby said. He sipped his coffee and then threw the dregs into the fire.

"Come on Chunk, let's do what we came to do."

Bobby walked around the knoll and saw the body. It was on a more or less level stretch of ground in an area some twenty feet wide that transitioned from the foothill to the stream. It was between a twelve-, maybe fifteen-foot-high bluff and Whipsaw Creek, dressed in a blue nylon parka-type coat with the hood up and wearing matching insulated pants. Winter boots, with the waffle-style tread, were on the feet. It lay face down in the snow at the foot of that bluff. It was straight and inline; the arms were outstretched. Except for the fact it was face down, and dead, it could have fallen over to make a snow angel. Bobby stopped and looked at it for several seconds. The snow seemed pristine. There were no tracks or marks of any kind hinting how the body wound up where it was.

"You think someone dropped it, like from an airplane?" Chunk mused while standing at the Sheriff's shoulder.

"I don't know," Bobby replied, "but I don't think so. If someone had dropped it, it would be deeper in the snow. The snow is not that firm. If we walked out there, we'd be in almost to our knees. Plus, I don't think it would have landed like that."

He glanced at Chunk, "Not that I've seen many bodies that have fallen from airplanes."

"This makes no sense," the Deputy complained.

"Not yet, it doesn't," Bobby agreed, "but we'll figure it out."

Bobby studied the area for several moments longer, and during that time, he asked Chunk to photograph the area and the body.

"Don't get closer than we are now, but I want you to use the telephoto lens so you can get as much detail as possible." he had instructed the man.

He wasn't afraid of it, but he suddenly realized he had no clue what he was doing. The Durnings watched him and he knew they would share what they saw. He couldn't blame them; if the roles were reversed, he'd do the same. He didn't know Chunk. Oh yeah, they had had coffee together and talked sports, but he didn't know if the man knew any more about what was expected of them than he did. Asking such a question, in front of the Durnings, was not about to happen. He might be ignorant of his job, but he wasn't without pride. Why didn't he ask Lucas to come with him? That would have been the smart thing to do. On more than one occasion, Bobby had admitted he wasn't bright. Now, he had proof.

He rubbed his chin with his gloved hand and saw Chunk looking at him out or the corner of his eye. In a low voice, the man said, "Whenever you're ready Sheriff, I'll follow your lead."

Not sure what Chunk meant by the statement, Bobby hoped it meant the man wouldn't make him look foolish. Besides, the Durnings knew no more about policing of dead bodies than he did. How would they know if he did it wrong? It was the blind leading the blind, or at least watching the blind. He looked at Chunk and felt a surge of confidence. He could do this; he would do this.

"Grab our snowshoes and the sled, if you would. Let's take our time, move slow and careful and try not to mess up the snow any more than we have to."

"You got it, Bobby," Chunk said, and the stocky Deputy seemed to find confidence in being told what to do.

The body turned out to be a female. Working on each side of her, the two men slowly lowered her arms, and rolled her over. It surprised Bobby she wasn't frozen stiff. He reminded Chunk to continue taking photos, lots of photos, as they prepared her for travel. The deputy was happy to have something to do.

The woman--who by a rough estimate was in her mid to late twenties, maybe early thirties--had dark hair, a round face, and both her eyes were closed. She appeared to be sleeping. Her skin held a smooth complexion, showing no signs of decomposition.

"She looks peaceful," Chunk observed, and Bobby nodded, then pointed out areas he wanted photographed.

After they had lifted her onto the sled, the two men worked themselves out of the immediate area that Bobby had decreed the "crime zone." When they were next to the Durnings and the fire, Bobby felt through the woman's clothes trying to find anything that offered a hint as to who she was. Due to her semi-frozen condition, and Bobby being unsure how to treat a corpse, the search was superficial at best. It revealed nothing: no wallet, no identification, no cell phone, no change. Nothing.

They placed her into the body bag which was then zipped up. Bobby made sure she was centered in the sled and then secured her there with straps. Chunk attached the sled to his Arctic Cat and turned back to the Sheriff.

"I want you to head back to Wapiti," Bobby told the Deputy. "When you get a few miles out of town, contact the office and have them schedule a flight to Billings for her. I want to get her into the morgue before she thaws out."

"You mean by chopper?"

"That's exactly what I mean. Have King stay on top of getting that flight here. Tell him to keep you informed as to the location to meet up."

Chunk nodded, "Okay."

"If..." Bobby continued, "If the flight can't make it, take her to the Medical Center. If that's the case, have King contact my sister and tell her we want this woman placed into a freezer, not the regular body bins in the morgue."

Chunk frowned, "You think she might be like, contagious or something?"

Bobby shook his head, "I have no idea what she is. I want her in a controlled environment before she thaws out. I think it might help the medical examiner if she's in the condition we found her. That's all. Just trying to be careful, Chunk. Trying to do the job right."

The Deputy smiled, "You're doing a good job, Sheriff. All of us think so."

"Really," Bobby grinned, "including Stewart?"

"Well, maybe not Stewart, but we don't count him."

"Thanks for the vote of confidence. Now get headed back."

"What you gonna do?"

"I'm going to set these snow poles around where the woman was. Make a circle about twenty feet round. Then I'm going to string the crime scene tape from pole to pole. After the snow melts, we'll come back out here and see what, if anything, is uncovered."

"You think it will be left alone till then?"

Bobby shrugged, "I don't know. You volunteering to guard this place for the next ninety days?"

"No Sheriff, I was not," Chunk chuckled.

"We do the best we can. Somebody wants more,   they can have at it," Bobby said.

Chunk climbed aboard his machine and fired it up. As he headed back to civilization, he wondered if the Sheriff's last comment was directed at Stewart.

CHAPTER 4

It was late when Bobby pulled into the Sheriff's Office. He had marked the site as planned and then rode back to his place, arriving late afternoon. He fed the horses and checked on the cattle. He ate a warmed-over bowl of chili and then headed into town. It was dark by the time he got there, and the streetlights illuminated the snow. When he walked into the office, he found Stewart, Nixon, and King there.

"Did Billings get over here and pick up the body?" he asked in general.

"Yeah," King answered. "Chunk notified me, I called them. They were only on the ground about fifteen minutes by the time he got her here. They landed the chopper in the football field. Couldn't have gone better if we had practiced."

Bobby nodded, "Sometimes it pays to be lucky."

He took off his coat and asked King for the department's camera. While King went to get it, he looked at the other two deputies.

"Everything go okay today, Nixon?"

"If you mean, did we have a crime spree? No."

He studied her for a second and then asked, "Make any headway on the stolen cattle and stock in Cold Camp?"

She shook her head, "No, I never got up that way. We were

busy here with minor fender benders, thank you Mother Nature. You'd think people who live in Montana could drive better on snow."

Bobby nodded, sighed, made no comment, and shifted his gaze to Stewart.

Undersheriff Stewart was a tall man who shaved his head. Maybe he was losing his hair or maybe he thought it made him look tough. Bobby didn't know, and more to the point, didn't care. The two had never gotten along; Bobby didn't know why. Stewart had been appointed acting Sheriff when the elder Trent was murdered. But later the county asked Bobby to take over the reins and pushed Stewart aside. They told Bobby the appointment was a show of respect to his father. He wondered if maybe they didn't want Stewart and figured a way to save the cost of finding an outsider. There were days he wished he'd turned them down.

"What are your plans tonight Stewart?" he asked the man.

Stewart glared at Bobby as if being asked such a question was out of bounds.

"I'll patrol the county, just like I do every night when I'm on the overnight shift."

Bobby was tired and his back and his injured hand ached from the pounding the Arctic Cat had given him. He had been cold most of the day and the worry he felt about the body was more than he expected. He was careful not to respond to Stewart's baiting.

"Find time to get up to Cold Camp and do surveillance of the feedlots. Maybe you'll get lucky."

Stewart stood to make sure the Sheriff remembered he was the taller man. His eyes held a challenge as he said, "I know how to do my job."

Bobby didn't bite and the man turned and left the office. Nixon looked at Bobby and almost said something, but she caught the slight shake of his head. "Another time," it reminded her. She turned as well and walked from the office. Bobby was watching her walk away when King returned. He too noticed the woman leaving.

"Been a long day Sheriff, are you sure you shouldn't get

some rest?" the older man asked.

"I won't be here long," Bobby replied. "I just want to go through the photos we took today and maybe print a few off."

"Chunk said we don't know who she is."

"I don't know, that's for sure, and moreover, I don't know what she is."

"I don't understand," King said.

"By her complexion, what little we could make out, she could be white, Native or Hispanic. I don't have a clue. I'm hoping the autopsy will help us."

"Any sign of foul play?" King asked as he took the memory stick from the camera and inserted it into the computer.

"Only if being found dead in the snow of the Montana wilderness is considered foul play," Bobby answered

Within seconds, the screen was filled with thumbnail-sized images and one after another the men enlarged and examined the photos. From time to time, Bobby would say, "That one, print that one."

Other than that, the men worked in silence.

After an hour, the two men had assembled a hard copy file of some fifteen photos. Some showed the woman in total. Some showed a close-up of her face or other parts of her. Some showed how she had been found and Bobby printed three photos of the snow around her head and feet. Once they were finished, he gathered them up and headed for his office.

"Thanks for the help, King. You should have called it a night a long time ago."

"No worries; I sleep little these days. I might as well putter around here as in my house."

"Still, we've already talked about the county not paying overtime."

The man laughed, "I don't do this hoping to get paid overtime. I do this because I want you to succeed."

Bobby stopped and turned back to face the man.

"What do you mean by that, exactly?" he said.

"Nothing sinister, Sheriff. I've worked here long enough to have had five different Sheriffs, you being number five. I've had the honor of working with your father, who was the best of the five. I've also worked for a couple of real knot heads. Couldn't wait to see them leave. You, if you stick around for a few years, will be my last one. I want to go out with a winner."

"You think I'm a winner?" Bobby chuckled.

"I think you can be. You need more seasoning, some training, and of course, experience. But I think you have it in you to be better than your father, and just so you know, I thought the world of your old man."

Bobby moved to one of the six desks that lined the long rectangular room and leaned against it. It turned out to be Nixon's desk.

"King," he said, "Don't blow smoke my way. I worry about getting through every day. When I got to the body today, I realized I didn't have a clue what I was doing out there. I even thought I should have sent Stewart. The man is a pain in the ass, but he knows law enforcement. I don't have the training, I don't have the management skills, and I'm not sure I'm smart enough to get the job done. On top of all that, if you want the complete truth, I've got one deputy I want to sleep with and another I want to knock the crap out of."

Bud King gave a gentle chuckle and then said, "Bobby, the other deputies work for the county. What I mean by that is that if you got fired, or quit tomorrow, they'd keep working. That's how it should be; they have families and responsibilities. They have to make a living." Bobby scowled, "Yeah, I get that. I'm not sure where you're going with this."

"Where I'm going is that, unlike those, I work for you. I leave when you leave. I've been here a long time and there's not much I haven't seen. Most I don't want to see again. After my illnesses, your dad allowed me to come back and I told him I'd work as long as he did. Neither of us figured on what happened, so I'm transferring my promise to him to you. I'll help you become the best you can be and I think you can be one of the best sheriffs in Montana. You got the heart for it, and moreover, you got the hard-headedness it takes."

Bobby grinned, "Thank you. I've got another year or so until Dad's time is up. Let's see how things are going then."

King studied Bobby for a bit and then said. "There is one

condition I must insist on for me to help you."

"What's that?" Bobby asked.

"I won't be the deputy you want to sleep with."

Bobby grinned, "Deal. If you don't mind, and only if you plan on being here awhile, print two copies of the entire set of photos we took today."

"That's gonna be a bunch of photos, Sheriff. Digital images don't cost. The price goes up for the paper."

"I know," Bobby said, "but the photos are all we now have of the death scene. I'm hoping the camera may have caught something that neither Chunk nor I saw."

King thought about what the Sheriff said and then nodded.

"For what it's worth, Bobby, it's that kind of thinking that's gonna make you a great Sheriff if you decide this craziness is for you. Your dad, as good as he was, would not have thought of that. He followed the rules, the procedures; he was good because he was consistent. Stewart, well, he wouldn't think about it, and he'd have called in the state by now. Mostly, he'd worry someone might criticize him."

Five hours of sleep later, morning chores done, a hot shower and coffee for breakfast, Bobby was on his way to the Northern Cheyenne Indian Reservation. He carried a folder with the pictures he had printed out the night before. As he drove, he called the office.

"Sheriff's office, how can I help you?"

"Bud?" he spoke into the device.

"Yeah, morning Sheriff."

"Hey, I'm headed out to see Lucas. Keep an eye on things until I get back."

"Will do."

"Did Stewart get up to Cold Camp last night? Was there anything to report on the missing stock?"

"I asked for the morning report and he said he didn't get up that way. He said he was too busy."

Bobby shook his head, "I see; and what was he busy doing?"

"He didn't say, Sheriff, and he didn't list any activities in his patrol log."

"Okay," Bobby sighed. "I'll take care of it when I get back. Have Nixon drive up that way and check with the ranchers that have lost stock. Have her find out if more have been stolen."

"Won't they report it if they have?" King asked.

"Yeah, they might, but by my count, around a hundred head of stock are missing. Most of it is sheep, but at least thirty head of cattle. If someone stole cattle from me, and I had the impression the Sheriff didn't care, I'd take matters into my own hands. All those boys have rifles, they know how to shoot, and it's not like we don't have trees enough to hang someone."

"You think it could come to that?"

"I think there is a number, a magic number, and when the stock stolen matches that number, someone is going to hang. The trouble is, it might not be the right someone. You know how these things can get. If we don't get proactive real quick, I think there's gonna be another dead body in the woods, this one hanging from a noose. If it were my stock being stolen, I'd invite the others to the first vigilante meeting. Get a hold of Nixon and have her drive up there. Tell her to make contact with as many ranchers as she can and make sure she touches base with all who have reported stolen stock. Let's try to get ahead of this mess."

"You got it, Bobby."

"Oh, and one last thing..."

"Yeah?"

"Call Billings and see if we can get a date when the autopsy will be completed. I want an officer there to witness it."

"Will do."

Bobby walked into the office of Lucas Black Kettle. Lucas, a little taller than Bobby, wore his hair long but tied back with a simple band. A quiet man with sharp, handsome features, he was a leader in his own right as the Chief of the

Tribal Police. Lucas and Bobby had been friends since boyhood.

"Good morning, *Viho*," Bobby said as he walked into the office of his friend. *Viho* is Cheyenne for Chief.

"Good morning, Sheriff," Lucas returned and then laughed.

The office was in the Tribal Building, which held the various offices working to administer the needs of a society. Not unlike a city hall whites are familiar with, the building held council rooms for the various representatives to meet and discuss the concerns of the tribe. The building was new and well kept. Most floors were carpeted, and those that weren't were made of wood plank. Various pieces of art depicting the history of the tribe adorned the walls. The Chief of Police's office was to the west end of the building.

"What's so funny?" Bobby wanted to know as Lucas led the way through the doorway.

"Just us, my friend. Do you remember when we were boys, playing in the backyard of your home?"

"I do."

"Would you have thought those two renegade children would grow up to be not only leaders in their communities but the highest-ranking law enforcement officers as well?"

"In all honesty," Bobby grinned at his friend, "the smart money would have been placed on you. You were always a step or two ahead of the rest of us. Me, I was a surprise finish at best."

Lucas shrugged, "Be that as it may, *ne'se'ne'*, you have, nonetheless, made the grade. I am a Chief, and you are a Sheriff."

Bobby chuckled, "I guess we're still playing cowboys and Indians, and still friends, still *ne'se'ne'*."

Lucas nodded, "Yes, I believe you could say that."

He looked at the folder in Bobby's hand and pointed at it with his chin.

"What have you got there?" he asked.

"Two days ago, Royal Durning and his son Samuel stumbled across a body north of the Yellowstone."

Lucas shook his head, "I do not know the Durnings."

"Grouchy old man," Bobby said, "owns a good-sized spread on the north end of the county. Runs mostly cattle, but also a few sheep. He and his boy were up there checking snow depth trying to figure when to move cattle to the range."

"And they found a body?"

"Yeah," Bobby nodded, "a woman, mid-twenties, maybe thirty. I've got a picture of her. I'm hoping you can see something and help identify her."

Bobby slid the picture of the woman across the desk to Lucas. He studied the full-face photo for several seconds. Bobby sat quietly as the Chief did so. It was Lucas's nature to consider all things before responding. Bobby was familiar with the trait.

"This woman looks as if she could be Cheyenne," Lucas said pensively.

"I agree," Bobby said, "or she could be Hispanic, or Latino, or even a white. KC has many of the same traits this woman has."

"Possibly," Lucas nodded, as he pointed to the photo. "Where is she now?"

"She's in Billings. She's scheduled for an autopsy there. We have no idea how or why she died."

"She had no identification?"

"None."

"Any marks or tattoos? Any scars?"

"None noted, but to be honest, she was still mostly frozen when we sent her by helicopter to Billings. We didn't disrobe her, so much of her was never examined."

Lucas stood and looked out the window of his office.

"You should not have done that, Bobby," Lucas said without turning around.

"Should not have done what?"

"You should not have sent her to Billings without checking with me first."

Bobby scowled.

"Why would I need your permission?" he asked. "I have no idea how she died, and I felt I needed to get her to experts as quickly as I could and in the condition I found her."

"I don't disagree with that," Lucas said, and then he turned. "But this woman could be Cheyenne, and we do not allow autopsies, except in the rarest of occasions. If one is to be done, some traditions must be honored. You should have checked with me before you arranged to have her shipped to Billings."

Bobby didn't like criticism, but he had tolerated it from ministers to high school teachers, from parents to girlfriends, and now, his friend. He and Lucas had been friends as long as either could remember and over the years that bond had been tested by a few arguments and even a couple of fights.

"You must forgive me, oh wise Chief," Bobby's voice was bitter, "I'm a slow learner, and I haven't gotten to the part in the Sheriff's manual where it says I need to check with you before doing my job."

Lucas kept his expression bland, "I didn't mean it that way, but is it too much for you to show an ounce of respect? Cheyenne people rarely approve of autopsies, and only after deliberation. To remove organs from the body is to desecrate it. Such an action cannot be taken without the approval of the council, and then the procedure is done in the Shaman's presence. He must be there to comfort the spirit."

"Lucas, we don't even know if she is Cheyenne. How do you expect to determine that?"

"You are correct," Lucas argued, "but why did you bring the photos if you thought she is other than Cheyenne?"

"That's just it; I don't know who or what she is. I'm showing this to you to find that out. I'm also going to put photos in the banks in town, the cafes, and anyplace else that will let me."

"And in your rush to answer a question that will not change with time, you have possibly desecrated a Cheyenne woman. Must everything be done on the schedule of the white man?"

"Lucas, you know I did not do this to hurt your people."

"The amount of harm done to my people without effort by yours is staggering," Lucas countered. Bobby glared at the Chief, afraid if he spoke he would not be able to walk back the words said. The silence was loud between them for some time.

"When is the autopsy set?" Lucas asked, his voice lowered, but tense.

"I don't know," Bobby said. "King is handling that end of the investigation."

"Would you call him and find out?" Lucas looked at his friend. "As you assumed she might be other, I must assume she is Cheyenne. I have to make arrangements."

"Can I borrow your phone?" Bobby asked.

"Of course."

Bobby spoke with Deputy King only for a couple of minutes. When he hung up the phone, he looked at Lucas. The conflict of emotions registered on his face.

"She has no identification of any kind on her. None at all. No tattoos, no scars, no moles or birthmarks. She appears to be a well-nourished woman twenty-five to thirty-five years old, with no bruising or any sign of foul play. The suspected cause of death is a heart attack. King said the autopsy report would say she died of Sudden Death, something or other. I'm sorry Lucas."

The Chief grew cold, his expression hardened.

"They've already done the autopsy." It was a statement, not a question.

Bobby nodded, "Yeah, finished about an hour ago. They had scheduled her to be done later in the week, but something came up. King wasn't told what, but she got bumped to the head of the list."

"Were they able to identify her race?"

"They're not positive, but they think she is Native American."

Lucas sat down heavily in his chair and allowed his head to fall back against the headrest. He looked at the ceiling, and remained so for several moments. During that time, Bobby sat silently opposite. Bobby knew Lucas was fighting to control his emotions. He gave his friend the time he needed.

"I think you should leave the reservation," Lucas said, not looking at Bobby.

"*Viho*, I would do nothing to purposely insult you or your

people. You know that."

Lucas looked at Bobby and said, "If that is so, your insult is made without thinking. What I know is that a Native American woman, possibly Cheyenne, was butchered at the hands of the whites, not unlike thousands before her."

"Lucas, it was a medical procedure. The woman is dead," Bobby responded.

"Her spirit lives, and she was insulted, molested, desecrated without her spirit guide present to protect her or provide her peace. This will not sit well with the people."

Bobby stood and glared at his friend, "I don't know what you expect of me. The body was at the far end of the county, almost on the government land. She was nowhere near the reservation, and there was no more sign she was Native than any other race. I get it. You're upset that I angered the spirits, or whatever. But let me share something else with you."

"What's that?" there was no expression on the Chief's face.

"She didn't die by any heart attack. That makes no sense whatsoever."

Lucas arched his eyebrows, "So, now, besides being a Sheriff, you are also a medical examiner? If you're so confident regarding the cause of death, why did you send her to Billings to be brutalized?"

Bobby studied Lucas for several seconds. At times, he grew tired of all the spirit world gibberish of his friend. He wanted to tell the man to be more white. It became obvious he would not be the support the Sheriff had hoped for. He reached into the folder he'd brought, pulled a few copies of the photo of the face, and slid them onto the desk.

"I've already apologized if she turns out to be Native. There is nothing more I can do. If you can bring yourself to do your job, share these and let's see if we can find out not only what, but who, she is."

"Do not presume to lecture me on my job. Unlike you, I studied many years to get to where I am."

Bobby glared at Lucas. Both knew the reference to his murdered father was a low blow. If he regretted making the comment, it didn't show on the Chief's face.

Lucas ignored the photos; Bobby turned and exited the building. He muttered to himself most of the way back to Wapiti.

His mood was sour, his stomach twitched from too much coffee and not enough food. He was in the perfect mood to see Marcus Kettling.

CHAPTER 5

T he Lodge Pole County Jail was located in the basement of the courthouse. At one time, the Sheriff's Office also resided there, but even backwater counties like those in Montana grow. With growth, new demands are placed on public service. Several years earlier, the county bought a section of a strip mall building, and the Sheriff moved. Now, the department had an auto parts store and a drugstore as neighbors, both who shared the parking lot.

The jail, which was expanded, was run by jailers separate from the deputies. They were called corrections officers, and they worked under the umbrella of the District Attorney and funded by the state through the DOJ. To say there was a certain amount of competition between the two would be an understatement.

Bobby entered the control center of the jail, which was a room with a sign-in desk, a row of lockers, and a walk-through gate that used electronics to search the person entering for possible hidden weapons. He turned and while facing the lockers, selected one that was empty, removed his sidearm, his badge, his wallet and truck keys, then placed them all inside. He closed and locked the door, taking the key with him. Then he turned to face the jailer on duty, a man named Rogers.

"Well, if it isn't Bad Bobby Trent gracing us with his presence," Correctional Officer Rogers said. Rogers was an overweight man sitting behind the counter, watching security videos and eating potato chips. Bobby stepped to the counter and noticed the man's shirt gapped between buttons. Rogers also wore three days' growth of beard. Bobby wondered if the man was trying to look dapper with the beard, or if it was just another sign of his slothfulness. He considered the repercussions of commenting on the man outgrowing his shirt, and he wondered if he should point out the broken potato chips littering his stomach. In the end, he let everything go; there was nothing to gain with petty bickering.

"I'd like to see Marcus Kettling," he said.

Rogers leaned forward. Potato chip pieces tumbled down the front of him. He noticed them and brushed more aside with the back of his hand.

"I'm not sure we can accommodate you, Sheriff. It would have been better if you had called ahead and let us schedule a time for you to meet with the inmate. Inmate Kettling has planned activities."

Bobby nodded and gritted his teeth to keep from lashing out.

"I'm sure that is the case. Marcus seems like the type who would enjoy an hour or two dedicated to the finer arts of knitting."

Roger's grinned, "See, I knew you'd understand. Why don't you come back in, say, a couple of hours?"

Bobby nodded, "Yeah, I guess I could do that, but what would I do in the meantime? I'm sure the county would expect me to be productive."

He glanced around the room, as if pondering the question, then turned back to Rogers.

"I know," Bobby said, "when I was walking across the parking lot, I noticed a truck parked in a handicap zone. It didn't have a decal. While I'm waiting, I think I'll go ticket that vehicle and have it towed. I'd guess it would only cost the owner a few hundred, what with fine and towing fees."

It took Rogers longer than what Bobby thought it should

have to realize the Sheriff was talking about the jailer's truck.

"Wait a minute," the man said, "you can't ticket me. I'm not in the handicap zone."

"But you are," Bobby replied. "At least a quarter of your truck is parked in the spot designated for handicapped use."

"Yeah, but that's not my fault. It's the pile of snow. There wasn't any room."

Bobby nodded.

"Yeah, I can see that point. The snow is high and has been plowed into piles, thus reducing the number of parking spots. I get that. Being the conscientious public servant you are, you naturally take the closest spot, even though it subtracts from the handicap spots. Heaven forbid you park on the second or third row. You might have to walk an extra thirty feet."

Bobby motioned at the man, "I can see how the extra few dozen steps would worry you."

"How far I walk is none of your concern."

"Agreed," said Bobby, "I couldn't care less how far you walk. But you're still parked in the handicap zone. My course of action is clear; I have to write the ticket."

Rogers looked around as if he was trying to find something to make this pest go away. When nothing was found, he looked back at Bobby and said, "You know, I think I can work you in to see Kettling, if you still want to?"

"That's why I'm here," Bobby suppressed a grin.

"Give me a second, and I'll have him transferred to an interview room."

"Appreciate it," Bobby said.

"How much time, oh, never mind, you take whatever time you think you need with the man."

"Thanks again," Bobby said. "Interdepartmental cooperation is a good thing, don't you think?"

"Yeah," Rogers nodded, "it's a good thing. Give me a minute."

Bobby nodded, and the man was as good as his word. Within a couple of minutes, another jailer stuck his head through a door and motioned for Bobby to follow him.

"Sheriff," Marcus Kettling said, as Bobby walked through the door. The room was square, made of concrete and painted white. A metal table was bolted to the floor in the center, and three chairs surrounded the table. Marcus sat in the one on his side of the table, with his hands handcuffed to a metal ring welded to the table. Two other chairs were on Bobby's side and he chose one and sat down.

"Your brother came to see me the other day. Wants me to figure out a way to get you out of here."

"Yeah, he told me. I thought you'd be here yesterday."

There was a hint of challenge in his voice and Bobby nodded.

"This might be hard for you to understand, but try," Bobby said. "It's like this; you're not listed as number one on my dance card. Rest assured though, I'm working down to you as fast as I can. Besides, it's not like you're going anywhere. I always know where I can find you."

Bobby smiled. Marcus did not.

"You've always been a prick, you know that Trent? And I don't care if you're Sheriff or not. Isn't it about at this point we go out back of the schoolhouse and knock each other around?" the big man asked.

Bobby shook his head, "Not anymore. I'm not in your weight class any longer. I'd have to cheat."

"You cheated back in the day," Marcus reminded him.

"Only once."

"You hit me with a stock cane made out of hickory wood."

"You were already as big as a horse. Got your attention."

"Yeah, that it did. That sucker hurt."

"Well," Bobby said. "I have an idea that might, and make sure you understand this, might, keep you out of the state pen. As it is, the charges against you could put you in for a decade or so. There's no point in that. So, here's the deal."

The big man leaned forward and gave his full attention.

"First," Bobby continued, "you will hire KC Sims as your lawyer. You'll pay her the full fee, not the pennies on the dollar the county pays public defenders."

"Why have I got to do that?"

"Because if this idea comes to be, she'll be the one arguing for you in front of the judge. She deserves to be paid."

Marcus shook his head, "That's not it. You're still sweet on her and you're thinking this might get you back in her good graces."

Bobby glared at the man, and then continued.

"Second, you will apologize to the redhead, in Stetsons, on a Saturday night, with a full house. You will also pay any medical bills she might have incurred though I think mostly it was her pride that was hurt."

Kettling shook his head, "Bobby, you know I never meant to hurt her. She's a sweetheart."

"Agreed," Bobby said. "You okay with the conditions so far?"

"I am."

"My deputies will waive the charges for battery on a police officer if you agree to resisting arrest. You'll do thirty days of community service, under my direction."

"What you gonna have me doing?"

"Every nasty job I can think of."

Marcus asked, "Can I take back that part about you being a prick?"

Bobby smiled, and after a hesitation, so did Marcus.

"That brings us to the damage done to Stetsons. I hear you're a better-than-average carpenter. You know how to handle a saw and hammer."

The man sat a little taller and nodded.

"I built my house. You can judge the quality of my work."

Bobby nodded, "I have. So, here's the deal. I get Stetsons to drop charges, and in return, you repair all the damages. You cover the cost of the labor and the materials."

"How am I going to do that? I ain't got that kind of money."

Bobby shook his head, "You, your brother, your friends, I don't care. It's up to you to raise the money and short of robberies or selling yourself on the corner; I don't care how you do it."

Marcus shook his head, "I have no idea how I'm going to raise that kind of money."

"I get it," Bobby said, "but it's not right to expect Stetsons

---

to wait for months on end for you to get the repairs done. You did damage out there, Marcus. It has to be answered for and corrected. Whatever you have to sacrifice is a damn sight less than doing time."

"Yeah, I know that. I just don't want to say I can do something when I can't."

"I understand. Why don't you talk to your brother and see if the two of you can come up with a plan? If you can, we'll run it by Paul and see if he agrees."

"Paul?" Marcus asked.

"Paul Adams, he's the owner of Stetsons," Bobby said, and the man nodded.

"Can I ask you something?"

"Sure," Bobby answered, "What's on your mind?"

"Have I got to sit in here until all this is resolved? If I'm in here much longer, I could lose my job. I need that job."

Bobby nodded, "I get that. If, and this is a big if, I get you released on your own accord, you give me your word you'll show up for court?"

"I do, Sheriff, I do. I give my word."

"Understand it is not up to me, but if I go out on a limb for you, don't be breaking it off after me. You be there for your court date."

"On my word of honor, Sheriff."

"All right, I'll take you at your word, and I'll see if I can do something," Bobby said, and then added, "no promises."

Marcus nodded, and Bobby thought he saw tears in the big man's eyes. He stood up to leave, but Marcus called him back.

"Sheriff, why you doin all this for me? I know you don't have to; it ain't like we're friends."

Bobby shrugged, "I might decide to run for election. If I do, I'll want your vote. Besides, sending you to prison isn't doing anyone any good; not you, not your family and certainly not Lodge Pole County."

"Thank you," the man said, and Bobby heard the catch in his voice.

As Bobby gathered his weapon and other items back in the control center, he looked over his shoulder at Rogers.

"So that we understand each other, tonight, at the change of shift, I will direct the deputies to pay particular attention to the handicap zones. I think it's only right to make sure they are accessible to those who really need them, especially with the snow and all. It would seem to me, walking with crutches or some other device would be a lot harder on ice and snow."

Roger's face blanched, and he started to speak. Bobby held up a hand.

"I don't want you to think we're picking on you. I will enforce the order throughout the county."

"But I thought we had an agreement," a confused Rogers blurted.

"What agreement? You did your job. Now, I'm going to do mine and make sure my deputies do theirs. Because of today, anyone illegally parked in a handicap spot will receive one warning. You've had yours."

As Bobby crossed the parking lot and the intersection separating the courthouse from the Sheriff's Office, his phone buzzed in his pocket. He dug it out and placed the device next to his ear.

"Trent," he answered.

"Sheriff, it's King. You need to get back to the office as quick as you can."

"Trouble?"

"It's brewing."

"I'll be there in a couple of minutes."

He disconnected the phone and shoved it deep in his pocket.

"Now what?" he glanced up at the sky and asked Montana.

Bobby heard the commotion before he entered the office. He stopped on the sidewalk and listened to several voices shouting, each trying to outdo the other. He could also hear King and Nixon's voices as they tried to restore verbal order. They were losing ground.

The thought crossed his mind to turn around, cross the square, walk into the office, and give DA Franklin Blue the badge back.

"Try it on for size, you told me. I feel like I'm a captive," he muttered to himself. The thought was fleeting; he'd never quit anything in his life. He tugged his hat lower on his head, squared his shoulders, and walked into the fray.

When they saw him, they seemed to be a stampeding herd of cattle, as they all came at him at once, all of them trying to talk louder than the others.

"Stop," Bobby barked, "Shut up and let me get my bearings."

He had to say it twice, but on the second command, the group stopped talking and stood staring at the Sheriff.

"All right," he said, in a measured tone, as he removed his hat and coat. He turned to look over the group, and once he recognized who they were, he also figured out the problem.

James Wood, thick-chested man, grey-haired, bearded, early sixties, liked to strut when he walked. He owned a ranch on the north side of the county. All the visitors did.

David Hill, also in his fifties, thin, vain, dyed his hair to keep it brown, used to be a screenwriter in Hollywood, then gave it all up to be a rancher, and was making a go of it. He also had a small spread on the far north end of the county and was still learning the craft.

The third man was Ernesto Torres. He was small, quick-tempered and tough. The shortest of the bunch, his deep brown eyes missed nothing. He was quick to move and quicker to fight when he was intoxicated. He had immigrated from Spain and rumor was he had been some sort of bullfighter over there and ran a man through with a sword who was seeing a woman Torres liked. Folks liked to ask him about the stories and, to date, he had always refused to answer either charge with any detail.

The fourth man was a woman though her gender would be hard to discover going by the manner of her dress. A brimmed hat pulled low, a fleece coat, jeans, and boots, Roberta Gomez stood as tall as the other men, taller than Torres by a head, and she could out swear any of them. She took in abandoned lambs, bottle fed them, and raised sheep.

"Bud," the Sheriff said, "have you offered these folks coffee?"

Torres interrupted, "I did not come here to drink coffee."

Bobby nodded, "Okay, Bud, bring everyone but Torres coffee. I figure you're here to talk about missing stock. You all come over here to the waiting area and sit down. There isn't room in my office. Let's have a chat."

"Not missing," Torres again butted in, "stolen."

"Yeah, I agree with Ernie," Wood said, his voice deep, and his rate of speech slow. "The stock has been stolen, Sheriff. We want to know what you're doing about it."

Bobby nodded agreement and waited for Bud.

"If it was your stock being stolen," Hill added, "I bet you'd have one of these deputies riding night owl on your herd."

Bobby glared at the man, and his eyes grew cold. Hill knew he had stepped over the line.

"I'm sorry about that. It came out wrong, but you know how it is. You run a ranch. Lose a few head to winter, a few more to wolves, a couple just due to dumb bad luck, and before you know it, you're not covering your expenses, and then you're working on some other guy's ranch."

He turned and pointed to Gomez.

"Roberta has lost close to thirty head of sheep."

Bobby looked at the woman, and she nodded her head and said, "Twenty-three to be exact."

"Whatever," Hill said, "the number is too damn high."

Bud returned with cups and a pot of coffee. Torres reconsidered and took the cup offered him. Bobby waited until all had been served and then he stood.

"Right now," he said, "with Nixon, King, and me here, you have more than half the personnel of the Sheriff's Office. The overnight shift comprises one deputy for the entire county."

"Sheriff, if you're telling us we have to put up with the theft of our stock because the county has you shorthanded, that ain't gonna fly," Hill snapped. "You wouldn't tell the store owners in town to suck it up if they were getting robbed every few nights."

"Sheriff Trent," Roberta said. Her voice carried just a hint of the Hispanic ring to it.

"Ms. Gomez?" Bobby acknowledged her.

"It is not that we don't understand, but you also have to understand. I carry both my shotgun and my rifle with me at all times. If I catch someone stealing stock, I will handle it myself."

"I have no doubt you will, and I don't blame you. I think you all are doing a bunch of patrolling through the back roads at night."

"Every night," Torres said.

"I can't remember the last time I slept a full night," Wood added. "We're watching our places and the places of our neighbors. It would be nice to see a Sheriff's patrol car up that way every so often."

Bobby glanced at Nixon, who looked to her boots and he caught her blush.

"Folks," he said, "there's never a cop around when you need them to be. But you need to believe me when I tell you we are patrolling up there."

"Well, we never see them," Hill challenged.

"Then you'll have to take my word for it," Bobby replied. He then took a sip of his coffee and stepped to where he could see each rancher better.

"Look, I get it. If my place was being hit--and to my knowledge, it has not--I would be just as angry as you. I expect you to patrol your properties, and I'm not going to tell you not to carry your guns. If you find someone, I hope you'll call us, and allow us to handle that. I don't want to see any of you getting hurt."

"You ain't tellin us what you're gonna do to stop this, Sheriff," Hill challenged.

Bobby looked at the man.

"Aside from promising more patrolling of the area, I'm not in a place right now, to answer that. But more effort on our part," he motioned to the deputies, "is on its way."

"That's all well and good, Sheriff," Woods said, "but what are you going to do about the City of David clan? You and everyone else knows they're the ones stealing the stock."

Bobby leveled his gaze at the rancher.

"You talked to Mr. Phillips about this?"

"Hell no, I ain't talked to him about this. You know, well as me, he's got snipers in those trees surrounding that camp of his."

"I heard he had buried landmines around the perimeter," Torres added.

"What makes you think the Phillips clan is behind this?" Bobby asked.

"Who else would it be?" Torres replied. "They got a bunch of mouths to feed up there."

"Well," Bobby said, "I'll take a ride up that way and talk to Phillips. I'll ask him if he has been stealing stock."

"Don't you think he's smart enough to hide them?" Woods demanded.

"As you pointed out," Bobby said, "I'm also a rancher. If he has cattle and sheep up there, I'll find them."

"You be careful," Roberta Gomez said. "That old man Phillips is crazy. It won't bother him to shoot a Sheriff."

"That's right, Bobby," Hill chipped in, "and that son of his is even crazier."

"I'll be careful," Bobby promised, as he stepped to the nearby counter where he had laid the folder with the photos of the woman. As he did so, he heard the ranchers mutter. It sounded as if none of them were happy with his offer. He selected a copy, the same one he left with Lucas, and turned back to the ranchers.

"A couple of days ago, this woman was found dead along the Yellowstone," he said as he showed the ranchers the photo. "Any chance any of you know who she was? Or, maybe, where she comes from? Any chance you know her people?"

The ranchers gathered and looked at the photo, a couple held it, but each of them shook their heads. All denied knowing the woman.

"Well, it was a shot in the dark," Bobby shrugged and returned the image. He again turned back to the ranchers and took a moment to look at each one of them.

"I know how lame my promises sound to you. They sound the same way to me. But, don't give up on us, not just yet. There's only a few of us, and there's a lot of land to search, but give us our chance."

He held out his hand as if he was cementing a bargain with the ranchers. One by one, each of them took the hand,

Hill being the last.

"It ain't that we don't trust ya, Sheriff. But as for me, I don't have the finances to last if I lose too many head of stock. The stealing hurts all of us. But me, if I lose many more, I could lose my place. I won't stand by and let that happen."

Bobby nodded understanding.

"I don't expect you to. Give me some time. We've got good officers," he said.

"I, for one," Hill said, "will hold you to that."

Bobby stepped back and toward the door.

"While you're all in town," he said, "stop over at Lilly's and grab a slice of pie. She makes some of the best. Tell her I'll be by later to settle the bill."

Roberta Gomez chuckled and then said, "Trying to buy our votes already, Sheriff?"

Everyone joined in the chuckle, except Bobby, who remained stone-faced.

"No," he said, "just offering you all a slice of pie."

After the four ranchers left, Bobby motioned for King and Nixon to follow him into his office.

"I'm open to ideas on how we can make some headway on this," he said.

Nixon and King looked at each other and back to him.

"No?" he quizzed again, "Neither of you coming up with anything?"

"I'm sorry, Bobby," Nixon apologized, "What more are we supposed to do? We patrol the area when we can, but I don't know what more we can do."

"I agree with Dori," King said. Bobby saw Nixon glance and scowl at the older deputy, but she said nothing. Bobby knew she hated being called the nickname but didn't feel it was his place to stop the others. Instead, he said, "Well, I've got a couple of ideas to get us started."

Both nodded they were paying attention.

"Okay, Nixon, starting tomorrow, you will drive Unit One."

"What?" she said. "That's your vehicle."

He motioned for her to be still.

"Tomorrow it will be your vehicle and we'll rename it Unit Five. Since it's a pickup, it can carry the snowmobile in the bed. I want you to spend at least half your shift driving the back roads of the area where the stock has gone missing. Some of that area, you'll need the machine."

"I don't own a snowmobile," Nixon said.

"For the time being, you'll borrow mine. Just make sure you dress accordingly."

She grinned, "Of course, Mother."

He grinned but remained serious.

"Look, I'm not sending you up there for a joy ride. To our knowledge, neither the cattle nor the sheep have been sold at auction. We have no idea where they're moved to, or were taken from, for that matter. Stock leave signs in the snow. That's what you're looking for. I expect you to find it."

She nodded.

"Before you clock out today, please move your gear to Unit One, and move whatever I have in my truck to your SUV?"

She nodded again.

"Thanks," he said. Then, he turned to King.

"With Nixon spending so much time in the northern end of the county, we will have to prioritize any requests for assistance that come in."

"I was wondering about that," King said. "With Dori that far north, the response time for calls in the southern part of the county will suck. Don't forget, Sheriff, the southern part of the county has ninety percent of the people. We can't ignore them in favor of cattle."

The old deputy grinned good naturedly, "Ya got to remember, cattle don't vote."

Bobby raised a hand motioning the deputy to stop.

"That's enough of that. I've got another year on Dad's term before I even think about doing this in my name. I will not spend the rest of the time I'm here worrying if they'll let me stay longer."

"I get it," King said, "but a year will go by faster than you think, so if there is a chance you might want to run, you better start making plans."

"Yeah, well, we better find some missing livestock, or all bets are off."

King grinned, "You find the cattle. I'll start thinking about your campaign."

Bobby shook his head, "No, I've got other things for you to do."

"Such as?" the deputy asked.

"You will buffer all the calls that come in over the day shift. You're going to decide which calls can be handled by the complainant coming into the office and which ones need a deputy on scene."

"I don't understand."

"An example then," Bobby said. "Say two people have a fender bender due to ice: damage to the vehicles, but no injuries. Every driver out there carries a camera on their phone. Direct the drivers to take as many photos as they want and exchange information for insurance purposes. Then, ask them to come into the office to make the report."

"Okay," King said, "who takes the report?"

"You do," Bobby answered.

"I do?"

"Yeah. Why not? You're the best report writer we have on the department. If the drivers show up with the photos, all you need to do is save copies to the computer and then take the report."

The older man stood a little taller and smiled.

"You're going to let me be a full deputy again?"

"If you want it. I know Dad brought you back after the medical stuff you went through. I know you've been on a light duty kind of thing. Right now, I need more from you, if it won't put you back in the hospital."

"Does that mean you will let me carry a weapon again? I mean, if I'm doing the job, I should be ready to do the job."

"Nixon," Bobby said, as he looked at the woman, "later this week, take King to the range, and check him out. Get him qualified to carry."

"Bobby, doing weapons quals is Stewart's job as the Undersheriff," she reminded him.

76

"Yeah, it was," Bobby nodded.

Her expression voiced question, but she said nothing.

"Now," Bobby continued, "back to the new way we do business. King, a call comes in. You decide if, one, the report can be handled in the office. If it can, it belongs to you."

"Got it," King said, still grinning at being looked at as more than an administrative assistant.

"Two," Bobby continued, "if the report needs to be taken on site, you will determine who will handle it. Based on where Nixon is up north, it could take her as long as two hours to get on scene. If that's the case, dispatch me."

"Dispatch you?" King asked.

"Yeah, why not? You been telling me what to do since I came on board."

"Only with your best interests at heart," the old man grinned.

"Yeah, I trust you," Bobby said. "Now, if I'm out of the area, say, in Billings yelling at a medical examiner who didn't notify us of the autopsy change, I'm not going to be able to respond."

"I guess I'll have to roll on it," King offered, as his grin grew.

"No," Bobby said. "If you roll on one call, just one call, I'll fire you that day. Your job is to bring as many complaints into the office as you can. Because there is a chance the complaints might be angry and hostile. I want you armed, for protection, but you do not leave this office."

"I don't understand," he said, "if both you and Dori is out of the area, who handles the calls?"

"Either Fisher or Stewart," Bobby said.

"What?" The two deputies spoke in unison.

"Yeah, you'll have to decide who is called in during their time off. You'll have to consider the time of day and how long the man has been off. Also, you'll need to try and figure out how long it will take to handle the call."

"Stewart isn't going to like this change," King said.

"I'm not sure I like this change," Nixon admitted.

"Look, I get it. In so many words, time off duty is not really time off, because there is always a risk of being called in. The good news is most of what we do at a scene can be handled in the office. I know there will be times we will be called in. In fact," he looked at King, "I want you to change the duty roster, so one day off is identified as standby day for call in. On that day, the officer can't drink alcohol and can't leave the confines of the county."

"Sheriff, it would work better if you let me put myself on that roster," King said.

"No, absolutely not," Bobby was adamant. "We have to have some stability here; the county wants to know we have someone on duty. That face of the department is you, Bud. But, I want you to put me on the roster."

"What about those days you have to go to Billings to smack down an M.E?" Nixon asked.

"I'll have to be more precise as to scheduling my travel plans," Bobby replied.

He looked at the other two and waited for questions. It pleased him there were none. He knew he was asking a lot of them, and he felt confident they would step up. He would figure a way to repay them, though at that particular moment, he didn't have a clue as to how.

"We good?" he asked.

"Just one thing," Nixon smiled.

"What's that?"

"I need your keys."

He returned her smile and dug into his pocket.

Thirty minutes later, Nixon knocked on the Sheriff's office door and entered without being invited. Bobby was looking through the photos of the dead woman.

"What are you hoping to find there?" she asked as he looked up.

"Honestly Nixon, I don't know. It's the best representation of the death scene I have. I keep thinking it will tell me something if I look hard enough."

Nixon stood and studied her boss as he lowered his head and returned to the photos. She slid the keys to her SUV onto the desk.

"I brought you the keys to your new unit," she said.

"Thank you." He didn't look up.

She remained where she was for some time.

"What's on your mind, Nixon?" Bobby asked and leaned back in his chair so that he could meet her gaze.

"Are you really going to go up to see that crazy, Phillips?"

He nodded, "I don't think he stole the cattle, but we can't ignore the possibility. I think there's a bigger chance one of them may have seen someone or something."

"What makes you think they will even let you on their place? You know they claim they have seceded from the United States."

Bobby grinned, "I'll be on my best behavior. They won't be able to resist me."

"When you go," Nixon said, not amused, "I'm going with. Don't leave here without me."

Bobby looked at her for some time and remembered the beating she had taken from men who wanted to hurt him. She had not only survived, but had shot one of the attackers to boot. Nixon was tough.

"I promise," he grinned, "you get to come with."

"I'll hold you to it," she said.

CHAPTER 6

Touch he hell I will," Stewart said when Bobby explained to the Undersheriff the change in the workload. The two of them were in the Sheriff's office with the door closed.

"I've got my days off, and I'm not about to sit around and wonder if King is going to call me or not. I have a life outside of this department."

"As do we all," Bobby agreed, "but for the short term, this change goes into effect."

"Tell that old man not to call me, because I won't show."

Bobby shook his head, "I was hoping we didn't have to get into the threat area, but if he calls you and you do not show, or if you take an extremely long time to show up, you'll be terminated."

"You power hungry little puke," Stewart glared, "I've been a lawman for half your life. You come in here and think you can order me around?"

"The fact of the matter is, I can order you around. I didn't ask for this; the county asked me to fill in for my dad until his term was up. I took the badge out of respect for him. Having said that, I will do what I think is necessary to get the job done. Right now, we need another deputy, but we don't have time to find one, nor the funds to pay one. That means, we all sacrifice a little. That means we do more with what we have."

"Maybe, I'll just quit. I'll tell everyone how you ran me off. With you down even another deputy, you'll really fall on your face. The next election will be mine for the taking."

Bobby calmly nodded, "Yeah, it might go that way, but you might want to rethink that plan. I haven't decided if I'll run or not. But whether I do or not, I'll make sure everyone in this county knows how you walked out on this department when we needed you the most."

Stewart glared.

Bobby smiled, and then said, "You do what you think is best."

The man said nothing and stood to leave the office. Bobby called him back.

"One last thing: when you are told to patrol a certain area, you damn well better patrol it. You need to spend close to half your time up north trying to get a handle on the missing stock."

"What about the stores and businesses? If we have nobody around, don't you think the bad guys will figure that out?"

"They might, and we'll have to reallocate as best we can. But we need to find out where that stock is going."

Stewart slammed the door when he left.

Bobby stepped out into the clear and cold Montana night. It seemed to be distorted daylight. The streetlights, the store lights, but mostly the moonlight, bounced, glanced and ricocheted off the snow and anything that had a shine to it. He smiled when he saw Nixon's SUV waiting for him. He'd always been a pickup truck guy but, "we all have to make sacrifices," he told himself.

On his way home, he had to pass Stetsons. He stopped to see Paul Adams, the owner, and the little redhead.

"Bad Bobby Trent," she squealed. "How long has it been since you been to see me?"

Without waiting for him to answer, she ran the half a

dozen steps separating them and launched herself into his arms. She wrapped her legs around his middle, offering her bottom for him to hold her by. Her arms were around his neck, and after a quick smile, she kissed him full on the lips.

"That's the best part of my workday," she said when she pulled back.

"You are something else," Bobby returned her smile and he bounced her just a little.

"Are you putting on weight?" he asked.

Her mouth went round, but she quickly recovered.

"I'll have you know I have worn these jeans since I was fifteen," she declared.

"And each year that passes, you fill them out just a little better."

"Is this part of your job, Sheriff?" she asked, "Holding up unsuspecting women?"

The patrons of the bar cheered as he carried her in place until they were under a light.

"Let me see your face," Bobby said. "Are the bruises gone?"

"To the point where I can cover them with makeup. I'm good Bobby. It's nice you asked, though."

He gently sat her down. Bobby was not a tall man--he had to stretch to make five foot nine--but still, the little redhead only came to his shoulders.

"Have you got a couple of minutes and is Paul in tonight?"

She smiled and her blue eyes sparkled.

"Yes, on both counts. Anything for you Sheriff."

"Be careful when you say that," Bobby teased. "I might stick around until after closing."

"Any night you feel lucky," she teased, and then she stopped, and her eyes got wide. "Why Sheriff, I think I just offered you a bribe. You might have to arrest and frisk me."

"Or, I could let you off with just a warning," Bobby countered.

"Chicken," she pouted. "Let me deliver these beers and I'll get Paul. Why don't you meander over to the bar? He's working tonight and we'll have to all talk over there."

Bobby nodded and found a stool to sit on. He watched the

little redhead as she walked away, balancing six open bottles of beer on a tray at her shoulder.

He admired her walk and her sense of balance. He was impressed with her graceful strength.

"Sheriff, I'm told you're waiting to see me."

Bobby nodded.

Paul Adams was a man of average height. He wore his grey, shoulder-length hair tied back with rubber bands. The man wore glasses and the style he chose were round and tinted. Wearing tinted glasses while working in the subdued lighting of a bar always struck Bobby as strange, long before he was Sheriff. Now, he wondered if the man was always stoned.

Adams had migrated to Montana from California, where the rumor was, he'd been a hedge fund manager. He'd made a killing in the investment field, and one day, woke up and traded the lifestyle away. People said he traded a Maserati for a Jeep Wrangler, and a yacht for a snowmobile. He exchanged three-piece suits for jeans and tie-dyed shirts. He got rid of his Dami crocodile loafers, threw away his socks and wore sandals. And he bought Stetsons. He had discussed changing the name of the bar when he first arrived, but a threatened boycott from the patrons changed his mind.

"You still on duty, Sheriff?" Adams asked. "Should I offer you a beer or coffee?"

Bobby hesitated for a moment and then asked for a beer.

"Been one of those days," Adams observed.

"That it has," Bobby agreed. "Make it a short one though, if you don't mind."

"Not at all."

Within moments, the mug was in Bobby's hand, and he enjoyed the feeling of the cold frothy liquid falling down his throat.

The little redhead walked over to Bobby and linked her arm through his.

"Now, I've got you," she said.

Bobby sat the beer on the bar and nodded.

"Yeah, you do," he said, "I'd like you to tell me what you

think should happen to Marcus Kettling for knocking you around the other night."

Reflexively, she glanced at her boss as she touched the side of her face. Bobby noticed it was still a little swollen.

She smiled, "I've worked with drunks a long time, Bobby, and mostly I handle them well. Now and then one gets too loud, too mean, or just plain too far out of control. Marcus didn't mean to hurt me. He just lost control."

"That doesn't answer my question," Bobby said. "What should I do about it?"

"Bobby, when you competed, did you ever get kicked or stomped on by one of those bulls or horses you ride?"

He held up his left hand, which had been stepped on. The result was three broken bones.

"You know I have. Why?"

"Did you punish the horse?"

"No," he shook his head, "but I'm not sure it's the same thing as a drunk knocking you across the floor."

"My point is, what happened comes with the job. Like a dentist getting bit, or a hair stylist getting a cut finger. There're risks, Bobby. You know that."

"I do, but we can't allow men the latitude to knock people around because they were drunk."

She smiled, "Do you have any idea how much money I made that night in tips?"

Bobby studied her and then shook his head.

"I have no idea," he said.

"About three times what I make on a normal Saturday night. I know it was because I got knocked around, but I didn't give it back."

"Nor should you have," Bobby said.

"So you see, Marcus stung me, but in the end, I came out way ahead."

"He's still got to be held accountable. I can't go to the DA and say one victim wants bygones to be bygones. Help me out."

She thought for a minute and then said, "Tell you what, when Marcus can come out and play again, he has to buy a round for the house. If he does that, I'll consider us square."

"He also has to apologize to you in the bar," Bobby said. "My condition."

She squeezed his arm.

"I like that," she said. "Now, I've got to skedaddle. There're thirsty boys and girls out there."

She pulled herself as tall as she could and kissed Bobby on his cheek.

"Just in case I don't see you when you leave," she smiled.

"Paul," Bobby said, "the same question for you. What do you want to square this with Marcus?"

Adams motioned after the redhead with a nod, and said, "After how gracious she is, I'm going to sound like a real hard-ass."

"I know you've got damages that need to be fixed."

"Yeah, and unfortunately, mine won't heal themselves."

"I know they won't. Sending Marcus away won't get them fixed either. I don't know if you have drunk insurance, but somebody has to pay. If Marcus is sent to Deer Lodge, it won't be him."

"Deer Lodge? Sheriff? Remember, I'm a transplant."

"Sorry. Deer Lodge is the location of the state pen. Marcus, if convicted, can do some serious time."

"I see," the bartender said.

"I don't think it serves a purpose to use that route," Bobby explained. "If Marcus goes down that hard, he loses everything. His family, his house, his job, and for what?"

Adams canted his head and studied Bobby.

"Don't get me wrong," the Sheriff continued, "Marcus must be held accountable, but it makes little sense to permanently take from a man when the damage he did is temporary."

"Since you feel that strongly about this," Adams observed, "I'm guessing you have a suggestion for a solution."

"I do," Bobby agreed.

"I'm listening."

"Have Marcus go the expense of fixing Stetsons and have him do the work."

"What if halfway through, he decides he doesn't want to finish the project?"

Bobby shook his head, "He won't have that option, not really. What I propose is that Marcus sign an agreement to do the work, buy the round, apologize to the bar, all as a condition of not going to the pen. If he fails, in any of those areas, he goes directly to jail."

Adams thought for a few moments and then asked, "What if I say no? What if I say I want the man to pay a heavier price?"

"Then there is no bargain and Marcus goes to court with no agreement. We're back to square one."

"Why are you doing this, Sheriff? This Marcus, is he some kind of friend or relative, or something?"

"No," Bobby said, "he's nobody special to me. I hate to see a family ruined when it doesn't need to be, and truth be told, I've done a few foolish things in my life. I was just lucky enough not to get caught."

"If I do this, you give me your word the bar gets fixed quick? Look, the place is still a mess."

Bobby observed the broken windows covered with plywood, places where booths and tables should be but weren't because Marcus broke them.

"If you support this, I will see to it that Marcus addresses this damage first. He's a good carpenter. In another scenario, he could be the one you hired."

Paul Adams nodded and extended a hand.

"I'm on board," he said.

"Thank you," Bobby said and turned to leave.

"Sheriff?" Adams called, and Bobby turned back.

"What does the man get for roughing up your deputies?"

"Thirty days under my thumb."

Adams smiled, "That's a new take on community service. Doesn't sound fun at all."

"I hope so," Bobby grinned, as he left.

As he drove home, he enjoyed the moonlight on the snow. It was cold, clean and seemed to say there is a new season coming. He pulled into the yard and went to the barn while still bundled. He was late, and the horses would be wondering where he had been. He fed and cared for them and he took time to rub each horse down with his gloved hand. Each horse nickered at him and only Sophie's carried the tone of recrimination.

"Where have you been?" she seemed to scold.

"I'm sorry, old girl," he said, as he rubbed under her extended stomach. "That baby is getting heavy, isn't it?"

As he walked to the house, he heard the howl of a wolf. He stopped and scanned the yard and as far as the subdued light would allow. He saw nothing, yet he felt he was being watched. Was it the wolf? Was it someone, or something, else? Trying to appear nonchalant, he covered the distance to the house and was relieved when the door closed behind him. He decided not to turn on the lights.

The following morning, King and Nixon found Bobby in his office studying the photos of the dead woman. He had a to-go cup of Lilly's coffee on the desk beside the pile of photos.

"You bring that to work with you?" King said as he pointed to the cup.

"It would appear so," Bobby replied. "I believe there is a logo on it."

"So you drinking her coffee instead of mine?"

Bobby looked up at the deputy.

"Again, it would appear so."

"You're being mean, Sheriff. I don't mind you going over to her place to sneak a cup every so often, but to bring her stuff in here; well, that's just hurtful."

Bobby took a swallow of the bitter brown liquid and smiled at King.

"That may all be true, but her coffee is so much better than yours."

"Hurtful, just hurtful," the old man repeated.

"Did Stewart patrol the north end last night?" Bobby asked.

"According to this patrol log, yes," Nixon answered.

"Did he report anything?"

She shook her head, "No. Just recorded patrolling that

area."

Bobby sighed.

"You realize how lucky we're going to be to find these guys, don't you?" Nixon asked.

He looked at her.

"The area up that way is huge. Backroads, forested, and it runs all the way into Canada."

"You think the cattle are being taken to Canada?"

"I'm not saying that, but it is a possibility."

"True enough. You gonna be nice to my truck today?"

The blonde smiled, "Actually, I thought I'd give it a workout. Since you only drive it on asphalt, I planned to see what it could do."

Bobby nodded, "As long as it's in the line of duty, have at it."

He winked at her, and she mimicked a curtsy.

"Nixon," Bobby said, and the deputy turned back.

"Have you got time for a cup of coffee?"

"With you? Sure. You're my boss."

He grinned, and added a wink, "I am, aren't I?"

She grinned and he dug into his wallet.

"Please run to Lilly's and grab us three large coffees. You can also bring donuts if you want. I understand they are a tradition with cops."

She smiled, looked at the bills in her hand, and said, "I get to keep the change?"

"Sure," he said, "save it for the day you take me to lunch."

Before she left, he handed her the full-face photo of the dead woman. She could have been asleep, but Sheriffs don't put up flyers of people sleeping too often. Under the picture, Bobby had added, "If you know her, please call the Sheriff's Office." He also added the phone number.

"Ask Lilly to post this in a place where people will see it," he said.

"Will do, boss."

King was in the office with Bobby when Nixon returned with the coffee. She did, indeed, bring half a dozen assorted donuts.

"Oh, this is just cruel," King whined when he saw the cups.

"Don't think of it like that," Bobby said. "Think of it more like community protection."

"What do you mean?" the older deputy asked.

"How would it be if both Nixon and I got sick and the department of health discovered it was your coffee?"

"You're a cold man, Sheriff. I take back all the good things I said about you."

"All right," Bobby said, "let's go to work."

"I've been thinking about some of the comments you all have made about the missing stock. So, we're going to see if maybe we can get luckier than we have been."

"What ya got in mind?" King asked.

"I want you to get the largest map you can find of the county and then I want you to get a hold of the assessor's office. I want you to get the plat maps of the ranchers that have lost stock. You're going to copy over onto the larger map the boundary lines of those areas."

"Okay," King said and nodded his head.

"I want to be able to see what property lines are shared. Also, plot out all the neighbors, so we know who has not been hit."

King nodded again.

Bobby turned to Nixon.

"I want you to start at the Missouri Breaks Park border and work your way south. I want to see what roads are capable of having stock hauled over them this time of year. Of course, you're also going to look for any sign of the stock. They can't just have disappeared. They got to eat, drink and stock leave sign."

"Bobby," she pointed out, "that's about twenty-five miles north of our county."

"I know that, but we got to find which roads and trails are being used. I don't think the cattle will mind if we're out of bounds."

"Any road worth considering hauling stock, I can travel in my SUV. Why do I need the pickup and the Arctic Cat?" she asked.

"Because I also want you to ride fences between the ranches. Again, the stock has got to cross somewhere."

She nodded her agreement.

"When you get back into town, I want you to mark the roads as they can, or they can't, be used to haul cattle. I also want you to mark any spot where cattle can be moved from one property to another."

"And the sheep?"

He smiled, "Anywhere cattle can go, sheep can get there faster."

She stood, and he asked, "Have you got a map of the county now?"

"I've got the small one we all have. It's not much, but for general patrol, it works."

He nodded, "Use that one for today, but we'll make you a copy of the one King posts. I want you to have exactly what we all see."

She smiled, "I don't suppose you will let me check in as Unit One, just once?"

"I'm afraid that might confuse people."

"It would be fun, though."

"You'll be Unit One quick enough. Go to work."

She smiled again, saluted him, turned and left.

"King," Bobby called, and the older deputy came to the office.

"Yeah," he said.

"There's something else I need you to do."

"What ya got?"

"I need you to call the brand inspectors in Idaho, Wyoming, and Canada. Find out if they've had any loads of stock that just didn't seem right,any new shippers crossing state or country lines."

"Okay."

"Also ask for any lists of livestock auctions they have and then contact the auctions and ask them the same. Anything that wasn't just right or a little odd, branding-wise."

"You got it, boss."

"One last thing and make it your first thing today."

King looked at Bobby.

"Call the M.E.'s office in Billings and make arraignments to get that body shipped back here. I want it by the end of the watch. If they've got a way to transport, have them get her here. If not, get a hold of my sister Rachel at the Med Center and have them send an ambulance."

"Will do. Anything else?"

"No, get the woman home. Today."

"You got it, boss."

Bobby stood, looked at his watch, and then reached for his coat.

"I'm headed over to see KC about Kettling, and then I'm on my way to Billings. I want to talk to the M.E. who did the workup. Try to have the body on her way back before I get there. I don't want them holding her any longer than necessary."

King nodded, "Let me know when you roll that way?"

"Will do. But I'm off first to see our esteemed public defender."

King nodded, "I'm sure you think of her in that light, Sheriff."

Bobby grinned, "You be careful. I am your boss."

"And you made fun of my coffee," King replied.

"Good morning, counselor."

KC, her dark hair pulled back in a bun, looked up from her desk and saw Bobby leaning in her office doorway. He noticed the flush of emotion that colored her already darker than usual features. She looked radiant in the form-fitting, rust-colored business suit, and the blush of color heightened the effect. She stood, and Bobby allowed himself to linger over her form as she focused her anger.

"I pay good money for an assistant to sit out there, answer my phone, and stop people like you from interrupting me when I'm busy."

"Come on," Bobby said and grinned at her.

She scowled, which wrinkled her nose and Bobby remembered that expression. During better times between them, that expression had a secret meaning. Now, unfortunately, it just meant she was angry.

"Jeff," she called and Bobby stepped aside as a twenty-something-year-old man rushed through the doorway.

"I'm sorry, Ms. Sims," he stuttered. "He told me it was official business."

KC switched her glare back to Bobby.

"It's the truth," the Sheriff said, "I did tell him it was official business."

"Yeah," the lawyer said, "I have no doubt you did. But why are you here?"

"It's official business," Bobby said.

"Jeff."

"Yes, Ms. Sims?"

"Throw him out."

Jeff took one step toward Bobby, and the Sheriff smiled.

"That ain't gonna happen, Jeff."

"Ms. Sims," the assistant whined.

"I need to see you, KC," Bobby said. "It's about the Kettling matter. It won't take long."

KC stamped her foot, which was another move Bobby liked, but he kept the enjoyment to himself.

"It won't take long," he promised her.

"All right. Since you're here, come on in," she said. She motioned toward a chair.

"Sit if you must."

Bobby sat and waited for KC to follow his lead. When she relaxed and pulled out a yellow legal pad, he explained all he had done and who he had talked to trying to resolve the Kettling matter. He wanted her to see the lengths he had gone to to find a fair and workable solution for all parties involved. He was careful as to the words he used as he wanted her to see him as concerned and professional. He did not want to sound boastful. KC took notes and waited until he was finished. Then she glared at him.

"Well, since we, in Lodge Pole County, are so blessed to

have the miracle worker Bad Bobby Trent as our Sheriff, we might as well retire the court system."

"I'm sorry?" he asked. His confusion showed on his face. "I was trying to help. You were there the other day when Calvin spoke to me about it. Are you telling me I should have ignored him?"

"I'm telling you that making plea agreements and discussing sentences of felons fall under the purview of the court system, not some attention-seeking, Sheriff."

"You think I did this to get attention?"

"No. I don't know, maybe. That's not the point."

"What's the point?"

"The point is, you need to stay focused on your job and let those of us who know the legal system do our job."

"I see," Bobby said. "So you would have got him off on all charges?"

"I didn't say that."

"You would have copped to a plea that would have sent him away?"

"I didn't say that either."

"Do you even know Marcus Kettling?"

"No, I don't. What does that matter?"

"So you would have met him, read over the charges and then you and the D.A. would have gotten your heads together and hatched out a fair-for-all agreement. Is that how it works?"

"I don't know. That's how it works sometimes," she said.

"So explain to me what I did that was so out of bounds."

"It's not your place to decide guilt or innocence," she choked on the words in her anger.

Bobby looked at her and stood.

"There was no debating guilt or innocence," he kept his voice just above a whisper. "I simply tried to make the system work so a temporary happening didn't permanently damage a man's life."

"What about the waitress? Who looks after her?"

"I talked to her. She's fine with the plan. I talked to all of them. I wouldn't present something to you they all hadn't agreed with."

"You had no business interfering."

Bobby shrugged, "Well, we all know I don't know how to do my job. Don't know why they gave me the star in the first place. When you meet with Franklin, tell him of the deal, and then tell him if he doesn't like it, he can have the damned star back. Have him call me. I'm on my way to Billings."

He turned away from her and walked to the doorway. He turned back.

"This is probably not a good time to ask you to dinner. My place. I'll cook. You can see my new kitchen."

"Get out," she said.

"You look nice, by the way," he smiled.

"Get out."

"I'll cook pasta. I know you like pasta."

She threw her pen at him, and he swatted it aside.

She glared at him.

He winked at her.

CHAPTER 7

The drive to Billings was unsettling. It wasn't the road, though parts of it were still covered with the slush of partially melted snow that had not been plowed. It wasn't the clouds that were grey to almost black and heavy with the threat of more of the white stuff.

The confusion was a part of Bobby, and he couldn't stop his thoughts from behaving like the clouds overhead. His thoughts tumbled through his mind the way ping pong balls tumble in a bingo cage. He wished he was the one cranking the handle, but he knew he wasn't in control of even that much.

He replayed the scene with KC from that morning. He had envisioned her seeing him as committed, concerned and stepping up to wrong misdeeds. He had hoped she would see him as being committed to the community. Instead, she described him as intrusive and bothersome. He had wanted to impress her, to have her see he was becoming more than he had been. She saw him as meddlesome and a pest. He glanced in the rearview mirror and admitted to himself her rejection hurt. It hurt a lot, but he'd be damned before he'd let her know that.

His thoughts slipped from KC to Lucas, another who had let him down. Lucas, with all his customs and his rituals.

Didn't he realize Bobby was trying to solve an unexplained death? Maybe a murder. He'd been the Sheriff for less than a year, less than six months. Why couldn't Lucas have helped? Why couldn't he have been supportive? What right did Lucas have for jumping all over him, for crying out loud? And, they found the body on his territory, not the reservation. Lucas, for all of his boasting of being a professional law officer, didn't hesitate before crowing all high and mighty.

Stewart jumped into his mind, and for once the thoughts were clear; fire the jerk. He needed deputies willing to do what needed to be done. He didn't need someone on the team trying to bring him down. He could do that all by himself.

Who was that dead woman? How did she get out there where they found her? Why did she die? Did she die naturally or was she killed and if she was killed, by who? And how? And, again, why?

The freckled face of Nixon came to mind and with her, the memory of their kiss. That had been nice. That kiss they shared was the nicest thing in his life over the last two months. Would it be wrong to get close to her? It was obvious she wanted to as much as he did, maybe more. She'd felt good in his arms, lean, fit, rounded and smooth in all the right areas. He smiled. She'd be adventurous, he could tell. She'd be fun. They'd have fun.

The blast from the air horn of an eighteen-wheeled semi trucker forced him to focus, and he realized he had drifted into splitting the lanes. He guided the SUV back where it belonged and smiled at a driver brave enough to loudly tell a marked patrol car to get over. He looked at his speed and noticed he was some twenty-five miles an hour under the posted speed. Bobby inhaled deeply and shook his head. Time to get his mind focused on what was at hand.

"Dr. Carlson, thank you for taking a few minutes to talk to me."

Bobby leaned over the cluttered desk and reached for the

hand of the man on the far side. The man was round, in body and head, and the head was mostly bald. The doctor sported a ring of hair that reminded Bobby of the laurel head wreath the Caesars wore. The man ignored the offered hand and instead focused on a sandwich he held with both hands.

"Sit down, young man," Dr. Raymond Carlson, ME, said as he sucked food particles from his teeth.

"How can I help you today?"

Bobby moved half a dozen file folders from the chair next to him and sat. He held the folders and realized the man had yet to make eye contact with him. Instead, the man alternated between locating where to next bite the sandwich and reading papers on his desk.

Bobby took a moment and glanced at the desk before him. Certainly far from some kind of neat freak, Bobby still felt there was a place for everything and everything should be in that place. If Carlson felt the same, the top of the desk was where everything was to be. More folders than Bobby could count lay intermixed with menus from delivery sandwich shops, napkins, correspondence and what appeared to be subpoenas. Bobby bent forward and placed the folders on the floor next to the desk.

"You wanted to talk to me?"

Bobby glanced up at Carlson and the man was indeed, looking at him. The doctor's eyes were a pale blue and watery. Maybe he spent too much time looking through microscopes.

"Yes, Doctor, I'm the Sheriff of Lodge Pole County and I wanted to talk to you about the woman found dead there."

"Lodge Pole, you say?"

"Yes, I'm the Sheriff."

"Do you have other business in Billings, Sheriff?"

Bobby shook his head, "No, I came over just to see you."

Carlson swallowed what he had chewed and said, "You've wasted the county's gasoline and your time. I sent a report and questions could have answered by telephone, or text even."

The man took another bite.

"Doctor, excuse me, but you're telling me you know what

killed her?"

He shook his head, "I'm telling you nothing of the kind. I have no idea why the woman is dead. Read the report young man. The findings are plain: Sudden Death by Unknown Causes."

Bobby took in a deep breath and slowly let it out. Carlson took another bite and followed it by loudly sucking on a straw stuck through the top of a soft drink lid.

"How can the findings be plain if you don't know what they are?"

Carlson swallowed, belched, and sighed, "I didn't say I didn't know what they are, I said I only know the woman died of Sudden Death..."

Bobby raised a hand, "Yeah, I get it, Sudden Death of Unknown Causes. That tells me nothing."

Dr. Carlson set aside his sandwich and focused on the Sheriff.

"I get it," he said, "you have a suspicious death every hundred years or so out there in the sticks, or boondocks, or wherever you're from, and you want to solve it. You're the Sheriff who is lucky enough to have this major case on your watch. Much more exciting than neighbors arguing over who shot whose dog."

Bobby told himself to be calm.

"Here's the deal Sheriff: I'm not a psychic or a magician. I'm a medical examiner. I can't go hocus pocus and create a cause of death out of thin air."

"What do you need to find a cause of death?" Bobby asked.

The expression turned smug, and Carlson replied, "Well, for starters you could do your job with a tad more thoroughness."

"What are you talking about? I gave you all I knew about the woman."

"I have no doubt," Carlson admitted magnanimously, "but unfortunately for both of us, your report was still sadly lacking."

"What do you need? I'll get it for you."

Carlson chuckled, "Will you, now? Okay, make a list."

Bobby nodded and turned on the recorder app on his

phone.

"I need the woman's age," Carlson said.

Bobby scowled.

"I need her occupation."

Bobby's scowl deepened.

"I need to know her lifestyle. Did she smoke? How much alcohol did she use? Did she exercise? Did she use illegal drugs?"

"I don't know any of those things," Bobby complained.

"Hush. There's more," Carlson replied.

Bobby scowled again.

"In addition to the previously requested, I also need to know the circumstances of her death, as well as her past medical history. Did she suffer from past heart issues? What about respiratory issues?"

Bobby glared at the man, who paid the Sheriff no mind.

"You want me to do a job for you? I need the history of her family. Did they have heart issues? I need to know what medications she was taking and what she had taken in the past, both prescription and over the counter. Also any allergies she may have suffered."

Bobby watched the man as he took another loud swallow of his soda.

"Last, but not least, I would like access to any ECG tracing that was done during any resuscitation attempts."

"You know I can provide none of those things," Bobby said, the frustration easily heard in his voice.

"Of course I know it, and because I can't deduce knowledge from evidence I don't have, we are stuck with the bland, sadly incomplete and superficial, not to mention useful only to cover my ass, ruling of Sudden Death of Unknown Causes."

Bobby stood and paced the office.

"There's got to be more than this," he muttered. "This is next to nothing."

Carlson leaned back in his chair and took a deep breath.

"Look," he said, "maybe this will make sense to you. Every year, just over two million, six hundred thousand Americans die. They die for all sorts of reasons, many of them you are probably familiar with as a lawman."

Bobby sat down again.

"Now," Carlson said, "Out of those deaths, a certain number are like just what we have here. For women, there are fifty-seven deaths of unknown circumstances for every one-hundred thousand. For men, the numbers are a little higher. What I'm saying is this woman is not the only one. Usually, we can be a little more precise, but not always. Sometimes this just happens."

Bobby scowled and fidgeted in his chair.

"Sheriff, it's not as bleak as all that."

"What do you mean?" Bobby asked the Doctor.

"I can't tell you for sure what killed her, but I can tell you what didn't. That in and of itself can be a help."

Bobby looked at the man.

Carlson held up a hand and used his fingers to count.

"We know she didn't die from a gunshot wound. She wasn't killed by stabbing or BFT."

"BFT?" Bobby asked.

"Blunt Force Trauma, you know, beaten to death. I'd have thought you'd have seen one or two of those. It's a personal favorite of drunk husbands to use on wives."

"I haven't been the Sheriff that long," Bobby admitted.

Carlson nodded, "And yet, you're the lucky one to win the lottery?"

"Something like that," Bobby said.

"Okay, whatever. It's yours to solve, so let's get at it."

Bobby nodded.

"As I was saying, we know she didn't drown. She didn't fall down a cliff or steep slope. She wasn't strangled. She didn't die of exposure. She didn't die of carbon monoxide poisoning."

"Crap," Bobby said, "How many ways are there to kill someone?"

"Oh, we're just getting started, and these are the ways I know she didn't die."

Carlson thought for a moment and then added, "There's one more thing,"

"What's that?" Bobby interrupted.

"She didn't die where you found her."

"She was moved?"

Carlson's expression looked like he was talking to a six-year-old, "Yeah, that's what I said. She was moved post-mortem."

"How do you...?"

"Sheriff, if you're going to stay in this field, allow me to suggest some basic forensic medical training. Aside from that, when this woman died, she was on her back. As the body cools after death, blood falls to the lowest points. Thank you, Mr. Gravity. Once it's settled, it coagulates, just like blood always does. There were pools of blood in her buttocks and the heels of her feet. There were smaller pools elsewhere, but you get my point, I hope."

Bobby stood up to leave but stopped.

"There's one other point if you don't mind."

"You've interrupted my lunch, go ahead."

"Why wasn't my office notified in time to have an officer present? Isn't that the usual way of doing these things?"

Carlson shrugged and picked up his sandwich.

"I have no input into that. Talk to the administrative people."

"It's just that..."

"Sheriff," Carlson barked and then rummaged around on his desk. He picked up a sheet of paper attached to a clipboard. He held it out for Bobby to examine. It was a list of names.

"See that?"

Bobby nodded.

"That's a list of my customers waiting in the coolers. Now, it takes up to four hours to complete a full autopsy, but that includes none of the additional dictation, coordination with labs, or meeting with interested parties, like yourself."

"I..." Bobby started to say, but Carlson stopped him.

"My point is, the list you're looking at will grow faster than I can prune it. When I have a body on the table, I don't care in the least who else is or is not there. Regarding your girl, they told me a body that had been scheduled was canceled."

He shrugged.

"Something about the family refusing permission; I don't know, but they substituted your Jane Doe. I didn't choose her, nor, as you know, did I refuse her. Trust me; she didn't care if you were there or not."

Bobby nodded his head, and said, "Last question."

"You already asked your last question."

Bobby stared at the man.

"Okay, okay, what is your last question."

Carlson drew out the word last.

"Do you think she is Native American?"

The question seemed to stump the doctor momentarily, but then Carlson nodded his head.

"Without a doubt, she's Indian. What tribe? I don't know. But she is Native."

"Thanks," Bobby said.

"If you need better evidence than just my say so, I can have a DNA test run on a tissue sample we keep on file. It will take a few weeks, but I can put a rush on it...if it's that important."

"I'd appreciate that, Doctor. I'd appreciate that a lot."

During the drive back to Wapiti, Bobby's thoughts did not wander. No, he ruminated about one train of thought the entire sixty minutes: How was he going to tell Lucas?

Even though the winter solstice had passed, the sun still sat early in Montana. That being the case, the town of Wapiti was dark. There were the artificial lights of course, but compared to the brightness of the day, the town was subdued at best. Bobby stopped by the Sheriff's Office only to find it deserted. Nixon had turned the duties over to Stewart. He read her patrol report, but there was nothing of any interest.

He drove by Lilly's and thought about stopping for dinner. He decided against eating there. Lilly's was, to him, a morning place. He hated the thought of going home and eating alone. Stetsons was out. He had tempered his visits there since being appointed. He tried to balance being friendly but not being a regular.

He was headed out of town when another thought struck

him.

"Oh, Bobby," he said to himself, "there are bad ideas, and then there are really bad ideas."

He turned the SUV around and headed for Nixon's.

When she peeked around the partially opened door, Nixon was wearing a cotton sleep shirt that was to her mid-thighs. It was V-necked with buttons up the front and it was colored blue and orange in deference to the Denver Broncos football team. She was barefoot.

"Sheriff?" She asked cautiously.

"You busy?" he asked.

"No. Just watching a little television."

"Can I come in?"

She hesitated and then said, "Of course."

She stepped aside and opened the door to let him past.

Nixon lived in a one-bedroom apartment on the second floor of a three-floor building. The entire structure comprised six apartments and she was number four. The doorway entered a living room area that had a sofa, a television and a recliner. There were also a couple of small tables. On the wall were photos of Nixon, some of her and her family, others with soldiers and a couple of just her. In each picture, no matter the surrounding, Nixon was smiling.

To the left of the door was a small kitchen; not a kitchen really, more of a kitchenette. Past the living room was a bathroom on the left and the bedroom on the right end of a short hallway. The place was clean without being spotless and neat without being staged.

Bobby stood in the center of the living room and took in the surroundings. He stepped to the photos and studied each as if he was preparing for a test.

"Is there something you need, Sheriff?" Nixon asked hesitantly, and he turned to look at her. She stood with her arms folded across her chest.

"Am I making you uncomfortable?" he asked.

"No," she shook her head, then added, "Maybe," and then she shrugged, "a little."

"Should I go?"

"You don't have to. It's just that of all the people who might visit me, I never thought it would be you."

He turned back to the photos.

"You've got a very pretty smile," he said. "Why don't you smile more around the office?"

He watched the color rise along her neck and for the first time noticed how long her neck was.

"When I smile, I look like I'm twelve. None of the other guys would take me seriously if I didn't keep my war face on."

He grinned, "Your war face?"

"Yeah, didn't you ever see the movie, Patton?"

"No."

"Well in it, Patton tells the others he has a war face that intimidates those around him."

"I see," Bobby nodded, "and did it work?"

"Oh, sure. Patton had the best war face of them all. Anyone who has a war face patterns it after Patton."

Bobby nodded.

"Don't you have a war face, Sheriff?"

He looked at her and saw the tease in her eyes.

"No, I'm afraid I don't. I might have tried one, years ago, but I'm pretty sure none of the horses or bulls I went up against had seen Patton either. Probably wouldn't have impressed them."

She smiled.

"You should forget the war face. That one is much better."

The smile grew, "You're the boss."

She crossed closer to him, but still a professional distance apart.

"So, boss," she said, "other than to talk about my facial expressions, why are you here?"

"Have you got anything to eat?" he asked. "I've been running all day and never stopped to eat."

"Need I remind you of the kitchen you have compared to the kitchen I have?"

He studied her, "I didn't want to eat alone."

She nodded. She understood.

"Want to order in a pizza?" she suggested.

"Extra meat?"

"The only kind."

"It sounds great. I get to pay," he volunteered.

"I'll let you," she accepted.

She crossed to the sofa where her phone lay on the arm. She noticed him watching her legs as she passed and for an instant wondered if she should cover up.

What would he think if she suddenly ran into the bedroom and returned wearing a long granny sleep shirt, or even men's' bottoms? Would he take it as a sign he intimidated her, or would he think she was afraid of him? If she remained wearing what she was, would he think she was flirting? She had known for some time he liked her legs, no matter what she wore. She'd caught him looking before.

She placed the order and turned back to him.

"They said about thirty minutes."

"Okay," he said.

The silence between them was heavy and then she said, "Want to watch a movie? I have movie channels."

"What would you like to watch?" he asked.

She shrugged, "Whatever you want."

"How about Patton?" he suggested. "Teach me about war faces."

She smiled, frowned and said, "Grrrrr. Great idea. I'll order it in."

"Who are you?" he laughed, "Tony the Tiger?"

"No, I'm working on my war face. That was a growl of fierceness."

"Sorry," he said, "I missed that one."

"Of course you did. You haven't seen the movie."

"Do you have a beer, by chance?"

"They're in the fridge. Help yourself."

"Thank you. Can I bring you one?"

She hesitated and then said, "Yes, please."

The movie played and Nixon knew many of the quotes. She impressed Bobby with her inability to act like George C. Scott, but he gave her kudos for trying. They ate the pizza, and as they ate from the delivery box, where they started at each end of the sofa, they ended in the middle. Their thighs were touching. Both noticed, neither said anything and neither moved away. With the pizza gone, Bobby leaned back into the sofa and spread his arms along the top. Nixon still close, followed him, and by default, his arm was around her. She rested a hand on his chest.

"You're kind of fun to have over for dinner and a movie," she said.

"Thank you," he replied, "it's the company that brings out the best in me."

She shifted position, and her head now rested on his upper chest. He canted his head and looked at her where she raised her face to study him.

"You never told me why you stopped by," she said.

"I went to Billings today and spoke with the medical examiner who did the autopsy on our Jane Doe."

"And?" she said.

"And other than telling me what all I didn't know about what I was doing, I learned nothing. Well, that's not true. I learned all the ways she didn't die."

With the hand not around her shoulders, he reached for his beer and finished it.

"Nixon, to tell you the truth, I've had just about all this sheriffing nonsense I want. Franklin Blue wants me in uniform. The ranchers want their stolen stock found. There's a dead woman who we don't even have a name for, and the deputies and KC are angry because I ask too much or meddle too much."

She raised herself and kissed him. She continued to climb until she was across him and she held him to her with more strength than he thought she had. Earlier, he had smiled at the way she attacked the pizza; now she attacked him with the same enthusiasm.

He looked around her head to replace the beer and then wrapped her in his arms and held her to him. It felt good to be wanted by another human being. It felt good to be alive.

In time, she released him and while remaining across him offered a little space.

"Wow," he whispered as he looked at her.

"That's what you get for feeling sorry for yourself," she said.

"So was that a reward, or a punishment?" he asked.

She moved again and as space grew between them, she traced the contours of his chest over his shirt. His arm that had been on the sofa now rested on her side, and he allowed it to trail from her ribcage to her thigh.

"Do you remember high school?" she asked.

The question surprised him, so he mocked a frown and then said, "As much as anybody, I guess. Don't spend a lot of time thinking about it."

She studied him for a moment and then said, "The legend says you were the big stud in high school. It is said every guy wanted to be your friend, and every girl wanted to date you. Remember that?"

"Yeah," he hesitated, "I guess."

"Well, would it surprise you if I told you that was only partly true?"

"What do you mean?"

"I mean that for every guy who wanted to be your friend there were two that wanted to punch your lights out. For every girl who wanted to date you, there were two who couldn't stand you."

Bobby studied her face and raised his hand to trace her contours there.

"I remember I had my share of fights. I don't remember being turned down very often."

"The girls who wanted to go out with you made it obvious, Bobby. Those who didn't ignored you."

He smiled and said, "Yeah, I guess you're right. But I don't think the ratio was that high, not on the girls; maybe more like fifty-fifty."

She smiled and gave him a quick kiss, and when she pulled back, she said, "Okay, for your mental health sake, we'll say fifty-fifty."

He trailed the length of her jaw with his finger.

"I know you had a reason for bringing this up. Care to share?"

She smiled.

"My point is simple: you were the number one guy in school. Even those who didn't like you knew that. Why do you think you had all those fights? Guys were trying to knock you off your perch."

"I guess. I still don't see what it has to do with now though."

"What was your secret weapon back then, Bobby?"

"I didn't know I had one," he replied.

"Your secret was you didn't give a care who thought what about you. You did want Bobby wanted, period."

"Maybe that's why some people hated me?"

"You don't get it. Some people will like you, approve of you, and some won't. It doesn't matter what you do; some will approve, others won't."

"I guess," he said, not completely comprehending.

"Look, you've asked us to work longer hours, and you've explained why it's needed. Most of us, hell, all of us, will support you and only Stewart will complain. But, here's the deal: if you walked into the office tomorrow and told us we all got a twenty percent raise, Stewart would complain it wasn't thirty percent."

Bobby moved his hand to the side of her face and played with her hair.

"I know," she said, "it's a mess, but I wasn't expecting company."

"Nixon, it's beautiful. You're beautiful, and right now, I'm learning how smart you are."

She smiled.

"You think I'm smart?"

"Yeah, I do. Not to mention dedicated and hardworking. I've told you before; you're the best deputy there. I trust you more than anyone."

"Then trust me when I tell you this: Stop worrying about what all the others are thinking. They will either see how right you are for this job or they won't."

"I guess, but..."

"No buts, Bobby. Look, if Stewart had gotten a dead body like this, he'd get rid of it as soon as he could. He'd turn it

SNOW BLIND

over to the DOJ and forget it. If the ranchers came to him about the stolen stock, he'd pay it lip service, but he wouldn't risk getting every deputy angry by trying to put a man up there more often. He certainly wouldn't go to bat for Marcus Kettling."

"You heard about that?"

"Yeah. Jeff, KC's assistant, and I go out for lunch now and then."

"Oh," he said, "Is it serious?"

She shook her head, "No. Not yet, anyway. I think he'd like it to be more than what I do, but..." she shrugged.

"He seems like a nice guy, a little timid maybe."

"Yeah," she said, "and he's three years younger than me. I get to boss him around."

"He's going to law school, isn't he?"

"Yeah, kind of slow about it. Student loans, you know. He goes for a while, then parks his studies so he can work full time and try to pay down the debt."

"Wow," Bobby said, "he's intelligent and patient. He'd be a pretty good catch."

"Yeah, maybe," she admitted, "but he'll never be called 'Bad Jeff' though."

He hesitated, and then said, "Oh."

"Yeah," she sighed, "oh."

"I'm not the bet Jeff is," he reminded her.

"Stop it."

He stopped.

"Look, I know you're still hung up on KC, and I don't blame you. I also know KC is planning on moving away from here, and I know you never will. No matter how long you're Sheriff, you'll never leave. Your family is here. Your land is here."

"Nixon, I..."

"I told you to hush."

He hushed.

"I know you like me. Maybe not the same way as KC, but I've seen the way you look at me, and I've kissed enough guys to know when the guy likes me and he's just after a cheap thrill."

111

He looked at her but said nothing.

"The way I figure it," she continued, "I've got time. I'm not planning on walking in front of a bus tomorrow. Maybe KC will leave, maybe she'll wake up and realize what a special guy you are. Maybe you'll wake up and realize what a special girl I am. Maybe nothing will happen. I'm willing to play the hand as it is."

She wrapped her arms around him and held him close. He caressed her back, and her shoulders.

"I think I should leave," he said.

"I don't want you to. I want to hold you all night. I want you to hold me. I'm not talking about sex; I just want to be next to you."

He took her chin between his thumb and forefinger. "I would love that, but tomorrow, your neighbors will find two county cars here, and there's a chance Stewart will drive by on patrol. As much as I would like staying with you, that is not a risk I'm willing to take."

Her eyes teared, but she smiled. "That's one of the reasons you're special, Bad Bobby Trent. Not one guy in ten would care about tomorrow if he had a chance to sleep next to a warm body all night."

"When is your next RDO," he asked.

"Two days from now. The way King has done the schedule, we're on twelve-hour shifts. We have three days off, with the third one a standby day, where we're not allowed to drink any alcohol."

"Is it workable?"

"Well, we just started it, but I think it will be."

Bobby pushed into the sofa which gave him distance from her.

"That doesn't work. There's not enough of you to cover all the shifts."

She smiled, "No, it works. You need to look at the schedule since you're on it as well. You work permanent day shift, but you and King handle calls four out of the seven days."

He smiled and relaxed, pulled her close again.

"That old rascal. That's smart. That's a good use of the

manpower we have."

"Manpower?" she said.

"You know what I mean."

"Yes, I do," she grinned. "Come here."

He did as he was told and leaned into her.

CHAPTER 8

Te following morning, Bobby mechanically went about caring for the horses and the stock. His mind was on Nixon. He had not spent the night. He had stayed another hour and then, while neither wanted the night to end, she agreed to let him leave.

Creeping down the outside stairs of her apartment forced him to think back to some of his conquests in high school. They had, mostly, behaved themselves. Oh, they had kissed, and man, how that woman could kiss, and they had held each other. But, as he explained to Sadie when he fed the mare breakfast, he didn't even get to second base.

As he showered, he realized it wasn't about getting to this base or that. It was about connecting human to human. He had gone there thinking he wanted to talk about the autopsy. Not the obnoxious doctor, but what they were going to do next. This was a death that needed to be examined and investigated and he was in so far over his head, he couldn't see daylight. Unlike last summer, when Lucas helped him, he wasn't sure that help would be there. He had allowed a native to be violated.

Last night, he had been on the verge of walking. Turn the mess over to Stewart, whoever was dumb enough to take it, or whoever the county wanted. A pizza, a couple of beers, and a loving, caring woman who told him he could do this changed everything. He knew nothing more, had gained no more expertise, but a woman told him she believed in him. He smiled. It made a difference.

As he shaved and looked at himself in the mirror, for the first time in his life, Bobby tried a war face. He thought he looked silly.

"Needs work," he told the reflection.

Since being appointed, Bobby had worn the clothes he always wore. Boots, blue jeans, snap front shirt and his hat. It was the standard ranch hand cowboy fashion. No longer. He knew he would never wear the uniform; that wasn't him. If that was what they needed, they'd have to look elsewhere. But, maybe, just maybe, there was a compromise.

Wearing only his boxers, Bobby walked to the closet and rummaged through his shirts; found it. It was a solid Montana sky blue shirt. Western cut, of course, with long sleeves and pearl colored snaps up the front. He ironed it and put it on.

Returning to his closet, again he searched and found a pair of dark brown western cut slacks that were measured to hang to the level of his boot heels. He again ironed them and put them on. He looked in the mirror and liked what he saw. He brought out his pair of dress boots — the ones he wore to funerals, dances, on rare occasions, to church and almost all of his dates. They were now his work boots. He polished them and put them on. He slipped a bolo tie, one his mother liked, over his head and adjusted it so it hung right. One more trip to his closet where he picked out a sports jacket that matched the pants. Not a suit, but close, at least in that part of the country. Bobby stepped back and studied his reflection. Three more items and he'd be ready.

Number one was the Colt Python his father had carried. They had warned him against taking the "wheel gun," as it only chambered six rounds and was slow to reload. Good arguments, he admitted, but tradition demanded certain sacrifices. He unbuckled his belt and slid the high-rise pancake holster into place on his hip. The holster sat next to his kidney but canted the gun forward, so it was easy to reach. In front of the holster, he slid the speed loader carrier with the two loaders in it.

Number two required him to enter his father's room. He'd been in it several times since the elder Trent had died, but the spirit of his dad was still there. He could feel him. He had even talked to him. He didn't need the space, so why not let Dad have it for a bit longer? He had moved nothing out.

"Dad," he said, as he entered. His father always required a visitor to announce himself. "Dad, I need to burrow your duty wallet. Don't mind, do you?"

Bobby pulled open the top drawer of his father's dresser. Among the curiosities there was an old leather wallet: not a wallet for money, but identification. The crafted leather had a cutout that allowed the Lodge Pole County Sheriff's badge to fit perfectly. On the other side of the flap was the slot covered in clear plastic for the identification card. Bobby returned the badge to the cutout where it had been carried for almost three decades. The other side accepted the identification card as if it belonged there all along. After looking at the wallet, Bobby folded it over and slid it into his right rear pocket.

"Thanks, Dad," he said as he exited and closed the door behind him. In the hallway, he stopped, his hand still on the knob.

"Should I tell him about Nixon?" he asked aloud. He'd think about that.

The last item waited for him on the top shelf of his closet. Yes, he could have dressed and got ready for work without the fanfare and walking around, but this morning, the pomp and ritual, the talking to his father, his predecessor; it was all required.

From that top shelf, he pulled a box and from the box, he pulled a hat. Not just any hat; this was a Stetson Seneca model made out of 6X buffalo fur felt, the top grade felt in the world. It had a four-and-a-half-inch crown, which would make him look a little taller, and a three-and-a-half-inch brim, which would keep the sun out of his eyes, but not block his vision. The crown pinched into a gentle point, so it fit well with his face. He had bought it to wear when he returned to riding rough stock. He still planned to return to rodeo, but right now, he had all the challenges he could manage.

He stepped to the mirror next to the coat and hat rack near the front door. He put on the hat and settled it onto his head. Then he squared his shoulders and looked in the mirror. He smiled. He liked what he saw.

"Might not be a new Sheriff in town," he said to himself, "but the old one is new and improved."

He picked up his keys, another pair of speed loaders, which he would leave in the glove box of the new Unit One, and his sunglasses. Today was a bright day. As he walked to his vehicle, he telephoned Franklin Blue. He had things to talk over with the man and wanted to get on his calendar. Besides meeting with the District Attorney, Bobby had a busy day, and his first stop was at the Wapiti Medical Center.

Bobby unzipped the bag and walked around the body that lay still on the gurney. She was naked, and her clothes were in a plastic bag, sitting on top of her stomach. Bobby moved the bag aside. When she had been found, she appeared to be sleeping; frozen, but sleeping. That was no longer the case. Yes, her eyes were closed, but a nasty incision ran the length of her midsection. Dr. Carlson had needed access to her organs.

The cut was "Y" shaped and was two cuts merged into one. The incisions started just beneath each of her collarbones and joined in the center of her chest, just above the sternum. From there, it continued in a straight line, the length of her middle until it reached her navel. Bobby stared, in detached fascination, at the "C" shaped move the cut made so as not to disturb her belly button. From there, it was back online until it stopped, just above her pubic area. The wound, once held open with various clamps and tools called extenders, was now closed and held closed by a row of silver staples. Looking at the damage forced an image of a perverse one-track railroad of silver ties. He canted his head and thought zipper.

Bobby glanced at the woman's face. It retained the same level of serenity he had noticed when they first rolled her over in the snow. Dr. Carlson was correct; the dead did not seem to mind. She minded the killing part, of that he was sure. Just as sure as he was that someone had killed her. He'd bet she did not approve of that. But, like Joseph, she had crossed into something more, somewhere different and hopefully better. If she was angry at him for the torture of the autopsy they had forced her to endure, she did not show it.

"Thank you," he said, "I am sorry."

Bobby brushed aside a few strands of hair that had fallen across her face when he opened the body bag. He gently refolded the sheet she was wrapped in, as he wondered if she received comfort from it. He pulled close the body bag and zipped it shut to her chest.

"You look like the image of a papoose," he said. "Where is your mother?" he asked her. "How do I tell her what happened to you?"

The woman, of course, remained silent.

Conflicting emotions washed over him; pity, anger, guilt, rage, and then his cell phone chirped. He dug it from his pocket and looked at the screen: Medical Examiner–Billings.

"Sheriff Trent," he said into the device.

"I was wondering if you'd be on the job this morning. Thought maybe I scared you off."

"Good morning, Dr. Carlson. I'm just here looking at your handiwork."

"Ah," the doctor said. "Let me guess: you think I did a lousy job of sewing her up."

Bobby replayed the image of the zipper in his mind, and then said, "I would tell you it is the worst job I've ever seen, except that it is the first job I've ever seen."

"Well," Carlson continued, "I've seen over a thousand now in my career, and there is one thing I've learned."

"What's that?" Bobby asked.

"The dead don't care."

Bobby hesitated, and then said, "I guess you have a point there, but what about the families?"

"The families have no business seeing that side of death. I rely on the mortician to do his magic for the family. I'll bet you didn't notice the cut I made around the back of her head so I could fold the skin up and over her face."

Bobby looked at the woman's face, calm, almost serene, and said, "What cut?"

"My point. You didn't even know about it, didn't notice it. Look just above her ears and around the back of her head. You'll see a tiny cut. That's so we can pull her skin up and over her head and then remove the crown of the skull, or skull cap, and gain access to the brain."

Bobby leaned close to the face of the woman and bent and twisted trying to see the incision. It was there but was hard to see and more difficult to recognize for what it was. With one hand, he kept the phone to his ear, and Carlson continued to talk to him.

"After we remove the brain, we glue the top of the skull back on and then pull the skin back into position. We use that super glue stuff to hold it all together.

You checking that out, Sheriff?"

"Yeah," Bobby said, and his voice felt tight and uncomfortable.

"Look, on the one hand, I don't give a spit about what you think of me. On the other, I care deeply about what you think."

"How's that?" Bobby asked as he stepped away from the body.

"Well, a couple of reasons. First, I like your attitude. You remind me of me. You came over here yesterday and held me to task as best you could, seeing you know nothing. There's a possibility we will work together in the future. I want you to know, whether you believe me or not, that I will give you the best I got, one professional to another. I don't care what you think of me, but I want you to have confidence in my work."

"I see," Bobby said.

"On a personal level, I did some checking up on you. I examined your father last summer. I knew I had heard the name Trent before."

"And?" Bobby asked.

"I want to offer my condolences and tell you there was no midline incision done to your father. His cause of death was clear."

"After standing here this morning and seeing this woman, knowing that makes me feel a little better, somehow. Thank you, Doctor."

"You're welcome. One other thing, Sheriff, and the reason I called this morning."

"Okay, what's on your mind?"

"Well, after you left yesterday, I kept going over each of the findings and all the questions still out there about that young lady."

"Yeah?" Bobby said.

"Well, I wanted to tell you personally, I've changed the ruling on the Jane Doe case you got."

"What's that mean?"

"Well, instead of Sudden Death by Unknown Causes, I will rule it Sudden Death Under Suspicious Circumstances."

Bobby was confused.

"Thank you, Doctor, I guess. But I don't understand. How does that help me?"

"More than you might know. Everything concerning the government is about money. You should know that Sheriff. If you haven't yet locked horns with your county over your budget, you will."

"Doctor Carlson, I'm sorry. I have no idea what you're talking about."

The doctor chuckled and said, "Oh to be young again and naïve."

"That's not helping."

"The new ruling can open funding for the investigation from the state. If your county is like most, there's always a question of how much is something going to cost. With the new ruling, you can submit for funds from the DOJ to finance the investigation."

"I wasn't aware of that," Bobby replied.

"Of course you weren't. Aren't you glad I'm in your corner?"

Bobby chuckled, "I certainly am."

"Between you and me, Sheriff, we know someone killed that young lady. I can't put it on the report, but at the end of the day, we both know it."

"Yeah."

"Well, I'm doing all I can to help you find the bastard. If you uncover any of the information we spoke of yesterday, call me. I'll factor it into my analysis."

"Thank you, Doctor."

"Go get um, Sheriff."

Lucas looked up from his papers when Bobby walked into the office. Lucas wore the reading glasses that were sometimes a source of teasing between the two men. That wasn't the case today. Tense, a touch uncomfortable, Bobby stood, Lucas sat, and the two studied each other. The last time they met, they had parted angry.

"I could use a cup of coffee if you have any," Bobby started the conversation.

"I think I can find you a cup," Lucas replied.

"Thank you."

"Why don't you grab a seat. I'm sure you're here to discuss something."

"Again, thank you," Bobby said as he moved to the chair in front of Lucas's desk, and sat down.

As Bobby sat, Lucas leaned forward, pushed a button on a small box on his desk and spoke in Cheyenne. When he had finished, he sat back and looked at Bobby.

"I ordered two cups of coffee and told them to fix yours special."

Bobby grinned. He recognized the dry humor of his friend and blood brother.

"And would that be adding peyote or poison?" he asked.

Lucas smiled.

Things would be okay.

"I came to apologize," Bobby said, "but, I have to also say, I did the right thing with the woman."

Lucas' grin held a touch of sarcasm, "You whites always think you did the right thing when it comes to my people."

Bobby held up a hand and shook his head.

"Not today with the Indian Wars, Lucas. I need to talk to

you about a murder. This isn't red or white; this is one dead woman and who would have reason to make her that way."

Lucas leaned back in his chair, his brows pursed, and he studied the Sheriff; he then rocked forward.

"You put on a jacket and tie and suddenly get all serious. What happened to my friend Bad Bobby?"

This comment drew a tight grin from the Sheriff, "Oh, he's still here, and I'm glad you noticed the change in my attire."

A young woman, petite, Native, thick black hair to her beltline entered with a cup of coffee in each hand. Bobby didn't know her name; he had seen her previously, but never introduced to her. Rarely did she speak English, as she had a definite preference for Cheyenne. Bobby was smitten by her belts. She wore beaded belts, and she must have had fifty of the things, as Bobby saw a different one every time he saw her. Who made them? He didn't know, but the artwork was precise and beautiful. He guessed each belt told a story, but he was afraid to ask.

She offered the coffee in her left to Lucas, the cup in her right to Bobby.

"Excuse me," Bobby said, and she looked at him.

"Let me have that one, please." He nodded toward the cup offered Lucas.

After a questioning look, the woman gave the requested cup to Bobby.

"Thank you," he smiled at her. She returned the smile a bit timidly, gave the other cup to Lucas and left the office.

"Just in case you were telling me the truth about your Cheyenne gibberish."

"Gibberish?" Lucas said. "You call my language gibberish?"

"See," Bobby grinned, "I told you I'm still around."

The two sipped from their cups.

"Okay," Bobby said, "To business. First, I owe you an apology. It's almost certain the woman is Native, and you were right in describing the autopsy as butchering. What they did to her is indeed ugly."

"Do you feel what you learned was worth the insult she had to endure?"

"I know you won't like this answer, but yes, I do."

"What did you learn?"

"I learned she was killed elsewhere and transported to where the Durnings found her. I also learned she was not killed in an obvious method, so someone is trying to hide what he did."

"Any idea how she was killed?"

Bobby shook his head, "At this point, not a clue."

"Did the medical examiner rule the death a homicide?"

"No, he did not. He ruled it Sudden Death Under Suspicious Circumstances."

Lucas pursed his lips and nodded.

"What does that mean?" Bobby asked.

"It means you can get some help from the DOJ with the investigation. At least covering some of the costs."

"How come you know stuff like that, and I don't?" Bobby asked.

"Because I am the one who is by far the most intelligent," Lucas said.

Bobby grinned. Yeah, things were cool; they were friends again.

"*Viho*," Bobby used the Cheyenne term for Chief.

"I owe you and the Cheyenne people an apology. The examiner told me he is almost certain she is a Native, though he does not know what nationality. He did a DNA test, which has been sent off. It will be a few weeks before results are known."

"I see," Lucas said.

"Having said that, I don't think she is Cheyenne," Bobby said.

"Why do you think that?"

"I had the photo I gave you plastered all over Wapiti and a couple of other towns near the reservation. I know some of your people go into town occasionally, but so far, no one has offered any information. Not so much as 'I saw her walking down the road.'"

"And?" Lucas asked.

"Well, I'm wondering what to do with her, to be frank," Bobby said. "I know I have insulted your people with the autopsy; I don't want to make it worse by embalming her. On the other hand, there is little room in the Medical Center morgue. My sister, Rachel asked me when I thought she would be moved."

"You're asking me if you can bury her in the Cheyenne cemetery?"

"I'm asking you to help me show her the respect she deserves. Someone killed her, the ultimate insult. Then, as you said, she was butchered, another insult. She deserves better. I can keep her in the refrigerated unit at the Medical Center for a few more weeks, but ultimately, she will need to be laid to rest. To bury her, without family and surrounded by whites, is where she will end up if she is buried at county expense. Talk to the council on her behalf."

"I can do that," Lucas nodded.

"In the meantime," Bobby said, "I've had flyers with her photo sent to all the outlying reservations and all the newspapers in the three-state area."

"Make it four states," Lucas said, "Remember, there are native centers in the Dakotas."

Bobby nodded, "Good idea."

Lucas leaned back in his chair and rested the soul of his foot on the edge of his desk.

"So, old friend, tell me about the new look you are trying out on me."

"Just trying to be all things to all people," Bobby replied.

Lucas chuckled, "How's that working out for you?"

"Not as well as I had hoped."

"Which is usually the case," Lucas agreed.

On his way to town, Bobby used his cell phone to contact King.

"How's things today?" he asked the deputy.

"Going good, Sheriff," the man said.

"Good, do you know where Nixon is this morning?"

"Yeah she had a call, which she cleared and she's gassing up to head up north. Why?"

"Contact her and have her meet me in the office. You come

along as well."

"Will do. How long you figure?"

"Should be there in about forty minutes."

"See you then."

John Perez had not been as productive that morning as Sheriff Bobby Trent. He woke up, sober and without a hangover. An experience he had less often, but the morning still sucked. Most mornings sucked for John Perez and had done so for the last twenty years. He didn't mind the mornings so much anymore. The afternoons, evenings and nights sucked for John Perez as well. Money was scarce, and if not for the fireplace and wood he gathered, he would be cold. Food was understocked, meals infrequent, and clothes from secondhand stores.

He had risen that morning and managed to feed the few horses he had left on his place. John Perez had been a horse trainer by profession, and years ago, by most accounts, a good one. Now, not so much. Ever since the disappearance of his daughter, there wasn't much to John Perez at all.

He managed to keep a horse or two to care for and board, but his training days were over. People don't trust a horse worth thousands of dollars to a drunk. The people who still hired John did so out of pity and figured even he could feed the animals and clean up after them. He managed to make payments on his place, but not much else. The simple house needed repairs it would never receive and the barns weren't much better. His pickup had several dents and scrape marks. Each front fender was crumpled, the result of driving off the road while drunk. They'd never be fixed, either.

So, on this mid-morning winter day, John Perez sat at his kitchen table in yesterday's shirt, and watched the unknown car pull into his driveway with slightly less curiosity than interest. A lost traveler, no doubt, who would soon be on their way. When the car stopped adjacent to the house, John Perez stood, tucked in most of his shirttail, and stepped onto the wooden deck-like porch to send the traveler on down the road.

The traveler turned out to be a woman, and as she stepped out of the vehicle, John Perez recognized that she moved with balance as well as purpose. She didn't wear a hat or a cap, but her dark red hair was pulled back and away from her face. Her coat was grey suede leather with some fur on the inside that snuggled around her neck.

Not familiar with fashion, John Perez thought the jacket looked expensive. It hung to her hips and was tied around her middle with a matching belt. The effect of the hip length jacket, the belt and the snugness of the neck left no doubt, even to the blurry vision of John Perez, she was, indeed, a woman. He knew nothing of coordinated dressing, but he found the black slacks she wore enjoyable to look at. The woman rested her hand on the top of the car's still open door and he noticed her gloves matched the coat.

"Can I help you?" he asked hoarsely. John Perez rarely spoke to people.

"You can if you are Mr. John Perez." The reply was pleasant, feminine.

Her voice was mellow enough, but her diction was clipped and sounded unfamiliar.

"You ain't from around here," the man observed.

"Boston, actually," she said, and then asked again, "Are you, Mr. Perez?"

"What do you want with him? Does he owe you money?"

"Do you know Mr. Perez?"

He nodded once, "Yes, I know him."

"How can I get in touch with him? Where can I find him?"

"What do you want?"

"Mr. Perez, I want to talk to you about your daughter and the man who killed her. In a month will be the tenth anniversary of the execution of Justin Stovel and I'd like to talk to you and your wife about it. I'm a journalist, Mr. Perez."

"There's no one here who wants to talk to you, lady, not about my Kanti," he said.

"I'm sorry," the woman said, "I thought her name was

Kathy."

"Her name was Kathleen, but she liked the name Kanti, and so she was called, by family and friends."

"I see. That's a pretty name; it's different."

"She was a pretty girl, and different."

"I came a long way to talk to you about her."

"Then, you have a long way to get back. I think you should start."

John Perez turned and walked back to his house. Without a backward glance, he closed the door behind him. That was that, and he sat to finish his coffee.

"Mr. Perez, it's cold out here. Even being from the northeast, I think your Montana winter is cold. Let me in, even for just a few minutes. Let me talk to you, please. Let me talk to Mrs. Perez."

"You and I have nothing to talk about and Mrs. Perez isn't here."

John Perez turned and looked through the window in the kitchen door. The woman stood looking back at him...looking at him and tapping a gloved nail against the window. She had followed him back to the house. He turned away from her. He attempted to show her his back, ignore her, but she called to him.

"Mr. Perez," she coaxed, "I flew into Rapid City last night, from Boston. I arrived early this morning, rented this car, and drove up to see you. I've had way too much coffee, not enough sleep, and I'm starving. Spend an hour with me, to talk; we'll have breakfast, my treat. All you have to do is tell me where there's a good place to eat."

The offer for food was tempting. John Perez rarely did breakfast anymore. Early morning meals didn't mix well with hangovers. It was another one of those things lost after the death of Kanti. He hesitated and pondered her proposal. Would it be so bad to spend a little time talking? Whether or not he spoke, the girl was always in his thoughts. Eggs, over medium, toast, sausage patties; how long had it been? He realized how hungry he was.

"There's a place in Wapiti. It's as good as any and better than most. It's called Lilly's."

"Wapiti?"

He opened the door, but refused her entrance.

"Yeah, Wapiti," he nodded, "it's French for elk. Legend says the first whites in this area were French fur traders and they started the town of Wapiti. It used to be nothing more than a trading post, a place for the annual rendezvous. Now, it's our county seat."

"How far is it?"

He motioned to the west with his head, "About half an hour."

"You say they serve good food?"

"If you like breakfast, yeah. If you're into eating weird stuff, you're not going to like it."

"Hurry Mr. Perez, I'm starving."

King, Nixon, and Bobby sat in the office. The door was open in case someone walked in. Bobby had already suffered through the "looking good today," comments from King and the "Oh, lookin' hot," from Nixon. He had brought coffee from Lilly's and focused the meeting.

"I know it's only been a couple of days, but I want to get this scheduling thing settled so that we can focus on the issues at hand."

He glanced at Nixon and saw the smile she was wearing the previous night. It induced one of his own.

"Something going on here I don't know about?" King asked.

Bobby shook his head and refocused his thoughts.

"Is there anything that needs to be changed and are we getting the most coverage we can with what we have?"

"The only way we will get better coverage is to hire another deputy. We're down two from what we had a few years ago. The county won't approve a larger budget," King said. "I remember your old man going round and round with the commissioners over this thing. And they are not about to open their wallets to an interim Sheriff, no matter what his name is."

Bobby surmised, "I have nasty thoughts at night that the money is one of the reasons they offered me this position. It kicks the can of budget increase down the road."

King studied Bobby for several seconds, long enough that the Sheriff became uncomfortable.

"What is it?" he asked the older deputy.

"Just amazed at some of the things that come out of your mouth," King said. "If I didn't know better, I'd think you've been dealing with public service all your life."

"I had a man tell me that every service provided comes back to money," Bobby said. "So, we got what we got, and we'll make do."

"Bobby," King said.

"Yeah."

"Your old man promised me a position as long as I wanted and was able. He created this in-house position so I'd have something to do. What I'm trying to say is I won't hold you to your dad's promise. It makes sense to let me go and hire a man who can do the full job."

"That's kind of what I'm thinking," Bobby said. "It's too bad you have slowed down so much."

"Bobby," Nixon broke in, "Don't even go down this road. We can make this new shift idea work. It won't be forever, just until we catch the stock thieves."

King shook his head, "Don't blame Bobby. Both my knees have been replaced, so I have rebuilt wheels under me, but my ticker is not what it once was. I'm not going to be chasing down many bad guys unless they come equipped with a walker."

"That's an idea," Bobby said, "We can post you down next to the nursing home and have you set up a speed trap. Some of those old ladies build up quite a head of steam coming down that ramp and we'd add the violation money to our budget."

Both men chuckled; Nixon did not.

"The two of you, knock it off. I was there when Sheriff Trent promised King he could stay as long as he wanted and could do the job. I'm not standing by here and letting you run him off over a couple a dozen head of cattle."

"Well," Bobby said, "no matter how we cut it, we need another patrolman for the south end of the county during the day shift. I know you have built a slot for me, and I will try to staff it as best I can, but if I had been needed this morning, I would have been out of pocket. I was at the Med Center with the body of the dead woman following up on autopsy findings, and I just got back from discussing those findings with Chief Lucas Black Kettle. If I had been needed to respond to a call, I couldn't have been there."

"And," King said, "no matter how you cut it, the people of Lodge Pole deserve better."

"They do," Bobby agreed.

"Bobby," Nixon said, "if you fire Bud, go ahead and fire me as well. If you don't, I'll just quit."

"Why on earth would you do that?" Bobby asked.

"When I returned home from the Army, I applied for a job here. I'm not talking bad about your dad, but in all honesty, he wasn't too keen on hiring a female. He was doubly worried as I'd be the only female."

"So why did you get the job?"

"Because Bud talked him into it."

She glanced at the old man.

"He showed me the ropes and I was there when your dad made the promise. I mean it, Bobby, if you fire Bud, I walk."

Bobby kept his eyes on Nixon as he sipped from his coffee.

"Well, I guess it's lucky for me that I had no intention of firing him."

"What?" Nixon asked. "What was all this about?"

"Actually," Bobby said, "since we need an extra deputy, for days only, I'm thinking of putting Bud in the field."

"What?" both deputies said.

"I'm thinking of giving Bud Unit Five as his patrol car."

He looked at King, "Sorry, but I don't see you on a Snow-cat."

"Are you serious, Bobby?" King asked. "You're going to let me back on patrol?"

"Yeah, why not? As you said, you got your legs back, though at a slower speed, so why can't you work dayshift patrol and respond to report-only calls. You know, vandalism, lost pets, burglaries, that kind of stuff.”

“And the more serious stuff?” Nixon asked.

“The more serious stuff will have the north end patrolman and me. If it’s bad, we’ll have three who can work together to get it under control. We don’t have to mess up the RDO’s anymore.”

“Wait a minute,” Nixon said, “If Bud gets Unit Five, what unit will I drive? I mean that has always been the Sheriff’s unit, so am I left afoot?”

Bobby shook his head, “No, the pickup will remain Unit Five as long as you want it or until we get new vehicles.”

“So what are you going to drive?” she asked.

“I’m going to have lights mounted in the grill of my personal truck, along with a radio. My truck will be the new Unit One, and Bud in your old SUV, will be the new Unit Three.”

“And, while I love the idea of having the truck full time, you’re telling me I’m stuck in the north end forever?” Nixon did not look pleased.

“For the short term, you will be spending a lot of time up there,” Bobby nodded, “but if my plan works out, you’ll have reinforcements.”

“Who?”

“In time, Nixon, in time. As for today, you need to make your run to the north end of civilization. Bud and I can handle this end.”

Nixon stood and looked at both men, “I always knew it would take two guys to equal the work I do.”

She smiled her smile from last night, turned and headed out. A few minutes later, they heard her over the radio, reporting “10-8, in service.”

“And you talked Dad into keeping her,” Bobby said to King.

“You notice how she’s smiling a lot more this morning?”

“No,” Bobby said, “I hadn’t noticed.”

Bud grinned, “I say this with all due respect, but you’re a liar, Sheriff.”

CHAPTER 9

The two men drank coffee in silence for a few minutes and then Bobby directed the new conversation.

"I need to hear you tell me you can do what I'm asking of you, Bud. I need you to say you can handle road patrol."

King looked at his boss and replied, "I can handle road patrol."

Bobby nodded and drank from his cup.

"I'm going to talk to Franklin about getting part-time filing help over here. They've got ladies that come in to file in the courthouse. Thinking from their perspective, it would be cheaper than hiring a new deputy. I think he'll go for it."

King nodded.

"Also, you will keep your responsibilities here, overseeing the report writing and making sure everything is correct legally and following procedure. At least while you're training the new file clerk."

"Of course," Bud nodded.

"I don't expect you to patrol, per se, only respond to calls and only those you're sure you can handle. Don't hesitate to call for backup."

"I know what you expect, and I know what I can and can't do. I get what you're doing, and I'm happy, thrilled in fact, that you're letting me be a part. I told you the other day: I want to see you succeed."

"Good. Are you willing to bend a few rules?"

The old deputy's eyebrows rose, "What are you talking about, Sheriff?"

"The medical examiner called me this morning and he changed the findings on the death report. The new finding lets us request support and funding from the state DOJ to help solve the crime."

"Okay, how does that help us?"

Bobby led Bud to the large wall map the older deputy had mounted. Bobby pointed to the area where the body was found.

"Now, we know according to the autopsy that they moved the body after death."

"I'm not with you, Sheriff."

"Hear me out," Bobby said.

"Okay."

Bobby pointed to another area on the map, roughly five miles away from where the body had been.

"Somewhere in that area, there is a trail that is allowing the cattle rustlers to get the stock out unseen."

"Yeah?"

"I want you to request a drone from the state narcotics boys to fly this area to look for disturbances in the snow."

"You want a drone to fly over the forest and look for cattle tracks?"

"Yeah, that's about it. Look its winter; they're not using it to look for illegal pot farms this time of year."

"I get that, but you can't request a drone from the state on a case of a dead woman and ask them to look for cattle tracks. The request has to be for the case authorized and cattle rustling ain't allowed."

"Bud, I get that. The request will be to look for disturbances in the snow that would indicate the route taken to dispose of the body. It's not our fault cattle rustlers are also using a route for their own purposes in the same area. A flyover for one thing, will pick up images of all things, will it not?"

"You're misappropriating state funds and resources, Bobby."

"I don't see it that way. A flyover of the area in question may help us learn something more about Jane Doe. If that same flyover helps us close another investigation, how is that wrong? The way I see it, I'm trying to get double the benefit of the state's money."

"I'm not sure your old man would agree with you and I know he would never pull something like this. Do you want to think it over before I go ahead with the request?"

Bobby shook his head, "No, I wanted the flyover yesterday. Get it in the works. Not a word to anyone until we get the green light."

Bud frowned.

"Look, this is something possibly never done before. If people learn about it, they will want to talk. Somewhere, out there," Bobby swept his arm in the direction of outside, "there are a couple of thieves. They don't need to know our plans, not until we have them dead to rights. Then we'll show them pictures,"

"You want the drone to take photos?"

"Damn straight," Bobby smiled, "I watched a war movie last night and the generals were always looking at photos from observation planes. We want photos we can study."

Bobby glanced at his watch and swore.

"I'm about to be late for a meeting with the DA. Do me a favor and call him, tell him I'm on my way."

"Will do. Not that you've asked, but it would be a good idea to brief him on your drone plans."

Bobby had grabbed his coat, but now he stopped.

"You think I should tell him what we're going to do?"

"I think if anyone in this town can be trusted, Franklin Blue can and he can give you the lawyer's opinion. It would be a good idea."

"Okay, I'll brief him on that as well. Call him, okay?"

"Will do."

"Hey, one other thing: call Boss at the truck stop. Tell him I'll buy him lunch if he'll come to town and meet me at Lilly's in about an hour."

King frowned, "Is he going to have a part in this?"

"No, but I'm going to have him install the lights and the radio in my truck. He'll get it done faster than the county, and he's been the only mechanic my truck has ever allowed under her hood."

"Well, a truck has to be careful nowadays," King laughed, "I'll have him meet you."

Blue was waiting for Bobby and he rose and extended a greeting when the Sheriff entered.

Bobby accepted and the two men shook hands.

"I'm sorry I'm late," Bobby said. "I apologize. Being on time has never been a strong suit of mine, but I'm getting better at it."

"Speaking of suits," the DA said as they released their grasps and each took a chair. "You been to a dance or a funeral today?"

Bobby grinned, "Neither, but this is one of the reasons I wanted to see you."

"How so?" Franklin asked.

"Well, the truth of it is, I can't wear the uniform, not now anyway, and maybe not ever. When I put it on, all I see in the mirror is my old man. You have to remember, he wore that every day for most of my life. When I put it on, I feel like I'm trying to be him. I can't do that. Chalk it up to a father and son thing."

"I see," Blue said.

"Anyway, I got all dressed up today to offer a compromise. I know wearing the old jeans and looking like a drifting cowboy won't cut it. I apologize to you and the county for looking like a bum these past five months. You were right to call me on it a few days ago."

Franklin grinned but said nothing.

Bobby grinned in return, "You know I was pissed at you for a few days over that?"

"I figured," Franklin nodded and then shrugged, "still had to be said."

"It did, and the simple answer would be for me to wear the

uniform. But I just can't. What if I make this my uniform? What if I wear this?"

Blue took his time and checked out Bobby.

"To include the tie?" he asked, "I like your tie."

Bobby nodded, "Just as you see me now, with the exception there will be times I'll need to dress down. Right now, we got some stock stealing going on and if we ever get a lead, I'm not wearing this into the woods to drag the thieves out."

"That only makes sense," Blue agreed.

"So, with that exception, what do you think? Will the county go for this?"

"And your badge?" Blue asked as he looked over Bobby.

"In my pocket, in the wallet Dad carried."

"Nice touch," the DA grinned.

Bobby nodded.

"Well, I'm not sure if you look more like a Sheriff or more like a cattle buyer, but I like it. It upholds the standard we want to show the citizens and the tourists, and I believe it will let you be you. While we offered you this position as a show of respect for your father, I want you to know it's you we want in the office, not someone pretending to be Trent Senior."

"That's good to know," Bobby smiled.

"One other thing," Bobby added, "I need a few more of these shirts and pants. I only have one go-to-a-funeral, go-to-a-dance set. I thought a couple of different colors so that folks will know I'm changing my shirt."

Franklin Blue grinned, nodded his head and said, "That will be fine Bobby. Pick them up next time you're in Billings."

"On another matter," Bobby said. "Did KC speak to you about Marcus Kettling?"

"She did," Blue nodded.

"I know she wasn't happy at what she called, my interfering. I want you to know that wasn't my intent."

"What was your intent?"

"Nothing more than to find a solution that worked for

everybody."

"And you think this plan you've cooked up does that?"

"Yeah, I think so, unless we're just out to slam it to Kettling."

"How do you mean?"

"Kettling has a couple of misdemeanor convictions on his record. Nothing too serious, a little pot use mostly, but that was a long time ago. When he married Wendy, he settled down and became respectable, or at least as close as he can."

"You know him, I take it?"

Bobby nodded, "I do. We used to try to knock each other's heads off every few days all through school."

"Not friends then?"

"Not friends, but Wendy and I were. What happens to her and their two kids if Marcus gets sent up to Deer Lodge? "

"What if what he did was more serious? What if he would have hurt somebody, or worse yet, killed somebody?"

"That would be a different conversation, wouldn't it?"

Franklin Blue got up from his chair and walked to his window. His office was on the third floor of the courthouse, so he had a good view of downtown Wapiti. He stood for some time looking over the area. It was warmer than a few days ago, but still cold. The few people that were out were out for a reason, and while they greeted each other as they passed, they did not stop to converse. That would wait for another day. A handshake, a quick hug, and they were on their way.

"I find you a strange man, Robert Trent," the DA said, as he turned around.

Bobby shrugged, "No stranger than any other, I would think."

"No, you'd be wrong. I didn't know you when you were growing up. I moved up here while you were on the rodeo circuit. Oh, I'd heard stories of the Bad Bobby Trent, and they have told me a few of your legends. Frankly, when the commission voted to offer you the Sheriff's job, I was the only one who voted against you. I thought it was a mistake. I'm glad to say I was wrong."

Bobby smiled, "You might want to withhold that judgment

for a bit longer. There are a couple more things I need to talk to you about. One has to do with the use of manpower and the other about an investigation and getting help from the state."

Blue grinned, "No, I think we got the right man for the job."

Bobby was satisfied after the discussion with Blue; the man had been more receptive than Bobby had dared hope for. He had been much more enthusiastic than King over the use of the drone. He felt the vibration of his phone, dug in his pocket to see King had texted him, "Boss was at Lilly's."

"Heading there now," he sent back.

Lilly's was but a five-minute walk and a walk in the crisp air of a Montana mid-morning would be good for him. He inhaled deeply through his nostrils. Even in downtown Wapiti, a man could smell the ponderosa pines.

He stepped into Lilly's and was momentarily blinded by the change of light intensity. He blinked a few times and recognized the large owner coming toward him. The lunchtime crowd was present. The place was loud with overlapping conversations and laughter. He glanced toward his usual booth and saw a couple occupied it.

"Morning, Sheriff," Lilly greeted, "or at least what's left of it."

He nodded and smiled to the woman, "I've got a lunch date."

"Oh? Who's the lucky girl?"

He shook his head, "No girl, Boss from Jessie's truck stop."

Lilly nodded, "He's got a table in the back. Follow me."

She turned and led, and Bobby followed the woman in front of him. As they made their way through the crowd, Bobby glanced at the other tables and booths. Many of the customers smiled or nodded, and a few greeted him verbally. In every case, he smiled and nodded in return. As he passed his usual booth, he glanced at and recognized the occupant.

"Good morning, Sheriff," the man facing him said.

"Morning, John Perez," Bobby returned, and his eyes captured the back of the head of dark red hair.

"Have you got just a minute?" John Perez asked.

"Just barely, I'm already late for lunch."

"I'd like to introduce you to Nicole McCarren; she's a reporter from Boston."

The head of red hair turned and raised, and Bobby was greeted by the bluest eyes he had ever seen. He momentarily forgot where he was and stared at the woman. Her skin held no flaw, her lips were full and painted a shade of red to match her hair. Bobby glanced at the coffee cup she held having just finished a drink. Her lips marked the rim.

"I prefer the title journalist," she smiled at Bobby.

"I'll remember that," he said.

"Nicole," John Perez broke in, "this is Bobby Trent; he is our Sheriff."

"It's nice to meet you, Ms. McCarren," Bobby said.

"And you, Sheriff."

She offered him a hand with manicured nails each painted to match her lipstick.

"Are you really a Sheriff? Like, Wyatt Earp?"

Bobby chuckled, "Anyone around here will tell you I'm not much when it comes to history, but I believe Wyatt Earp was a Marshall."

She kept possession of his hand, kept the smile and asked, "Is there a difference?"

"Well, they appoint a Marshall, and they elect a Sheriff, at least usually. In my case, I was also appointed."

"So you are like Wyatt Earp."

Her smile was captivating and he struggled, but managed, to look back to the horse trainer, and free his hand.

"John Perez, I don't normally see you in town. How're things?"

The man shrugged, "I manage. Can't promise more than that."

"I'm going to need some help, come spring, getting the herd out. You interested?"

The man nodded his head, "Let's talk when the snow goes. I imagine I'll be available."

"Good," Bobby said and turned back to the woman. "Nice to meet you, Ms. McCarren."

"And you, Sheriff. Maybe, I'll see you again while I'm here."

"It would be a pleasure," Bobby said, as he tipped his hat, then he turned to find Boss.

Nicole McCarren watched the Sheriff walk away and cross the room. His movements made her remember dancers she had seen. On lesser men, it would be called a strut. But this man, he moved in balance with the universe. Nicole had been around men most of her adult life, journalism being dominated by them, but this one: he looked special. Unknowingly, she grinned as she remembered the hat tip. No man had ever done that to her before, other than doormen, and they didn't count, as they were paid to. It's funny, she decided, how a simple gesture from one person can cause uneasy feelings in the stomach of another. She promised herself she would get to know him better even if she had to prolong her stay. She forced herself to refocus on the man across from her.

"Mr. Perez," she started.

"You can call me John," he said.

She studied John, and reflexively, compared him to this Bobby Trent. She forced herself not to shake her head. It seemed cruelly unfair to Perez to assess the two.

"I noticed that," she said, "but why are you called John Perez?"

He smiled and said, "You may have noticed this is not a large community. Most of us have known each other all of our lives. My graduating class in high school had only thirty or so boys in it."

"I'm not following," she said.

"Out of the thirty, give or take, three of us were named John. There was John Williamson, John Sodderburg, and me, John Perez. To keep us straight, we each had a different name, Williamson became JW, Sodderburg was just called

John, and I became John Perez."

She smiled, "What happened to you all? Do you keep in touch?"

He shook his head, "No. JW was killed in a car wreck a few years after graduation, and Sodderburg moved away. I think he lives in Idaho Falls."

"So, that leaves just you."

He nodded, "Yup, just me. But I'm still, and most likely always will be, John Perez."

She motioned for Lilly and asked the woman to clear the plates, do a quick wipe of the table and bring fresh coffee. Once Lilly had finished, Nicole produced a notebook and a recorder from her handbag.

John Perez noticed and asked, "Doesn't your recorder work?"

She looked at the device as if she needed to examine it, then smiled.

"No, it works just fine, and I'll record us if you don't mind. Recording helps me be more accurate."

John Perez nodded but said nothing.

"And," she continued, "I always use a notebook. I'm kind of old school that way. Notebooks allow me to jot down questions before the meeting, you know, from my research. It helps me stay focused during the discussion and I write down spur-of-the-moment questions that come up during the interview."

"I'm still not sure I want to do this."

She nodded, "I can understand that. How about we talk, I'll take notes and record our discussion? When we're finished, if you don't approve of what I have, you can tell me no."

"And if I tell you not to use it, you won't?"

"Mr. Perez, much of the story is public record. The law allows me or any other journalist the latitude to use what is in the public domain. That means there will be a story written about your family and the man who killed your daughter."

"He didn't kill my daughter."

"He didn't...? Justen Stovel? He was convicted of killing

your daughter and executed."

John Perez shook his head.

"That's not true. They convicted Justen Stovel of kidnapping, raping and murdering two girls. He was caught shortly after killing a girl named Karen Collins, in Tacoma, Washington. Karen was fourteen when he took her. She had dark brown hair, thin to the point of looking like a boy, hadn't developed a woman's shape. He was tried and found guilty."

Nicole nodded, "Yes, I know that, but your girl..."

John Perez ignored her. He had started to tell his story and the emotional dam began to give way.

"At about the same time the Collins girl disappeared, just a few weeks before, to be exact, they also found a girl in Missoula, dead. Her name was Susan Morris; she had been sixteen. They found her dead and, according to the evidence, she had also been raped. She resembled the Collins girl, long dark hair and a boyish figure. You have to remember this was before DNA was being used, but semen and blood found on the body of the girl was linked to Stovel. Montana requested he be extradited and Washington agreed. Leading up to the Montana trial, Cynthia Anderson from Milwaukee, Linda Hill of Minneapolis, and Donna Lewis of Spokane, all of them fourteen to sixteen years old, all of them with long dark hair, and all of them slow developing were found and linked to Stovel. Later on, he confessed to the kidnapping, raping and murdering of all those girls."

Nicole scribbled notes but said little. She had been doing this long enough to know: when a subject wanted to talk, let them talk. Details, inconsistencies, and contradictions could be worked out later. It was apparent, despite his earlier apprehension, John Perez wanted to talk.

He took a break and drank some lukewarm coffee, and when he lowered his cup, Nicole refilled it from the pot Lilly had left on the table. The trainer nodded his thanks.

"As the trial in Missoula was coming to a close, Stovel realized they would convict him, I guess. He started taking credit for more killings. I never understood that, but I guess if you're going to be remembered as a serial rapist and murderer, take credit for as many as you can. I'm told Ted Bundy did the same thing."

He drank coffee.

"Anyway, he claimed credit for three more girls. Their bodies were never found, but he claimed to have killed a Cheryl Foster at roughly the same time as he killed the Anderson girl, in Milwaukee. He also bragged about killing Patricia Wright, also in Milwaukee, and a young lady named Debra White in Tacoma."

"Didn't he take credit for Kanti?" Nicole asked.

John Perez shook his head, "No, he never did."

"What do you think happened to your daughter, Mr. Perez? Surely, after all this time, you have some thoughts."

The man studied his coffee cup, which he cradled in both hands. She watched his jaw work as he fought to keep the words from coming out of his mouth. He canted his head to one side to give him more leverage to fight the words, but he lost the battle. John Perez talked about Kanti.

"You'll hear what I have to tell you, but you won't understand. I don't think it's possible to understand unless you have gone through the same torment. I think God protects parents by not allowing them to even understand the pain a missing child brings. It's worse than having a child die. With death, you know where they are, and you accept that they have gone to heaven if that is your belief. Even so, you have a marker, a gravesite where you can place flowers every Thursday if that's your thing. How do you accept, just missing, just empty, just gone?"

He slowly turned the coffee cup in his hands as it rested on the table. He refused to look at her, but focused on the cup. She wondered if he knew where he was, or if he was lost in his own tormented thoughts. She said nothing and waited him out.

"In some ways," his voice was low, "it's like a sick magic trick, you know? First, she is there, and then she is not. Now you see her, now you don't."

He glanced at her and then away.

"There was no warning on that last morning; it was like every morning before. We got up, we did our chores, grabbed breakfast, and Kanti left to fish the Yellowstone. She loved to fish. There were no long, tear-filled goodbyes. She promised to be back before lunchtime."

He raised his eyes and looked at McCarren, "But she wasn't. Lunchtime came and went, but she didn't show. We thought nothing of it. She'd been late before when the fishing was good. But then, she wasn't there by evening and then she wasn't there by dark."

He rubbed his hand across his face.

"All these emotions start getting jumbled inside you. You worry, and then you get angry. How dare she be this late? Then you get scared. What if something happened to her?"

"What did you do?" McCarren asked.

"When it was close to dark, I saddled a horse, took the strongest flashlight I had and rode the river. I called her name hundreds of times, but she never answered. Finally, I came home. I felt I had abandoned her."

"And that first night? What did you and Mrs. Perez do?"

"That first night? We sat up, waiting for our daughter and told each other things would be fine. We kept saying how smart Kanti was and how she knew to take care of herself. We told ourselves she had gone further than planned and was camping overnight until she could follow the river back home. Of course, we prayed, and then we blamed each other. Kanti and I loved to fish, and most times we fished together. I should have gone. I should have taken the day off and went with her."

Again, for the moment, he watched his cup, as if it might disappear. Then he raised his eyes to look at the journalist.

"If I had made that one decision different, Kanti would still be here. She would be here, a grown and beautiful woman. If I'd only chosen this instead of that."

How many times, in the thirty plus years of the girl being gone, had the father tortured himself with that logic, McCarren wondered.

"Mr. Perez," she said and indicated a change in the topic. He welcomed it.

"Yes?" he said.

"Earlier, you told me Stovel didn't kill your daughter. How

do you know?"

John Perez frowned and for a moment, McCarren wondered if he'd refuse to answer.

"You have to see what I'm about to tell you from my point of view."

She nodded.

"At the beginning, Kanti was not linked with the other girls at all. She was simply a girl missing and later, a girl lost in Montana. Never did anyone around here think an outsider had come into our mix and abducted her. You have to understand that as horrible as what happened to those other girls were, that was all separate from what was going on here."

McCarren nodded again.

"It was only after the trial and the conviction of Stovel that Kanti got linked to him. He claimed the other girls I mentioned, and he was keeping himself on the front pages and on the top of the news by making wild claims. He claimed he was going to write a tell all book and he wanted special meals. He did all this to keep himself relevant to the public. But it was the investigators from the DOJ that linked Kanti to Stovel. He never claimed he killed her. He never even gave an account of finding some girl on the Yellowstone. At the time, I believed the investigators. If nothing else, it offered an ending to her story; it was better than not knowing. I believed them. I wanted to believe them. I needed to."

"What changed that belief?" she asked.

"The night they executed Stovel, I was one of the witnesses. I wanted to see the man who had taken my life, be forced to lose his. All through the years of his appeals and legal wrangling, I held on to the image of him dying, of him begging for mercy, but dying just the same. I would sit for hours and play that scene out in my mind. Sometimes I imagined they asked me to push the plunger of the poison that killed him. I had elaborate fantasies where I arrived to witness the execution, but the man who was scheduled to work the apparatus couldn't make it. He was sick, and the warden needed someone to substitute. I volunteer and the warden thanks me."

She stared intently and didn't realize she had squinted her eyes until he looked at her and said, "Yeah, I know, sick."

"I'm sorry," she quickly said. "I've heard nothing like that."

He shook his head, "No offense taken. I spent so much time imagining killing Stovel, I actually killed myself."

"What? I'm not following," she said.

"I sat around, so consumed in pretending, imagining me killing that man, that I killed myself. I wasn't riding the horses they hired me to ride, so my business died. I wasn't paying attention and blamed my wife to the point our marriage died. I couldn't pay my bills and my reputation died. Finally, I crawled inside a bottle and with a little bit of luck, the job will be finished in the not-too-distant future."

They sat in silence for several seconds. McCarren hoped John Perez would continue on his own, but he did not. Finally, after making a show of checking her notes, she asked, "You haven't said how you know Stovel didn't kill your daughter."

John Perez looked at her and said, "He told me so. He told us all."

"What?"

"Yeah," John Perez repeated, "He told all of us. They strapped him down on the gurney and the needles were in his arms. Then the warden asked him if he had any last words."

The man stopped and took several deep breaths. He closed his eyes.

"Justin Stovel admitted killing the girls they convicted him of killing. He admitted killing the others they never charged him with. He admitted killing the three girls they never found and then he looked at us sitting in that cramped little room and said he did not kill Kanti Perez. He said he had no idea who she was or had been. He denied ever being in Wapiti or the surrounding area. He said he was about to meet God, and he would not go without refuting something he had never done."

Nicole McCarren sat there. She didn't know what to say, to ask. She didn't need to. John Perez wasn't finished.

"Stovel smiled at us. He bragged about having so much crap on his plate to square with God, he wasn't about to take the blame for something he didn't do."

He blinked, sipped cold coffee and finished the story.

"After that, they turned the gurney away from us, and a few minutes later, pronounced him dead."

"You obviously believed him," McCarren said.

"Why would he lie? At a time like that, why would he lie?"

"To cause more hurt, more pain, to remain relevant, as he had done for years."

John Perez shook his head, "No, not with me. I was nothing to him. I doubt he ever heard my name. Why would he pick a no-name horse trainer, who lived in nowhere middle of Montana to pull a last cry for publicity? If I was a rich businessman or a somebody, then maybe, but not me."

He looked at her and watched her expression. He knew she didn't believe him.

"Miss McCarren," he said, "Have you ever hunted deer?"

She shook her head and glanced at some of the mounted heads around the diner.

"When you hunt in mountain country, like around here, one tactic to get the deer to move is to roll rocks."

"Roll rocks?" she repeated and scowled in confusion.

"Yeah," he nodded. "When you think deer are down in a valley or a canyon, and you're above them, you choose a rock and roll it down the hill. As the rock picks up speed, it crashes into trees and brush and just keeps going. The deer spook and when they move, you might get a shot at one."

The woman shook her head, "I don't understand. What has rolling rocks got to do with this?"

He held up a hand to stop her.

"The secret to rolling rocks, if there is such a thing, is to roll a big one. A big one picks up speed and momentum. It will crash into things and keep going. It has what it takes to get all the way to the bottom of the canyon and once there, scare the deer that might be down there. A small rock never picks up speed and is stopped the first time something gets in its way."

"I still don't understand," she said.

"Why would Stovel use me if he was trying to scare up more publicity? I'm just a small rock."

She studied the man.

"I see," she said and nodded, finally understanding.

"Would you mind taking me home now? It's not like I got a lot to do, but what little I have, is there."

She nodded again.

CHAPTER 10

It was a little after eight the following morning when Nicole McCarren walked into Lilly's. Only six or seven other patrons, all local men, were there, and each one turned and watched her enter except one.

The man who didn't notice her, was sitting in the booth she and John Perez had been occupying the day previous. His head was down as he studied papers on the booth table. She allowed a small smile when she noticed his dark brown and curly hair. She imagined grabbing two hands full of the stuff and shaking him; playfully, of course.

She liked the pale green shirt he wore, with the bone-colored snaps that held it closed and secured the two pockets. The color looked good on him; better than the blue he had on the day before. She noticed the felt cowboy hat sitting on the table next to him.

Standing just inside the door, she kept her eyes on the man while she removed her grey leather coat. He never looked up, but she enjoyed the attention paid her by the others. Nicole McCarren knew she was an attractive woman. She had realized long ago, it never hurt to make an impression. Many times such an investment paid dividends. Who knew? She might wind up interviewing one of these clod hoppers and if they remembered her movements, so much the better. When it came to men, she was used to getting her way, and with that thought in mind, she waved aside the request of help from Lilly and approached Bobby Trent.

"Good morning, Sheriff," she greeted, as she extended her hand. She enjoyed watching his reactions. He lifted his head, saw it was her, flipped over the photo he was looking at, checked her out from top to bottom, or as far down as the table allowed, and then stood and took her hand.

"Good morning, Ms. McCarren. I'm having coffee."

Her smile widened. He was like a little boy caught with his hand in the cookie jar. She thought him to be adorable.

"Mind if I join you?" she asked, as she slid onto the bench across from him.

"No. Not at all," he said as he retook his seat.

"Do you mind if I have breakfast?" she asked.

"Nope."

She picked up the menu and glanced at it, and asked, "So what's good?"

The man shrugged, and she noticed his shoulders. Shoulders big enough to lift her, or hold her down, whichever she preferred.

"Just about anything, depending on your personal tastes, of course," he said.

"Personal taste?" she wondered if he read her mind. "What are you talking about?"

"Well, I'm talking about breakfast," he was slightly confused, "If you're coming in here looking for yogurt or an egg white omelet, you'll most likely be disappointed. If you're a girl who likes bacon, sausage, ham, hash browns or pancakes, you're in the right place."

Lilly arrived before the redhead could respond. The waitress refilled Bobby's cup and filled Nicole's.

"Are you having breakfast, Sweetie?" Lilly asked.

The woman nodded but kept her eyes locked onto Bobby, as she said, "Two slices of dry wheat toast with strawberry jam if you have it. If not, anything you have that I can spread will work."

Lilly nodded, "We have strawberry; I'll be right back."

McCarren noticed Bobby's smirk.

"What's that about?" she asked.

"Nothing. I just expected you to be a little harder to please."

Her smile displayed her close-to-perfect white teeth.

"Oh, I am hard to please, in things more involved than breakfast."

Their eye contact was unwavering for several seconds.

"So, Sheriff," she said, "what are you looking at?"

"Photos," he replied.

She smiled, "I guess every state is the same. Every cop must have to attend a class on how not to talk to the reporters."

Bobby returned her smile, "I wouldn't know. I haven't been trained yet."

"What?"

"It's true," he continued, "the old Sheriff quit, and nobody in town wanted the job."

She looked at him, and her eyes narrowed.

"Anyway," he shrugged, "they held a raffle, and I won, or lost, as the case may be. I have to be the Sheriff for the next two years."

"What did you do before becoming Sheriff?"

"I was the town drunk. That's why I think they rigged the whole thing."

"I don't believe you."

He shrugged and then looked up at Lilly as she delivered Nicole's breakfast.

"Lilly, settle a debate for us," he said.

"If I can."

"Was I elected Sheriff, or was I appointed."

"You were appointed, I guess." She looked at Nicole and continued, "All I know is he showed up in here one day with the badge on his shirt."

Bobby looked at the woman across from him and raised his hands in the "I told you so," sign.

Nicole looked from one to the other as if she was trying to figure out their secret code.

"Where was I just before they made me Sheriff?" Bobby

asked the waitress.

"Oh, you were in jail," Lilly said. "He got drunk out at Stetsons and got in a fight. They arrested him."

"Stetsons?" Nicole asked.

"It's a bar outside of town. They serve pretty good burgers and hot wings," Bobby said.

"Their burgers ain't as good as mine," Lilly interjected.

"And that is the truth," Bobby closed the discussion.

He sipped his coffee while Nicole doctored her toast and he watched her as she ate. She soon had jam on her fingers, and he enjoyed watching her remove it.

"So," he said, "my turn to ask you questions. I saw you talking to John Perez yesterday. What are you doing here in Wapiti?"

"Why do you want to know?"

She flashed him a practiced, mischievous, but coy smile.

His return smile was relaxed. She could see he felt he was in charge. Whatever advantage she had gained by walking up on him unannounced, he felt he had nullified.

"I'm the Sheriff. I'm supposed to ask these kinds of questions, or so they tell me."

She liked his smile. It wasn't just his mouth. It took in his entire face, and his eyes glittered with a tease. His smile was contagious in that she wanted to smile back. She wanted to talk about things other than her business. She wanted to flirt.

"It's the tenth anniversary of the execution of Justin Stovel," she finally said. "They charged him with killing Perez's daughter."

Bobby nodded, and while his smile stayed on his face, it left his eyes. She wondered if she had touched a nerve.

"Kanti Perez," he said.

"You knew her?"

"No," he shook his head, "she disappeared a couple of years before I was even born, but we were all raised with her in mind. Even years later, when kids got home late, their parents were on them, and poor Kanti was the justification."

"That must have been weird," she said.

"Justin Stovel was the local bogeyman for a couple of decades. Most of it is forgotten now, or if spoken about, done quietly."

"Why's that?"

"Mostly due to John Perez, would be my guess. He's had a hard go. Never really got over it. As I said, it all happened before my time, but I understand he idolized his daughter."

McCarren kept her eyes on him as she sipped her coffee. Even without the smile, she enjoyed his face.

"Do you think Stovel did it? Do you think he killed the Perez girl?"

Bobby shrugged, "They say he did. I don't know more than that. Never really thought about it past that."

"Do you know with his last words he denied killing the Perez girl?"

Bobby shook his head, "No, I've never heard that."

She nodded to strengthen her point, "He did. He admitted killing the others, even said he'd killed others besides but denied killing Kanti Perez. He said he had to meet his God with a clean slate."

"So that's all it takes?" Bobby interjected, not overly impressed, "Admit what you did, and deny what you will and you get to meet God with a clear conscience?"

It was Nicole's turn to shrug, "According to Justin Stovel."

"I guess," Bobby agreed.

"What if I told you Mr. Perez doesn't think Stovel did it?" she asked

"What if you did?"

"What if I told you, I agree with Mr. Perez?" she smiled like she was sharing a secret.

He shrugged, "It happened a long time ago. Why would you want to open that can of worms?"

"If I'm right, there is a murderer out there who has gotten away with killing a young girl. You find that acceptable?"

"I'm telling you nothing of the sort. I'm telling you this isn't Boston. I'm an untrained and inexperienced Sheriff who runs a five-man department with no detectives, no evidence techs or any of the other stuff you see on television. Right now, I'm being outsmarted by a bunch of cattle rustlers. Give me one reason I would want to open a thirty-five-year-old missing girl case? A case, mind you, the courts have closed."

"We could work on it together," she offered and gave him a sideways look that hinted at the fun they would have.

He studied her and kept his expression mostly neutral.

"As tempting as that may be," he said, "I don't think so."

He placed his hand on the table and rose. She covered his hand with hers. He stopped. Her hand was warm and he liked the look of her perfectly filed nails covering his rough ones. He raised his eyes to look at her.

"Please wait for just a moment," she said. "Let me explain."

With some reluctance, he sat back down and nodded, "Okay."

Her smile was one of victory.

"Okay," she said, as she leaned forward to get closer and conspire. She did not remove her hand but acted as if she had forgotten where she placed it. Bobby hadn't. He knew where it was and he didn't mind.

"Just hear me out."

Bobby nodded.

"All the girls, including Kanti, were between the ages of fourteen and sixteen. All of them had long dark brown or black hair and all of them were boyish in build."

She stopped to sip coffee, using her other hand, and Bobby waited for her to continue.

"Here's the big mystery: Besides Stovel denying the killing, Kanti Perez was the only girl taken from an isolated location."

"What do you mean?" Bobby asked.

"Every girl, except Kanti, even those they never found, were taken from a public place. A few were at bus stops, some were at shopping malls, and two were walking down the street and seen getting into a vehicle."

"Where was Kanti taken from?" Bobby asked.

"According to her parents, she left the house to go fishing."

Bobby nodded.

"Does that make sense to you? What fifteen-year-old girl likes to fish?"

"More than you might think," he said.

"That makes no sense to me," was her reply, and Bobby smiled.

"You've never fished the Yellowstone."

"Okay, even if she was fishing, why would Stovel be out in the woods? That wasn't where he hunted for victims. He'd be as lost in the woods as I would."

Bobby shrugged, "I don't know. You'd have to read the old files, I guess. Maybe talk to any detectives still around who worked the case."

"Well, my editor sent me out here to interview people about the execution, but I think there is a much larger story to tell. I'm going to find it."

"You think you have a suspect?"

She nodded, "I do."

"Who would that be?"

"I think there is a chance John Perez murdered her and blamed it on Stovel."

The heat of her hand paled when compared to the cold that came over him. His eyes grew hard and any interest he may have had in her faded. He stood, and as he did, his hand slid out from under Nicole's. He reached for his hat and coat and then turned to face her.

"You know much more about this case than I ever hope to. You do what you think you must. I have work to do," and he motioned to the pile of turned over photos.

"Oh, yeah," her tone was snide, "you have to find somebody's cow."

"What?" he asked, "Don't the cops in Boston investigate grand larceny?"

"I'm asking you to investigate a murder."

He shook his head, "No, you're asking me to stir up old wounds that are just now healing. You're looking for a book deal, or a made-for-TV crime drama. I'll have no part in that."

"You haven't even looked at the evidence or the information."

"I don't have to," he said. "There is one part of this you don't know. You don't know John Perez. I never knew his daughter, but I grew up watching that man suffer. When I went to Sunday School, and they taught the story of Job, I pictured John Perez. I don't think I was the only one."

"Bobby, I…" she started to explain.

"It's Sheriff Trent," he cut her off. "I know John Perez, and if you harass him or make wild accusations like that around here, you'll be on your way back to Boston."

She lifted her chin in defiance.

"You going to run me out of town," and then added, "Sheriff?"

"On a rail," he said.

He gathered his photos, and as he did, Nicole caught sight of one. It was a woman's hand laying on snow. Then, it was gone, and once he had finished, he too was gone. Later, after she'd finished her toast, and forced herself to calm down, she also left. It was then she learned he had covered her tab with Lilly. She smiled.

Two days later, Boss showed up at the Sheriff's Office driving Bobby's truck.

"Here you go," he called as he walked into the office, and tossed the keys for Bobby to catch.

"You should have coffee for any man who delivers a freshly-modified Sheriff's cruiser," Boss hinted.

Bobby looked at King, "Do we have coffee on?"

"Of course we do," the older Deputy said, and he had a vague sound of hurt feelings in his voice.

"Great," Bobby said, "can you get Boss and I a cup, please. I need to talk to him for a minute."

Then he turned to Boss.

"I know you did a good job, but show me how to work what you've done."

"Grab your jacket and follow me."

The old biker walked Bobby through the location of the control knobs and where the toggle switches were located.

"I could tell you about the secret code you all cops use, but I ain't supposed to know that."

Bobby smiled, "Don't feel bad. I don't know it either."

When they had finished, Bobby invited Boss in for coffee. Once they were alone in his office, he closed the door.

"Boss, you're one of the few people left here that might remember the Kanti Perez mess. You mind if I ask you about that?"

The mechanic who, in his younger days, had ridden with a motorcycle club, and still wore his hair long and braided, shook his head. "I don't mind. But I'm not the one I would ask about that. Why don't you talk to John Perez?"

"I intend to, Boss, but I want to get some background about it first. No crime was reported, just a missing girl alert so there is nothing in the files except old newspaper accounts of searches attempted and who showed up to help."

Boss nodded, "Yeah, I remember that. Even the club showed up, and we busted our humps walking through the woods looking for her. Back then, there was a lot of hard feelings between bikers and cowboys. Around here, for that summer, all that was put aside."

"You ever hear any talk about who might have taken her?"

"Sure, it seemed for a while that everyone knew who took her, at least according to them. Some said it was bikers, of course. Some said Indians, and others said some guy riding the BNSF Railway. Everybody had their own favorite bad guy."

"I'm not accusing you, or any of your brothers, but why do you think that was?"

Boss shrugged, "Back then, I would have been in my twenties. Kanti Perez was a little sweetheart. She was just a girl, of course, but she liked to flirt and hang out. She was building a rep as a horsewoman, and she used to like to ride on our bikes. She was a bit of a daredevil. Some of the guys, myself included, gave her rides up and down the town. It made her feel special, a little rebellious, maybe. Since most of us thought old John Perez was stuck on himself, it was payback, of sorts."

"Payback for what?"

Boss shrugged, "Nothing really, just the animosity of the time between cowboys and bikers."

"And some thought the Cheyenne took her?"

"Yeah," Boss said, "Of course. The talk was some Indian came off the Rez and dragged her off. She was half Cheyenne, you know?"

"No," Bobby shook his head, "I didn't know."

"Yeah, her mother was full-blooded. I think she still lives out there. Her and John Perez split after all the fuss was over."

"Anyone else?"

Boss thought for some time and then shook his head.

"I don't know what you're after Bobby. There was a lot of names mentioned. They thought any stranger in town to be the guy for a while. They thought crews working in the hay fields could be hiding the girl; you name it."

"I see," Bobby said.

"I don't think you do."

Bobby said nothing and just looked at the man.

"They never found her, Bobby. So for all the people who thought this guy or that guy did her harm, there were just as many who figured the girl ran off."

"You think she could have done that?"

The old biker shrugged, "Who's to say? John Perez was a straight by-the-rules sort of guy back then. I mean, you could count on him if you made an agreement, but he was not an easy father. It's not like this is first-hand knowledge, but the way I heard it was the girl had to earn her hours on the horse. If she didn't get good grades, if she stayed out too late, if she got caught smoking a cigarette, she couldn't ride. I won't say he was a mean father, I don't think he ever beat her, or anything like that, but who knows? He was strict."

"You ever see him or hear of him losing his temper with the girl?"

Boss canted his head and looked hard at Bobby.

"Where's this going?" he asked.

"It's not going anywhere. I've just heard things about back then, and I'm trying to sort through them."

Boss shook his head, "Anyone who would even think John Perez could hurt that girl doesn't know Crisco from motor oil. He loved that girl, maybe even idolized her a little. John Perez grew up wearing hand-me-down shoes. His folks had nothing. Rhonda, born and grew up on the reservation, was probably worse off. If it was possible to have less than John, Rhonda managed it. When they married, they were two of the hardest working folks you ever saw. I mean John Perez was working twenty hours a day. He was working full time for the BNSF back then. Then he'd come home and ride horses trying to build his training business."

Bobby stood and looked out the window.

"I remember my old man saying much the same about him."

"I'm not going to sugarcoat it; John Perez was strict with the girl. Was he too strict? Who am I to say? Times were different back then, but he was strict because he wanted her to learn that there's no easy way in this life; not for most of us. He wanted her to understand that sacrifices had been made for her to have the quality of horse she was riding."

Boss stood and held out a hand. Bobby took it.

"Sheriff, I'm sorry if I got a little long winded about all that. Anybody who would think John Perez could hurt his daughter is crazy. He couldn't have done it by accident either. He wasn't that kind of guy."

"Thanks, Boss, and thanks for the work on the truck, too."

As the two men walked the length of the Sheriff's Office arranging payment for the work, King called to Bobby.

"Hey Sheriff, have you got a minute?"

"What's up?"

"The pilot of the drone is here and he wants to go over some maps and do some planning with you."

"Outstanding," Bobby said.

He turned back to the old biker and shook hands.

"Thanks again, Boss," he said.

"Go take care of business," Boss grinned. "I know you're new at this sheriff stuff Bobby, but weed don't grow in the snow. You'll be looking for hot houses."

Bobby grinned, "I'll keep that in mind."

CHAPTER 11

The meeting went well, and without telling the pilot about the missing cattle, Bobby directed the area the drone was to fly.

"I want photos, lots of photos. I want to basically search while still in my office just looking at photos."

The pilot, ex-Air Force, who had flown drones in Afghanistan, reminded Bobby that he knew his job.

"I'm sure you do," Bobby admitted, and then added, "Does this drone have the ability to track the heat given off by bodies?"

The pilot snorted, "Of course it does. It's called thermal vision, but why would you need that? The body is dead, and besides, it isn't even there anymore."

"Tell you what," Bobby said, "you fly the drone, and get me the images I want. That is your job. I will take the images and, if you're any good at your job, use them to solve a case. Does that sound doable?"

The pilot nodded, "Yes, of course it's doable."

"Great," Bobby smiled and slapped the man on his shoulder. He turned to King, "If he can get it done, I want the first flight tonight and every night after that for a week. Have the images sent to our computer."

King nodded.

"I'm going to drive up as far as I can and then take the Arctic Cat up to see the area where we found the body. Have Nixon meet me at my place in about an hour."

"Will do," Bud said.

He didn't have much time, but he wanted to drive over and see John Perez. He was glad to see the man's truck in the yard when he pulled up next to his house and stopped.

As he climbed out of the vehicle, John Perez stepped out of the house, and onto the three foot high deck that served as his porch. As a boy, Bobby sat, swinging his legs on that deck while John Perez and his father talked horses.

"How's it going, Sheriff?"

Bobby looked at the man who appeared older than he was. He needed a shave and his hair trimmed. He was back where he had started, wearing second-hand clothes. The disappearance of his daughter had destroyed not one, but three lives.

"John Perez," Bobby said and leaned against the grill of his truck.

"Until the other day, I hadn't seen you in some time. Feeling a little guilty about not stopping by."

John Perez shrugged, "The road runs both ways, Bobby. I ain't been over in your direction since before your father passed. You make the adjustment okay?"

Bobby exaggerated his shrug so that it could be seen across the distance between them.

"You know how it is; you do as best you can."

"Ain't that the truth of it, Bobby," the man nodded, "ain't that the truth."

"Got a couple of things to ask you, if you don't mind," Bobby said.

"Why would I mind?"

"No reason, just feel a little awkward."

"It's about Kanti, and that lady reporter from Boston, isn't it?"

"That's part of it. If she pesters you, I want you to let me know."

"Why would she pester me? What happened, happened. She can't bring her back. She can't change things."

"No, she can't. But still, everyone has their own take. If she bothers you, let me know."

"Thanks, will do. You said a couple of things. You got something else on your mind?"

"Yeah, I've gotta take a ride up along the Yellowstone to see where that body was found. Just want to check out the area and see if it's changed at all."

"Sounds like you're taking this Sheriff thing serious. Some folks around here didn't think you would."

"To tell you the truth, John Perez, I wasn't sure if I would."

"You're doing a good job I think, Bobby."

"Thanks. Could I get you to drive over to my place and feed the stock and the horses for me? Leaving this late in the day, it'll be way past dark before I get back."

"Sure, Bobby, be a pleasure."

"Thanks, John Perez."

Montana spring was still more of a hint than a promise. True, some snow had melted, but the white stuff wasn't quite ready to give way to warmer weather. Bobby walked the perimeter of the area he had marked with the fiberglass poles. He had used black electrician's tape to mark the depth of the snow. Now, that tape was almost a foot above the covering. In some areas along the Yellowstone, there had been more melting, but the area where the body had been found was deep enough in the valley and tucked up next to the side of the slope, that it remained in the shade a good part of the day. Still, a foot of melt was a foot closer to the ground, in anyone's book.

"What were you doing out here?" Bobby asked the space where the body had been.

In his mind's eye, he could still see her there; body face down, in a straight line, arms outstretched, almost as if she was on a cross. Was some religious cult involved with this?

"I don't think so," Bobby answered the silent question aloud.

Bobby had driven the snowmobile close to the enclosed

space, turned it ninety degrees and stopped. Now, he sat on the bench seat sidewise, reached in the pocket at the rear, and pulled out the manila packet of photos — the same images he had studied in Lilly's before being interrupted by McCarren. The same photos he studied every night at his house. The same pictures he was convinced would give him something, anything, to act on, and the same photos that had, so far, eluded him.

The photos sat in his lap, and one at a time, he lifted the top one to study it. They were in no particular order. He had hurriedly shuffled them together when McCarren had shown up and had not rearranged them. For the first two weeks he had the images, he kept them in various orders. The first was the order in which Fisher took them. "And you did a good job too, Chunk," he said to the trees.

That order failed. He spread them across his new tile kitchen floor and arranged them by the body area captured in the image. All headshots went first, followed by the right arm, the left arm, and so forth. Bringing order to chaos, he had called it, and he studied them in that manner until Lilly's. McCarren surprised him and he shuffled the pictures together without thinking. He acted only by impulse.

"Maybe that was the breakthrough I been looking for," he said. "Maybe the confusion created by a gorgeous woman will ignite my brain."

His mind wandered through the images ignited by that woman and those memories were strengthened by the remembered scent of her perfume. Part of it wishful thinking, all of it fantasy. He shook his head and laughed.

"Get a grip, Bobby," he chastised himself. "You're not some high school kid stuck on the girl from his homeroom class. She's just another woman."

He stopped, shook his head a second time.

"No, that ain't true. She's pretty much in a league by herself."

He nodded, grimaced, and admitted that was true.

"Still, it's not like I haven't known beautiful women before. KC takes a backseat to nobody. Nixon is tops in the girl next door category. Still, KC doesn't seem to want any part of me, and Nixon can't happen. Not as long as I'm sheriff and she's deputy."

He continued to look at the photos, flipping and holding them up, one at a time, aligning the reproduction with the area before him. Mentally fighting the images of McCarren, he stopped working through the photos and just thought of the woman. Thought of those hauntingly blue eyes, the lips in deep red. He imagined the smudges of those lips over his body the way they had left marks on the coffee cup.

"Would it be the end of the world if McCarren and I had some fun? It's not like she will be out here forever. How long will it take her to research and write this story? According to Boss, there's nothing to tell."

He flipped another photo; the image of the woman, on her back, just after they had rolled her over. He studied that face.

"Why did he or they or them or whoever the hell it was, kill you?"

He turned his face away and glared at the snow bunched in the snowmobile's tread. He followed the tracks made by his machine.

"How'd they get you there?" he asked. "How the hell did they drop you off and not leave a sign or a mark or a track?"

He jerked his head up and looked at the scene before him. Across the way, just outside the tape, sat the big, grey, alpha male, wolf. His yellow-green eyes bore into Bobby.

The eyes of the animal locked onto the human and Bobby felt the photos slip from his fingers. His mind silently screamed for him to pick them up; protect them from the snow. His hands refused to reach for them; his fingers failed to close. The gaze of the wolf held him captive.

He felt no fear. The wolf had visited before. Not counting the other night, it had been some time, and a part of him admitted he had missed the animal's silent and unexplained appearances. Was it real and not just a mental aberration? KC had seen it, so it wasn't just imagined, but Lucas had claimed it was a spirit animal. The combination of all wolves who had lived and those who would yet live. Bobby didn't know what it was other than what he saw: a large, grey, male wolf.

"What do you want?" Bobby asked and then realized only his brain was speaking. His lips hadn't moved.

"Why are you here?" Again, the silent, but anxious communication.

The wolf sat still, but the snow next to it moved.

First, the particles shifted but remained on the surface of the covering blanket of white powder. It was as if they were grains of salt that bounced when a tabletop was slapped. They moved like that. Then, the movements became organized. The bits of snow swirled in the same direction and the same speed. They moved faster, and it looked to Bobby as if the bits of snow danced. First, a waltz, orderly, in unison. The movements were silent, but the energy increased. They again, increased speed and frenzy as if the dancers' changed styles and tempo.

Bobby felt dizzy and realized he had forgotten to breathe. He filled his lungs, and the intake of cold air caused him to shiver. The movement of the snow increased again. The dancing particles now lifted from the surface and formed a funnel. Like a tornado, they raised themselves higher, and soon they towered over the wolf. The tornado grew and engulfed the animal, but it seemed not to notice the white whirlwind, nor care. He kept his eyes locked on Bobby, his fur as flat as if the day itself was calm and breathless. He was in the depth of the swirling storm but remained untouched.

The base of the column of swirling, spinning, churning snow grew larger, and Bobby felt the bite of the little frozen crystals as they attacked his face. He squinted and tucked his chin for protection, but remained determined to keep the wolf in his sight. He failed. He could see nothing but the storm of swirling, stinging, freezing snow. It pelted against any exposed skin and seemed to invade his core. He momentarily feared he was blind, snow-blind. He imagined his body frozen, next to where the woman had been found. He lowered his head even more and covered his face with his hands.

Then, it was over. As quickly as it appeared, the storm was gone. Bobby blinked the sting from his eyes, and slowly his sight returned. He felt his core regenerate heat, and the shivering stopped. He looked across the taped-off area, afraid the wolf would be gone. It wasn't. The alpha sat as unconcerned as he had before the storm. A man, a large man, stood beside him.

"*Homa'e Nestoohe?*" Bobby whispered. "Whistling Beaver?"

The man said nothing. He studied Bobby and slowly turned his head as he examined the wilds of Montana.

"Joseph?" Bobby whispered again.

The big man smiled and raised a hand in greeting.

"*Hania Chevey O,*" he said.

Bobby remembered the term, "Spirit Warrior," returned the smile, returned the wave, and blinked back tears of joy.

Joseph stood tall and strong, dressed in ceremonial clothingthe beadwork exquisite, the feathers unruffled. His eyes were bright, intense, his expression firm. In life, he had been a large man, towering over others, both in build and attitude. It was clear death had not changed him.

"Why you carry many troubles, my brother," he said, and Bobby heard the same deep, rich baritone voice that had previously called him *Kachada*, meaning white man.

"I have missed you, friend," Bobby said.

"Why? I have been with you always."

"I haven't seen you."

"Nor do you see the wind, but it is there."

Bobby nodded. Joseph was right.

"I ask again, why many troubles?"

"I have assumed the role of my father, and I fear I cannot walk that tall."

Bobby heard the man, or was it a spirit, snort a short and condescending laugh.

"Of course you can't. No man can walk in another man's boots. He must wear his own."

"And if I don't know how to walk? Whom do I follow?"

"The wolf, Bobby," the visitor said. "Look to the wolf, let him lead you, and follow the snow. Snow can blind you, but it can also help you see."

Bobby turned the comment over in his head. He looked at the snow encircled by the yellow tape. He looked back at

Joseph.

"I don't understand. What do you mean?"

Joseph smiled and again raised his hand.

"*N'ese'ne,*" the man said. "Friend."

Bobby too raised his hand, and Joseph was gone.

As if he had been nothing more than the reflection on a frozen lake, the man was gone. Only the wolf remained. Throughout the visit, the vision, the occurrence, whatever the hell it was, the wolf had continued to stare, silent and still, at Bobby. Now, those eyes blinked, and the wolf turned slowly and unafraid and trotted soundlessly into the trees.

Bobby watched the wolf until he disappeared into the wilderness. He allowed his eyes to trail back to the taped area, and then he noticed it. Neither Joseph nor the wolf left tracks. The snow where they had been, was undisturbed.

"What the...?" Bewilderment stopped Bobby from completing the sentence.

"How can that...?" he spoke aloud and hesitated for an answer that didn't come.

Bobby remembered the words.

"Look to the wolf, follow the snow. The snow will help you see."

What did it mean? He struggled to understand. Was he snow blind? Hallucinating? Or was the wolf showing him the way?

The ride home, both on the Arctic Cat, and later in the pickup, took the last of his reserves. He was glad he had talked John Perez into taking care of the stock for the afternoon feeding. He was sure the man had done as he said, so when he finally pulled into his yard, he went straight to the house.

It was cold as the temperature had dropped once the sun had settled behind the Rockies. His muscles were tense, and his head ached. He stripped off his clothes as he walked across the living room and into the bathroom where the shower awaited him. By the time he had covered the distance, he was naked.

The hot water ran over him and he stretched his shoulders, rotated his head, and arched his back. He stood with his eyes closed, and held on to the image of Joseph in his mind, while the water pelted his face. The man was dead. Yet, he stood before him. Joseph had been murdered months ago, yet today, they talked. What did he mean?

"Look to the wolf; follow the snow. Snow can help you see."

Bobby flexed his neck and let the water run down one side and then the other.

"Joseph, what did you mean? Why can't you just tell me?"

Thinking of the man brought a smile, even with all the frustration. It was like Joseph, the trickster. The three-hundred-pound imp. He could almost see the big man smile and hear his laugh. He missed his friend.

The cold throughout the day left his injured hand aching. Now, as he held it under the stream of water, he flexed the fingers. He opened and closed the hand as he studied it. He watched it move and wondered if it would ever be strong enough again, durable enough to ride bucking horses.

He wrapped a large towel around his middle and stepped out of the shower. He looked in the mirror and decided not to shave until the following morning. Entering his bedroom, he pulled on a pair of boxers and followed them with jeans.

Hungry, but too tired to prepare a meal, he padded barefoot into the kitchen. He rummaged through the fridge looking for something, anything, that could be consumed without thought. He found nothing. Joseph accompanied him no matter what room he entered. The big man's presence was palpable. He wasn't there, of course, but like the name on the tip of your tongue, or the tune stuck in your head with the unremembered title, he was there. Joseph was what you saw from the corner of your eye, but didn't focus on, or the missed line of dialogue in a movie. He was there, but he wasn't.

Bobby stepped into the living room and stood before the large window that looked out over the Montana prairie. As a boy, he had sat and looked out this same window. He had grown to manhood, and while other items seemed to get smaller, Montana never did. The horse that was too tall for him to ride one summer, he easily climbed aboard the next. The center pole in the fence that was too high to step over, yet too low to crawl under, he now used as a ladder. The bale of hay too heavy to lift, now wasn't.

It seemed every part of his life had changed their size to suit him as he grew — all of them, except Montana. Montana grew right along with him. There was always one more town to see. One more rodeo to compete in. One more stream to fish, one more ridgeling to crest and one more trail to explore. He would never outgrow Montana. Montana teased a man to be more, grow taller, reach higher, become better. That magic was just one of the reasons he loved her.

Somewhere, in the darkness before him, a highway ran. It lay in the snow-covered countryside and was usually invisible this time of night. On the best of nights, there was only the moon to illuminate it. From time to time, vehicle lights marked the way of the road as they passed his place, a quarter of a mile off that highway. As he stood and looked into the night, Bobby experienced an uncomfortable feeling, a feeling he rarely felt; he felt lonely.

Bobby was used to being alone, comfortable in fact. A nod of "hello," a smile of "how you doing?" was all he needed or expected. He never discussed politics. The weather was what he saw, and the only sport in his life was rodeo. He rarely considered tomorrow, or next week, in any other manner than to make sure he had entry fee money. Some people called him calloused or uncaring, some said he was conceited and stuck up, but it didn't matter. Bobby Trent was a man focused on now; he hated to think. He had lived as the discarded leaf that rides the currents of the mountain stream. He went where the ebb and flow of his life took him. Often he bragged that his concentration lasted no longer than eight seconds; the time required to ride a bull or a bronc.

Now, all he did was think. Who was the dead woman? Where was the missing stock? What prompted the appearance of Joseph? And what did the message mean? Thinking was uncomfortable, and it was work. Bobby had lived for the laughter. Now, the laughing had stopped. Unanswered questions left him stale as if he entered a room behind a long-closed door. The sensation of dry dusty air tickled his nostrils. A long-closed door? Where did that image come from? Was the answer behind a door? What door? Where was the door? And what room did it lead to?

Bobby cursed. Look to the wolf, he had been told. Follow the snow and let it help him see. The words of Joseph and now the image of a long closed room. "All this shit is giving me a headache," he muttered.

He stood looking into the deep black void before him and compared it to the vacuum he felt. A pair of lights turned off the highway and onto the snow-packed lane that led to his place. There was a bump in his heart rate, and a small smile grew on his face. Who would come to see him this time of night? Maybe it was KC. Maybe she wanted to be friends again. Perhaps she wanted to be more, again. The smile grew.

Nixon, the lights had to be Nixon. She would surprise him with pizza and beer. They would replay the night they had shared. Was this her RDO? He couldn't remember. He hoped so. She could stay the night. He'd start a fire in the fireplace. Turn out all the lights, and eat pizza and drink beer on the floor, wrapped in blankets. The smile caused his head to nod, and a sense of excitement, of expectation grew in his stomach.

Maybe it was the reporter, Nicole McCarren. All business, seriously intelligent, seriously sexy. A woman with many layers and he'd unwrap them all. He imagined her eyes in the fireplace light; intoxicating, hypnotizing. She'd be the aggressor; he'd let her. She'd want to claim him as a climber does a mountain. Bobby chuckled.

"Okay by me."

The lights stopped and then backed up. Once on the highway, they headed back the way they came — just a stranger turning around. Montana could be lonely.

Nixon looked up from the report sheets she was reading when she heard the main door to the Sheriff's Office open. The cold air rushed the room and beckoned her. Nixon stood and stepped to the counter that separated the entry from the work desks. She had never seen the redheaded woman before then, but her spotless complexion that did not have to contend with freckles was an indication they would not be friends.

"May I help you," Nixon asked and grew impatient as the woman took the time to remove her winter coat before answering. She displayed the sweater that had been hidden. The sweater was full, with graceful, yet body-hugging curves. Nixon decided the two of them would not be sharing girl talk.

Nixon glanced at the woman's hair. Deep red, it showed the strength of her character and yet seemed to reflect the sunlight.

"Is Sheriff Trent in?" the woman asked. Her voice deep for a woman, husky, maybe lustful, made Nixon cringe.

"No," the Deputy said, "He'll not be back until this afternoon. Can I help you?"

The woman gave Nixon a quick and superficial inspection, forced a small smile and said, "No, I don't think so."

The woman's superior attitude and dismissive expression made it too easy; Nixon didn't like her.

"Would you be a sweetheart and give the Sheriff a message from me?"

"I will."

"Would you tell him I would like to meet with him and continue our discussion from the other morning? I'm in the Crest Mountain Hotel, room 214."

"I'll be sure to tell him," Nixon said in a professional tone, through clenched teeth.

The redhead turned to leave, bundling her coat under her arm.

"Who should I tell him the message is from?" Nixon managed.

The woman turned back, slightly lowered her head and

looked at Nixon through the perfectly shaped and brushed eyelashes.

"Oh, he'll know. He'll remember. Don't forget, now; room 214."

The redhead turned, opened the door and left, leaving only the essence of her perfume.

Nixon was sure; she hated the woman.

"Lucas, I saw Joseph."

The Chief of the Tribal Police of the Cheyenne nation looked up and saw Bobby standing in his doorway.

"I might have to start locking that if you don't start checking in with my assistant."

"Did you hear me? I saw Joseph."

Lucas stood and walked around his desk so he could lean on the front edge. He motioned with his head for Bobby to enter.

"Yes, I heard you. I simply needed time to process what you had said. You must admit, it is a most uncommon way to start a conversation. Hi, I saw a dead guy."

Bobby sat on the visitor's chair.

"I never said hi," he reminded Lucas.

The Chief thought, and then nodded, "And so you did not."

For several seconds the two friends sat in silence and then Lucas said, "Are you going to tell me about it? You come to my office and make such an announcement and then tell me nothing. Must I drag it from you?"

"No, *Viho*. You need not drag it from me."

Bobby explained how he was convinced someone had murdered the dead woman. He had no idea how they had killed her, and he had no idea who, but someone had killed her.

"Bobby," Lucas said, "I'd be a liar if I told you I didn't wonder the same thing. It makes no sense, this woman, whoever she is, out in the middle of nowhere. Yeah, she was dressed in a coat and snow pants, but she wasn't dressed for cross-country hiking. I too think she was killed, but there is nothing to prove that, or even suggest that."

"The wolf told me, Lucas," Bobby said.

Again, there was silence, and when Lucas spoke, there was respect in his voice.

"When was this?"

"The night before I went out to the body. Durnings told us about it too late to fetch it the same day, and the old man had left Samuel to guard the site, so Chunk and I went out early the following morning. The night before, after I was all packed and ready to go, the wolf visited me. He told me."

"What did he say?"

"Damn it, Lucas, it's not like he says anything. I stare at him, he stares at me and thoughts form in my head. He holds me with his eyes. I stood in the doorway of my house and nearly froze before he let me close the door."

"What were you doing in the doorway?"

"Watching Nixon get back to the highway."

"She visited you?" Lucas asked and raised his eyebrows.

"Yes, Lucas. Nixon visited me, and we talked about the department and the deputies, and the body, and we had a bowl of chili. Then, I watched her drive back to the highway, to make sure she didn't get stuck."

"You should grade that driveway of yours."

"I came to that same conclusion right before the wolf appeared."

"And he told you she had been murdered."

"No, it's not like that. But he shared with me her death had been painful, almost torturous."

"She didn't appear to be tortured."

"I know."

Lucas circled his desk and sat down in his chair. He sat heavily like a man burdened with too much.

"Now, today you saw Joseph?" he asked.

"I did, and he told me to look to the wolf and follow the snow. The snow would help me see."

"Look to the wolf and follow the snow?" Lucas repeated.

Bobby nodded, "And the snow will help me see."

"What the hell does that mean?" Lucas asked.

"I don't have a clue," Bobby said. "I was hoping you could tell me."

"Why would I know? Lucas shook his head. "I'm not the one talking to spirits. I swear Bobby; I don't know if I'm envious of you or relieved it's not me going through what you are."

Bobby nodded, "I know. I've come to take you up on your offer."

"What offer is that?"

"To do a vision quest. I think a vision quest might help me understand. Will you talk to the shaman for me?"

Lucas studied his friend for several seconds. He had repeatedly asked Bobby to consider the quest. After the death of his father, Bobby had reported seeing and conversing with spirits of the wild and those who lived previously. Bobby had just as repeatedly refused Lucas's suggestions and in fact, laughed at what he called, "hocus pocus or witchy woo."

"I'll not approach the shaman if you are not sure you will go through with the quest," Viho said.

"I'm sure I will go through with it. I have to go through with it," Bobby said.

"Why?" Lucas asked.

"Why?" Bobby repeated, "Why what?"

"Why do you feel you must go through with this?"

"It's the only way I will figure out who killed the woman. I have nothing I can use to get close to those who killed her. Joseph knows the answers. He can tell me, but he will only talk if I reach out to him."

"You think you can communicate with Joseph during the quest?"

"Lucas, I don't know. I'll tell you what I know. I know I can't send Joseph an email. I know I can't call him up. I can't meet him at Stetsons for a beer. Maybe, maybe, I can reach him during a vision quest. Maybe he will agree to help me and not just torment me with bits of information that frankly, don't mean squat to me."

Lucas smiled at his friend's frustration.

"It's not funny *Viho*," Bobby complained. "Joseph didn't know me long. You should have told him I'm kind of dense. I don't do well with puzzles."

Lucas continued to smile.

"Stop it, damn you," Bobby said.

Lucas shook his head.

"Bobby, I've known you all my life. We grew up together, and yet, to see you now, it's like I never knew the real you. If I didn't know better, I'd think you cared for more people than yourself. It's a good look on you, cowboy."

Bobby stood up.

"Don't get all soft on me, Lucas. You know me just fine. This has nothing to do with caring about people. This has to do with me winning. I've always wanted to win. You know that. It doesn't matter what the game was, bull riding, or a three-legged race; I want to win. Same thing here, I'm the law and the law should win. nothing more."

"If you say so, white man," Lucas shrugged.

"You'll talk to the shaman for me?"

"I will," Lucas promised.

CHAPTER 12

Nixon felt angry. She was disappointed in her lack of professionalism. If nothing else, Nixon considered herself a professional law enforcement officer. Part of her job was to brief her supervisor, the Sheriff. She had not.

She had gone far enough to write the message on a stick-up style note and press it onto the frosted window in the door of Bobby's private office. She recognized her passive-aggressive nature when she stuck it in the exact center of the Lodge Pole County Sheriff circular logo. Then she tore it down. Pure anger motivated her to crumple the note and throw it away. She refused to help that out-of-state redheaded hussy meet up with Bobby.

While she prepared for patrol, she silently debated the pros and cons of giving the information to King, so he could deliver the message. She couldn't decide if she won or lost the debate, but in the end, she didn't share the info with Bud.

Now, as she patrolled the county and listened to the official radio, hoping for a call, the debate had deteriorated into chastisement. No calls were coming in. The people of the county were behaving. Nixon had nothing more to occupy her time than try to convince herself she was not petty.

"Unit five, Dispatch."

The radio worked. Nixon keyed the mic attached to her

"Dispatch, this is Unit Five. Go ahead," she said.

"Dori," the dispatcher said, "See the woman at Castle's Convenience Store. Unknown complaint."

Nixon frowned. "No idea what is wrong?" she asked.

"Unknown, Dori. The woman requested to see you."

"10-4, dispatch, but be advised I am thirty minutes away. Unit three is in the house. Per the Sheriff, Bud has been cleared to handle report calls and he is closer."

"Negative Unit Five; the caller requested you."

"She wants a female officer?" Nixon wondered if rape or some type of battery by a man was involved.

"Again, negative Unit Five, she requested you, personally."

"She used my name?"

"Not exactly Unit Five."

"What did she say, dispatch, exactly?"

There was a hesitation and then the voice came back.

"She said, and I quote, wants to meet with the pretty blonde deputy with all the freckles."

Nixon stewed the entire trip to Castle's, and the simmer turned to a boil when she pulled into the lot, behind the sedan...the one with the redheaded woman leaning against the left front fender, smoking a cigarette.

Nixon reported on scene and got out of her unit.

"You shouldn't smoke around gasoline pumps," she greeted the woman in a cold but professional voice.

Those haunting blue eyes went from Nixon to the pump, to the cigarette, and back to Nixon.

"You're right, of course. How silly of me. I was so deep in thought I forgot where I was."

Nixon pointed to the store, "There's a small coffee bar in there. Want to go in?"

"That would be nice," the redhead said, and Nixon led the way. McCarren dropped the butt in the ashtray canister at the door.

The coffee bar was little more than what Nixon claimed it to be. It was a twenty-four-inch-wide shelf, constructed of three-quarter inch plywood, and attached to the side of the wall. Most of the wall was windowed, which made it a touch more pleasant. The customer filled his or her cup from pump-handled cravats, added whatever extras, then took the mix to the register to pay. They could then retrace their steps to the shelf and sit on one of the dozen stools.

If the customer was not a coffee drinker, he or she could choose a soda from one of the cooling units along the back wall. Also, refrigerated, pre-made sandwiches could be selected and heated in the microwave. Small bags of various chips, plastic wrapped cookies, or a wedge of pie, could all be added to make the experience a complete meal. All of this was served on paper plates with plastic utensils.

The two women purchased their coffees, crossed back to the counter, and selected stools. Their perch along the window gave them a view of the gas island and the two doors leading to the restrooms. There was also a stack of forgotten tires next to the corner of the building.

"You called for a deputy?" Nixon said.

"I called for you," the woman clarified.

"How can I help you?" Nixon said, silently reminding herself to be professional.

The redhead started to speak and then stopped. She sipped her coffee through the small hole in the plastic cap and smiled.

"Let's start over," McCarren said. "I feel like we got off on the wrong foot."

Nixon said nothing but rewarded the idea with a nod of her head. The redhead removed her gloves and offered a hand to Nixon. The deputy couldn't help but notice the painted, manicured and close-to-perfect nails. She felt a stab of embarrassment when she accepted the woman's hand.

"My name is Nicole McCarren," the woman said, "I'm a writer from Boston."

"I'm Doreen Nixon, most people around here call me Dori, which I hate, though a few now call me Nixon, which I don't mind."

Nixon rotated McCarren's hand to admire the nails.

"That's very nice," she said with reluctant admiration.

"Thank you." McCarren accepted the compliment and then smiled, "I have a standing appointment at a place back home. If I were ever to move from Boston, I'd have to move them, as well. I can't go three weeks without my mani-pedi."

Nixon nodded, and with a sarcastic grin said, "We also have a place here. The guy who runs it does women's nails every other Tuesday."

Nicole scowled, "And what does he do the other days?"

"He's a farrier."

"A what?"

"A farrier, a guy who puts shoes on horses."

Again, Nicole scowled and then she smiled, "Oh, I get it, you're making fun of me."

"Not really," Nixon said, "you may have heard a touch of envy in my statement."

She offered her hand, and while the nails were clean, they were also clipped short and could have been mistaken for a boy's hand.

Nicole took the hand, rotated it, and examined the nails with a critical eye. With all the certainty in the world she said, "You could use a little help. Where would the closest nail salon be located?"

"Billings," Nixon shrugged, "though a few girls do manicures out of their homes around here."

"That won't do," Nicole decreed. "I have an immediate vision of the woman stopping every thirty seconds to chase down a trouble-making child who should be in pre-school. We will find a day and go to Billings."

Nixon smiled. It was nice to have a girlfriend and just as quickly suppressed the friendly response.

"I'm sorry," she said, as she took her hand back. "You called and wanted an officer."

Nicole dismissively waved her hand. "I wanted to meet up with you. I don't need an officer; I need you. I wanted girl talk. You know?"

"What will I know?" Nixon couldn't hide her confusion.

"What I want to know is if your boss is on the market or if some cowgirl has already branded him or lassoed him, or whatever you say out here."

"We don't say lassoed; the word is roped. We rope them."

Nicole grinned, "I like that. You rope them and that's just

one step away from tying them down."

"I guess," Nixon said, fighting to keep from showing how uncomfortable she was.

"So is he?"

"Is he what? Oh, is he spoken for?"

"Yeah, is he spoken for?"

Nixon blushed.

"See?" Nicole said. "You do know. I can tell by your face."

"I'm sorry," Nixon stammered. "I don't know, and if I did, I'm not sure I should be telling strangers about his personal life."

Nicole was momentarily puzzled and then caught on.

"Oh, like if I knew he was sweet on someone I could kidnap them or something and force him to do my will?"

"Yeah, kind of like that," Nixon said.

"This is nothing like that. If I get the chance to have your Sheriff do my will, it won't be through holding someone else hostage, believe me. I want to know if the coast is clear for me to make a play for him."

Nixon chuckled, "That would be a waste of your time."

"He's taken?"

"No, I wouldn't say that, though there are a few girls who would certainly try to change that, if he was agreeable."

"Ohhh, you mean he's gay."

Nixon blushed again, "No, no, that's not what I mean. He's not gay."

"Oh, good. For a second I thought we'd lost him to the other team."

Nixon was shaking her head, "You don't have to worry about that."

"Then why would it be a waste of my time?"

"Because you're from Boston and Bobby will never leave Montana."

"Why? I don't understand what...," Nicole was confused.

"Oh you think," she waved her finger as if pointing to the coast and back, and then she laughed.

"Nixon, you are such a sweetheart. I don't want to adopt the man. I don't want to take him home; I want to take him in bed."

For the third time, Nixon blushed.

"Your Sheriff is a Greek statue," Nicole concluded, "and he could give me many fond memories of Montana if he's as good as he looks."

As she parked Unit Five outside the Sheriff's Office, Nixon imagined Bobby as the model for Michelangelo while the master carved his work, David. True, Michelangelo wasn't Greek, but his work was impeccable, just like Bobby. Why didn't she tell Nicole to keep her east coast man-stealing hands to herself? Why didn't she tell the woman to leave Bobby alone? She should have claimed him as her own. That would have been a lie, she silently admitted, but it would have been satisfying to say aloud what she secretly wished.

She walked in through the back door, past the "male & Nixon" shower sign hanging on the bathroom door. She stopped and looked at the sign that had been put in place by the former Sheriff Trent. He had hired her after her return from service in the Army. She placed a hand on the sign and thought of the man with melancholy fondness.

She passed the lockers mounted along the hallway. The lockers were assigned and gave the officers a place to hang jackets, extra gear and a change of uniform. She passed the evidence room and the holding cell with the iron front and doorway. This was where she first got to know Bobby. She tased him, arrested him, and babysat him for nearly ten days — he on one side of the bars, her on the other.

"Welcome back," King said, as he looked up from paperwork.

Nixon said, "I was only gone a few hours."

King smiled, "Yes, I know. I was counting the minutes until we were reunited. Each minute of separation from you is like an eternity."

Nixon arched an eyebrow, "You know you're silly, don't you?"

King grinned, "Of course, but welcoming you back like that sounds better than just grunting you a hello. Besides, I can't talk like that to Stewart, or Chunk."

"Or Bobby, for that matter," Nixon giggled.

"Indeed, nor the Sheriff," King agreed. "See how special you are?"

Nixon kissed the man on his balding forehead.

"Thank you," she said.

"And thank you," King replied.

Nixon turned and looked to the far end of the office space.

"Is he in there?" she motioned with her head to the only office with a door, the Sheriff's office.

"Yeah, he's been in there over two hours."

"Bet he's looking at those pictures, again," Nixon said.

"Again? You mean still. I've never known a man to review photos of a death scene the way he is those."

Nixon stepped to where she could see inside the office, and just as the old deputy had said, Bobby was there, head down, forehead resting on one fist, looking at photos scattered on his desk.

Nixon superimposed the Sheriff as The Thinker, a statue she knew nothing about, except that it was a nude man, hunched over in concentration.

"You better get your head together, lady," she chastised herself as she crossed the space to talk to her boss.

She knocked on the doorjamb, and called, "Bobby?"

Bobby glanced up at her without changing positions, then back to the photos on his desk.

"You're in your boots, right?" he asked.

"Ah, yeah, I always wear boots on duty." She thought the question strange.

"But you got your running shoes in your locker, right?"

"Yeah, though I don't think I will run today. What's going on?"

He looked up at her.

"Grab your lace-up shoes, take off your boots and put the others on."

He returned his attention to the photos, then back at her.

"Please," he amended.

When she returned wearing the running shoes, he examined them carefully, then he called to King and asked if he was wearing lace-up shoes or not.

"Lace ups," the old man answered back.

Bobby asked the man to come to the office where he could examine his shoes as well.

After he'd finished, Bobby sat back in his chair and said, "thanks," to both deputies.

"Ya want to tell us what's going on, boss?" King asked.

"People tie their shoestrings the same," Bobby said.

"Yeah?" Nixon said, confused.

"What I mean is, we're taught to tie our shoes exactly the same. Our mothers or someone teaches us by saying something like left over right, make a bow, right over left."

"I think we all know that," Nixon interjected with impatience, "We're not, or at least, I'm not following where you're going with this."

Bobby picked up a photo of the dead woman. It was taken at the location where she had been found, and her feet were together.

"Look at this," Bobby said. "On her right shoe, the laces are right over left, make a bow, left over right. That's how a square knot and a bow knot is tied."

Nixon looked at the photo, and King looked over her shoulder.

"I'm sorry Bobby, I still can't see it," she said.

"Me neither," King agreed.

"Her right shoe is tied right over left, then left over right. But her left shoe is left over right then, right over left. Both are square knots, but they're exact opposites of each other."

Nixon studied the photo for several seconds and then nodded.

"You're right," Nixon said, and King agreed.

"What's that mean?" Nixon asked.

Bobby shrugged, "I guess it could mean a lot of things, but what jumps to my mind is that someone else tied the left shoe. See? If I was to tie your shoe, Nixon, it would be tied from the bottom side of your foot and not the top. I would be opposite of you."

Nixon smiled. She liked it when Bobby was figuring things out. Even if he was wrong. Known as a class clown through high school, accepted as not the strongest thinker, it felt good to see him concentrating.

"What does this mean for the girl?" she asked him.

Again, Bobby shrugged, "You're going to think I'm nuts, but I think she was poisoned."

"Poisoned? With what?" King questioned with growing interest.

Nixon's eyes were round, "Her shoes are tied differently, and you decide she is poisoned? That's a stretch, Bobby."

"Hear me out, before you certify me for the looney bin," Bobby said.

Both deputies looked at him with uncertain expressions.

"The cause of death is listed as sudden death. Carlson told me that phrase is the same as heart attack. So the woman died of a heart attack," Bobby said, and both King and Nixon nodded. "But she has no sign of heart disease or heart problems of any kind," Bobby continued. "No evidence of smoking, alcohol or drug abuse. Doesn't that raise the question if her lifestyle didn't cause the heart failure, something else had to?"

"You're thinking this because her shoes are tied differently?" Bud asked. "Wouldn't the poison be identified by the toxicology screen?"

"Maybe not," Bobby said. "If potassium chloride was the agent used, it may have been missed. Potassium is a mineral and is naturally in the body, so the presence of it wouldn't normally raise a red flag."

"Yeah," Nixon shook her head, "but it's poison. You can't just pick it up at the corner drug store."

Bobby nodded, but added, "It depends. Potassium chloride is also used as medication. It's prescribed for several medical conditions."

Nixon looked at King, and then back to Bobby.

"Okay," she said, "If, you're just trying to impress us, it has worked on me. I'm impressed."

King nodded, but Bobby waved off the jesting.

"Look, I've been reading up on this, and an overdose of potassium chloride can cause a person to have a heart attack. It's the drug the state uses in a lethal injection execution."

"Executions?" Nixon asked.

"Yeah," Bobby said. "The state uses a mix of three drugs, one given right after the other. First, they inject sodium thiopental that causes the criminal to become unconsciousness. Second, pancuronium bromide, which causes the muscles to quit working and the respiratory system to shut down. Then potassium chloride causes cardiac arrest, also known as a heart attack, sometimes called sudden death, just like what Dr. Carlson wrote on the autopsy report."

"You don't think her heart attack was just accidental? That it just happened?" Nixon asked.

Bobby shook his head. "Of course it could all be that simple, but I think someone murdered her," he answered.

"Why?"

"I don't know. I don't know why. I won't know why until I figure out who."

"And you figured all this out based on her shoes not being tied the same?" King interjected.

"Along with the findings of the autopsy," Bobby defended.

"Don't get tense," the old deputy said, "I believe you. I'm on your side."

"I'm headed over to the Medical Center; I want to look at our Jane Doe's feet. Her left foot to be precise."

"Why her left?" Nixon asked.

Bobby slid his chair back from his desk.

"Nixon, come sit on my desk facing me," he directed, and the deputy did. On the desk, Nixon's feet were off the floor, and Bobby took her left foot by the ankle and lifted it to set it on his right leg. He patted the foot.

"If I'm going to do anything to this woman's feet, give her a rubdown, paint her nails, inject her with potassium chloride, more often than not, I'm going to pick her left foot first."

"Why?" Nixon asked.

"Because most of us are right-handed, and we tend to favor our dominant side. My right side lines up with your left."

He patted her foot and released her leg. He smiled at her, and said, "Thank you for the prop. It helped with my show and tell demonstration."

"My legs are yours anytime you want them," Nixon said, and immediately blushed. "That's not what I meant. I said that wrong."

Bobby and King laughed, which helped her not at all.

"Doctor Carlson, this is Bobby Trent, do you have just a moment?"

"Bobby Trent?" The voice was uncertain, then, "Oh, Sheriff Trent, yes, but only a moment. I have patients waiting, and you know how the dead hate to wait."

"Ah, yeah, I guess," Bobby stammered, and then admitted, "No, doctor, I don't have a clue."

The medical examiner laughed hard enough to choke, then calmed down.

"Only a little morgue humor. How can I help you, Sheriff?"

"Strange you say that," Bobby replied, "as I'm standing in the Lodge Pole morgue as we speak."

"Strange place to hang out."

"I've got an idea, and I'd like your opinion and a little guidance."

"I'm flattered," Carlson replied.

Bobby explained the shoelaces and what he had seen in the photo. He reminded the doctor of their conversation about poisons and their effect on the body. Through it all, Carlson only commented with, "ah huh" from time to time.

"Now," Bobby concluded, "if my theory holds any water, there should be marks of some kind on the left foot. You know? From where they injected the potassium chloride."

"The great saphenous vein," Carlson interrupted, "it descends the ridge of the foot, then bends along where the toes attach. That would be the place to look."

"Great, what am I looking for?"

"That's the tough part, Sheriff. At most, you will see a pinprick. There will be no bruising, and after this amount of time, there will not be any blood showing. There might not have been blood at all, and if there was, the killers would have wiped it away. You can double check my report, but I don't recall any spotting of blood on her feet."

"So I might be wasting my time?" Bobby suggested.

"I didn't say that," Carlson said. "You've learned, or at least drawn some strong conclusions to those questions we had when Ms. Doe was here. I think you have something, but if the killers used a small-gauge needle, there might not be any sign."

"Wouldn't a smaller needle taken them longer to get enough poison into her to kill her?"

"Sure, they'd have to reduce the flow into her or risk blowing the vein which would certainly leave signs."

"That means she would have taken longer to die? Right?" Bobby asked.

"It does indeed, and if she was conscious, the death would be more painful. Heart attacks are not pleasant experiences."

Bobby shook his head, "I'm going to catch these bastards. You know that doc?"

Carlson chuckled, "A few weeks ago if you had made that claim, I would have chalked it up to male bravado. Now, if I knew who they were, I'd call and tell them to start worrying."

"Thanks, Dr. Carlson," Bobby said.

"Anytime, Sheriff."

"Aren't you gonna wish me good luck?" Bobby asked.

"Crimes aren't solved by luck, Sheriff," the man said, "skills and hard work are what you need."

"And if I have no skills?" Bobby chuckled, self-deprecating.

"More hard work. You're a cowboy, Sheriff; you're not afraid of hard work."

"Never have been," Bobby admitted.

"But, if you think it will help you; good luck, Sheriff."

Bobby leaned close to the foot of the woman and tried to see any mark or blemish that may have been caused by a sharp object. He knew Carlson had inspected the body, but just because another fisherman is ahead of you, doesn't mean you won't catch in the same spot later. His father had told him that, and the recollection brought a smile. He looked around and located the magnifying lens, the one with the lights to illuminate the area searched. As he moved it into position, his cell phone vibrated in his pocket. Only after fighting down the urge to ignore it, did he answer the page.

"Sheriff Trent," he said, not looking at the caller ID, as he was still working with the lens.

"Bobby, it's Nixon."

"Yes?" he said.

"We got an email saying they have sent the first batch of photos from the drone overflight. Thought you ought to know."

"Thanks," he said. "That is good news. Give me something to do tonight."

"You going to stay late and go through them?"

"I need to run by the place first, but, yeah, I thought I would. We need to find those cattle."

"Want company?" she asked.

"You offering to stay and go through them with me?"

"No, I was asking for King. Of course, I was offering."

"Oh yeah, you're the one who said I could use her legs anytime I wanted."

"Please never remind me of that again."

He laughed and then said, "Deal."

"So, you want me to stay?" she asked again.

"Hey, Nixon," Bobby said.

"Yeah?"

"Would you mind staying and going through pictures from a drone with me tonight? It won't be as fun as watching a movie together, but still..."

"And no beer," she said.

"Right, no beer."

"I thought you'd never ask," she said.

"Okay, I'll run by my place, take care of the critters, and I'll stop by and grab burgers and sodas? That sound okay?"

"Sounds great. See you in about an hour."

"You can start going through them if you want."

She snorted a laugh, "Yeah, we only got about five hundred of the things to go through."

"And," Bobby added, "hopefully one or two will show us where the cattle are."

While Bobby was trying to sort out shoelaces, and Nixon was trying to corral lost stock, Nicole McCarren was earning her pay as well. She contacted John Perez and asked the man to meet her for lunch.

"I'd like to go over some topics we touched on the other day," she told him.

"What more is there to tell?" John Perez asked her. "Kanti is gone, and Stovel is dead. According to the state, justice has been served. The story is over."

"You said Stovel didn't kill her. If that is true, there is a killer out there who has never been held accountable. Maybe the story will generate enough interest to reopen the investigation."

"Miss McCarren, I'm no big city guy. We both know you got more schooling than I do. I'm a simple man, but I know you don't give a hoot about me or my daughter. You're looking for a story that will make you more than you are. I'm not interested. Please, don't call me again."

"Wait, wait, Mr. Perez, why the cold shoulder? What have I done? I thought we got along fine when we met before."

"Yeah," John Perez said, "we did. Then you got along fine with several others in the county. Do you think we don't talk to each other? I heard about your speculating."

"Speculating?" McCarren asked.

"Yeah, you think I might have something to do with my daughter's disappearance."

"Who told you that?" she demanded, while she silently cursed the Sheriff.

"Doesn't matter. Any man who could do something like that to his own daughter is less than human, in my book. If you think that of me, we have nothing more to talk about."

Feeling more than a little desperate, McCarren said, "Wait, Mr. Perez."

"No, Miss McCarren, you wait. I loved my daughter, and

she was a teenager, so that means we had our squabbles. She wanted to stay out later than I thought she should. She wanted to date boys I didn't like; all the stuff that most girls that age go through, I guess. Kanti had two loves in life; she loved riding horses, that was number one, and she loved to fly fish. She was a good fisherman. She was patient and she was delicate when fighting the fish. One morning, Kanti left with her rod and her gear and never came home. That's the story."

"That must have been horrible," she said, trying to keep him talking.

"Unless you have lost a child, you do not understand. My wife Rhonda and I went through several evolutions over Kanti being gone. First, we prayed and asked others to do the same. We put up flyers, offered rewards, begged for information, and conducted and took part in searches along the Yellowstone."

"I see," she said, gently.

"No, you don't. When none of that brought our daughter home, Rhonda and I took turns blaming each other. One day, I'd blame Rhonda for allowing our daughter to wear makeup. The next day, she'd blame me for not letting her stay out later. It went back and forth, each of us blaming and accusing the other. Never, did we think something bad had happened to her. Never did we think she was dead. Not until the two investigators from Missoula came to talk to us. Until then, we hung on to the idea she'd come home."

"Was that the first time you heard the name Stovel?" she asked.

"I've already told you, I'm done. You're no more interested in the truth now than they were then. You have magazines to sell. That's all I am to you, a bigger profit. You want to write I killed my daughter, have at it, lady, but show me the respect not to ask me to provide the story. You can make that up all on your own."

"Please, Mr. Perez..."

The call was terminated.

As Bobby drove to his ranch to care for the stock, he placed a call to Lucas.

"Hey, *Viho*," he said when the man answered.

"Bobby, what's up?"

Bobby explained what he had figured out with the shoes and how disappointed he was not able to find any significant sign of an injection. He ended his recounting by telling Lucas he had no idea where to go or what to do at the point he was at.

"So, you come to your red brother for guidance and wisdom?"

"This will cost me, won't it?" Bobby said.

"I think that is a fair assessment."

"Okay, so how much have I got to grovel?"

"You can't ask me a question like that this soon. I have to think about that."

"Okay, do you have any suggestions on what to do next?"

"I do."

Bobby waited, but Lucas said nothing more.

"Well?" Bobby asked.

"Well, what?"

"Are you going to tell me your suggestion?"

"Yeah. You still have the woman's clothes, right?"

"Of course."

"Get her socks and come see me."

"What?"

"You heard me. Bring her socks over so that I can examine them."

"Don't make fun of me, Lucas," Bobby warned. "That doesn't go well; you know that."

"Yes, I know, and I'm not. I'm going to show you some magic, hopefully. Just bring the socks."

"First thing tomorrow?"

"Sounds great."

"Lucas?"

"Yeah, Bobby?"

"You're not jerking me around are you?"

Lucas laughed and then disconnected the call.

CHAPTER 13

Bobby balanced carrying the bag of burgers and fries, as well as the soda carrier, into the station. It was awkward getting through the doors, but he made it.

"Could have used help," he said when he spotted Nixon sitting at the one computer the department owned.

Startled, she turned and looked at him as if she had not expected him.

"What's up?" he asked her.

"I know where the cattle are and who's taking them."

He canted his head as if he had not heard correctly.

"We haven't gone through the photos," he said.

"You'll never see it in the photos," she said, "but you asked for thermal images, and it shows up like they drove the cattle down the main street."

"You said you know who?"

She nodded, and she looked uncomfortable.

"Yeah, the ranchers were right," she said.

"How so?" he asked.

"It is the bunch in the City of David," she answered.

Bobby nodded, set the bags of food on the desk, and pulled over a chair so he could sit beside her.

"Can you cycle through and show the images you are talking about?"

Nixon nodded, and the two of them sat shoulder to shoulder, thighs touching, for the next two hours reviewing both natural light images and thermal images. Nixon was right. The cattle and the sheep were all penned in a small box canyon.

Bobby pointed to what appeared to be a small plume of steam in a couple of the images.

"If I were a betting man, I'd tell you those are natural hot springs. I've heard there are several in those hills."

Nixon nodded, "I'd agree. Do you think the hot springs have anything to do with the gold strike they have up there?"

"Gold strike? What gold strike?" Bobby had never heard of a gold strike.

She looked at him as if he'd just woken up.

"That's how they make their money," she said. "I've heard it all my life. We all know old man Phillips went up there and claimed the land as separate from the United States based on political beliefs. But the truth is, he wants no one to know about the gold. I mean, look what happened in South Dakota when gold was found? Would you want that mess here?"

"I see," Bobby said, though his tone was doubtful.

"By claiming he is separate from the U.S. he doesn't have to file a claim and he's able to keep the secret," Nixon explained.

Bobby arched his eyebrows, "You have to admit that if it's true, there is a certain amount of sense to it."

"I was told that by my folks when I was in school."

"Really?" he said, "Once again, I wasn't paying attention. I never even heard about it."

She smiled at him. "You had your mind on other things back then, but my folks told me always to stay away from that place. They said Phillips would do whatever it took to keep the gold a secret."

Bobby sipped what was left in his soda cup, and the straw made a slurping sound. He studied Nixon for several seconds as he hunted with the far end of the straw for the last of the soda.

"You know," he said, "just having gold isn't enough. Somewhere they have to separate the gold from the ore and more so, they've got to have a place to trade it. You can't just walk into any old store and say, 'use my shiny rock for payment."

"No, I guess not," Nixon said, "he probably uses some guy in Canada for that."

Bobby nodded thoughtfully, "I guess he could."

Bobby clicked through a dozen images on the computer. Some were natural light. Most were thermal. Several, he sent to the printer. After a few minutes, he looked at Nixon.

"I'm not saying your folks were wrong, and maybe back then they were right, but it seems a man with money in the ground and a super need for secrecy has got to be out of his mind to steal cattle in the middle of winter. I mean, we know moving cattle leave a trail."

She nodded and smiled, "I guess great minds do think alike. I was wondering the same thing."

Bobby rose from the chair, walked to the printer, and retrieved the images and carried them to the desk. Instead of sitting back in the chair, he leaned on the front edge of the desktop. Nixon joined him, and once again, they were close together and side by side. He flexed his shoulder enough to rub against her upper arm.

"This could get to be a habit if we're not careful," he said.

She canted her head as if searching for a sound.

"I hear no one complaining," she replied.

Bobby sighed, "I wonder if we would, should this get out."

"People are small-minded," she sighed. "Trust me, we'd hear about it."

She rested her head on his shoulder, and the two of them stood in silence for several minutes. Both imagined their own version of how things could be if they were free to pursue their attraction.

After a time, Bobby patted her on her nearest thigh, "You are one heck of a temptation Doreen Nixon."

She raised her head and looked at him. She smiled, "And is that a bad thing?"

"Not at all," he smiled back.

From her eyes, he lowered his gaze to her lips and resisted

the desire to kiss her. She could sense the want in him, and stayed close, not shying away. He returned his gaze to her eyes, and said, "We need to focus on work."

She gave him a nod and a small, disappointed smile.

He shuffled the images and worked through them. As he brought one copy to the top of the bunch in his hand, he looked at the map King had mounted on the wall. Between the two of them, they identified where the two, map and image, matched up.

"Tomorrow," he said, "I've got to see Lucas on the Rez. He wants me to bring the socks the woman was wearing. He said he has some magic potion that can show if there is blood on them."

Nixon giggled.

"What's so funny?" he wanted to know.

"Not funny, just cute," she said. "It's not a magic potion; it's luminol. It's been around for a while now."

"What does it do?" Bobby asked.

"You can spray it on surfaces and then turn out the lights. If blood is present, it gives off a blue light."

"What? You're joking."

"Don't you watch crime shows on television?"

"No."

She laughed, "I don't know what the compounds are, but luminol counteracts with the iron in the hemoglobin causing the blood to give off a blue light."

"This might be interesting," he said.

"Why the socks?" she asked.

"I think a syringe was used to inject the poison in her foot. I can't find any puncture marks, but Lucas said we might find a spot of blood on the sock."

"I'd like to see that," she said, "mind if I tag along?"

"Not at all," he said. "I'm planning on driving up to City of David after meeting with Lucas, so come prepared for that."

"You're really going to go see them?" she asked.

"Of course I'm going to go see them. I don't see how we even have a choice now. The cattle are on land they claim as theirs. I want to hear how they got there."

"I already told you, I'm coming with on that trip."

He nodded.

"Get the socks out of evidence for me and be at my place first thing tomorrow."

"How early is that?" she asked.

"If you can make it by 0600 hours, I'll cook breakfast."

"Deal."

The moon was full and the cover of snow across Montana made the reflection all the brighter. As he drove along the highway headed home, he smiled as he remembered the winter nights of his youth. Several times, when taking girls home from dates, he'd turn the lights of his truck off and drive by moonlight only. He claimed it was the modern-day sleigh ride. Most of the girls liked the game, some more so than others.

On a whim, he did just that. For the briefest of moments, he could not see the roadway, but eyes do what eyes do, and soon the way was easy to follow. He rolled down the window of the truck, and the cold air rushed against him, which caused a quick intake of breath. For only a second, he considered raising the window, but he did not. He turned off the highway onto the lane to his house. Lit by the moon, with a backdrop of white, the darker-colored buildings stood out in the distance. He smiled, if only there were smoke from the chimney, he'd have an image fit for a Christmas card.

"Maybe next year," he smiled and muttered to himself. Then he saw the car.

He saw the car, parked in the yard, next to the spot where he usually parked his truck. Looked to be a typical sedan, four doors, nothing special. Yeah, he saw the car, but he didn't recognize it. Months earlier, people had tried to kill him, and even now, things out of place, like strange cars in his driveway, spooked him. Bobby stopped his truck, leaned forward to access the Colt Python high on his hip, and placed the gun on the seat beside him. Then he drove into the yard.

Stepping out of the truck, Bobby held the Colt low in his right hand, and kept his head on a swivel, as they say. He watched the car. No movement. He kept an eye to the shadows created by the evergreen bushes next to his house.

He silently reminded himself the bushes needed to be trimmed — something to do next spring. He looked to the corners of walls, then to the doorway where the shadows were the darkest. He tried to look everywhere at once as he crossed the distance from his truck to the car. Once there, he looked inside; no one, nothing. He touched the hood of the vehicle; cold. It had been parked there long enough for the Montana night to cool the metal. Trying to be cat-like, and not slip on the ice and snow, Bobby made his way to the front door of his house. Gently, he attempted to turn the knob; locked, just as he had left it that morning. Carefully, he made his way around to the back.

As he closed the distance to the back door, which was a sliding glass and opened onto his screened-in porch, he heard the music. He stopped and listened. The music was a mix of blues and jazz. He heard the saxophone, the piano, a guitar and the heavy and rhythmic beat of a drum. Whoever was in his house had pretty good taste in music he decided and he looked through an available window into his kitchen.

The woman had a full head of dark red hair that hung just past her shoulders. He'd never seen it loose before, and as she bobbed her head, the mane shimmied back and forth in time with the beat of the music. She had her back to him, and he took the time to look down her frame. She wore a sleek and sleeveless top, meant to be worn under sweaters, tucked into dark blue form-fitting ski pants that molded to her lower half and legs. Her feet were bare, as she had removed her boots, socks, sweater and piled them on a nearby chair. She shook, shimmied, and stepped in time with the beat, and for a moment, Bobby forgot to try to locate weapons. When he remembered, another visual exam of her shape convinced him there was no place where a gun could be hidden. He also realized she was standing at his cooktop. She was stirring something in a saucepan. She was cooking. Bobby stepped into the room.

"If I am in the wrong house," she said, without turning around, "I'm in a lot of trouble."

Bobby slipped the Python back into where it was carried.

"What makes you think you're not in trouble anyway?" he

asked.

She turned and studied him.

"Because I made dinner."

"It smells good," Bobby admitted, as he glanced to the island and noticed the place setting for two. He looked back at Nicole McCarren.

"John Perez refused to talk to me," she said. Bobby shrugged a small shrug.

"He said, I was using him to further my career, and that I didn't care if my writing caused others harm or not," she continued.

Bobby slipped off his jacket, laid it over the back of a stool and removed the holstered Colt. He sat it, along with his hat and speed loaders, on the island top.

"And you felt so bad, you broke into my house to cook away a guilty conscience," he said.

She turned back to the stove and stirred what was in the pan. Her arm movement clockwise swayed her hips in a counter-rotating manner. He liked watching her.

"I did not break into your house," she defended herself.

Bobby said nothing.

"I know it was you who told him not to talk to me," she continued. "I was angry and wanted to have it out with you. You're interfering with my work. I zealously protect my work."

She turned back to him. She licked sauce that had managed to find itself on the back of her hand. Bobby liked watching her do that as well.

"I parked and knocked and you weren't here."

"So you came on in," Bobby said, "makes perfect sense."

"No, I waited in the car, and had to leave it idling when the sun went down. It got cold."

Bobby nodded, "And not wanting to pollute the air, you then came into the house."

"No. I didn't come in the house until I saw the wolf."

"You saw the wolf?" Bobby asked.

"You've seen him before?" She asked in mild surprise.

"I have," Bobby nodded.

"Yes," she said, "I saw a wolf. So I snuck around the house and found the back door unlocked. That's when I came in."

Bobby looked at her and then asked, "Why would you do that? Why, after seeing a wolf, would you get out of your car to run around to the back of a house? That's a bit crazy, don't you think?"

She blushed, and the extra color to her face heightened her beauty.

"I read somewhere that country people lock their front doors, so people know they're not at home, but leave the back door unlocked in case someone needs to get in. You know, for emergencies. Like if they see a wolf."

"You got out of a car which was perfectly safe, and ran around to the back of the house, based on an old wives' tale?"

Bobby laughed, and she began to get angry. Her anger also colored her face.

"I guess it does sound kind of dumb," she admitted as she calmed down.

"What do you have on the burner?" Bobby asked. "It smells like it's burning."

"Oh," she spun back to the cooktop to see the sauce she was making popping and spitting onto the stovetop. It was too thick to boil, but it was making a mess, and was, indeed, being overcooked.

Bobby stepped around her, gently pushing her aside, and removed the pan.

"What were you cooking?" he asked.

"I saw the tortellini in the refrigerator and decided to make a sauce to go with it."

"I'll tell you what," he said. "You step over to the wine rack, pick one you like, and I'll take care of the sauce making."

Her look was dubious as she stepped where he pointed and found the wine rack mounted on the wall, away from the stove.

"By putting it over there," he explained, "it keeps the temperature more constant. Heat will ruin wine."

She studied the labels and looked back at him several

times as if making sure the man and the wine were not some kind of illusion. The rack was made of wood and wrought iron. It was a masculine rack, a frame that belonged in a ranch house. The bottles lay on their sides with the labels to the front where they were easily read. She used a finger to track from bottle to bottle as she quietly mouthed the names. She looked back over her shoulder and watched the man as he gathered a bowl, olive oil and several small bottles of spices.

"What are you making?" she asked.

"Something quick and easy. I've got bread, homemade, and it's only a couple of days old. We'll tear it into pieces and dip it into a dip."

"The dip is oil based?" she asked, again looking at the bottle on the countertop.

"Yeah, and we'll add a little basil, parsley, minced garlic, thyme, oregano, some black pepper, crushed red pepper, and lemon juice, salt to taste and have a terrific late evening dinner with no fuss and little muss."

"You rattled that off like you know what you're doing," she said.

He smiled, "I know what I'm doing."

She selected a bottle, held it for him to approve.

"I'm a sucker for a red," she said. "Sometimes, I forget who I am when I drink red."

He smiled, "Then red it is."

She crossed back to the island while he got the corkscrew from a drawer. He gave it to her, and she smiled when she took it from him, their hands touching for only a moment — a hint of what might be.

He mixed the sauce, dipped a finger to taste it and nodded. He lowered his finger again and offered it to her. She focused on his eyes as she tasted the mix and nodded approval.

Bobby stepped to a bread box and removed a loaf of bread. It was crusty, thick and heavy.

"Can I see that?" she asked, and he handed it to her.

She raised it to her nose and inhaled, "This is fantastic."

"Thank you," he said.

"I made it a couple of days ago," he said as he ripped the loaf into chunks and placed them on a platter. She watched his hands as he grasped, ripped and tore the bread apart.

"Wait a minute," she said. Bobby stopped, remnants of the loaf still in his hands and looked at her.

"Who are you, Bobby Trent?"

"I'm the Sheriff of Lodge Pole County."

"No, you're more than that. You know how to cook, by the looks of this kitchen, you know wine, you own a ranch. Who are you?"

"All the above, I guess."

"This kitchen," she looked at it, "you planning on a wife soon? I don't get it."

"A man can't have a kitchen?"

"I didn't mean that."

"Well, this is the kitchen of my dreams. I built it for me. I enjoy cooking, and I wanted a place where I had a chance to cook anything I felt like."

Bobby looked over the area, smiled and said, "Unless the recipe calls for someone to cook it in a zero-gravity environment, I think I can handle most anything."

She smiled at the man; she liked him. She imagined him wearing only an apron.

"You seem pretty sure of yourself," she said.

"In most things, not all. I'm not a particularly good Sheriff."

"Why do you say that?"

He shrugged and moved the food to the island top. He pulled out a stool for her and then sat beside her. He opened the wine and poured her a taste.

"Hmm," she said, "as good as I'd hoped. Now tell me why you think you're not a very good Sheriff."

Bobby picked up a piece of bread, broke it into smaller pieces and dipped. Bending over the table, he hurried the dripping bit into his mouth.

He nodded, "Good, if I say so myself." He dipped another piece of the bread and with one hand under it, offered it to her. Again, she studied him as she took it in her mouth.

He shrugged, "I feel like I'm in over my head most of the

time."

"But you said you had just started," she said as she chewed.

"Yeah, but who starts at the top?"

She dipped her piece of bread and placed it in her mouth.

"Well," she said around the chunk of bread, "it seems to me if the folks around here didn't like the job you were doing they would fire you and get someone new."

"Isn't that a comforting thought to go to work with every day?"

"I came out here to give you a piece of my mind," she said. "You had no right to interfere with my working with John Perez."

"What he said? Is it true? Are you just looking for a story?"

"My job is to write stories. I'm good at it."

"And if people get hurt?"

She shrugged, "I'm not cold-hearted. But people get hurt every day, whether or not I write about them."

"What you're doing here, this story about a freak long dead, and a girl long missing. How does that do anyone any good?"

"It's a human interest story. People are always interested in an unsolved crime."

"But it's solved. The killer is dead."

"Not according to John Perez. According to him, the man did not kill Kanti."

"So, in your mind, that means John Perez did? That doesn't even make sense."

"Admitted, it doesn't work except from the angle of the killer. Perez has played the grieving father right under the noses of an entire community. He has all of you fooled."

Bobby shook his head, "That's absurd."

"Maybe, but it makes a great story. I'm just telling the story. I don't have to prove it."

Bobby shook his head, stood, picked up his plate and took it to the sink. He set it down and turned back to face McCarren as he leaned on the counter.

"I didn't talk to John Perez. I haven't seen him. I might

have told him not to talk to you if I had, but I've been doing other things. That being said, if you hurt that man, if you rile up this community for nothing more than a brownie point from your editor, or publisher, or whoever in hell hands out such things, you will answer to me."

Her half-smile showed her eyeteeth, much in the way vampire movies do. Her eyes glittered as she slid off her stool and crossed to him. She pushed against the man, forcing him to remain trapped against the sink counter. She slid her hand along his stomach and onto his chest.

"I don't want you mad at me," she said. "If you're mad at me you might not take me to bed."

She was as tall as Bobby and she pressed against him. He stayed where he was, and she nuzzled his neck.

"Course," she whispered, "there are times the best sex is angry sex."

Bobby looked at the woman and as he looked at her, she moved in and kissed him. Her kiss was a mix of heat with a taste of garlic and thyme. The olive oil made her lips slippery; it was easy to slide across her mouth and onto her neck. She bit his earlobe as she pulled open his shirt, the snaps giving way one by one.

"Oh, these are fun," she murmured as the closures gave way. "I now see why you wear them."

Bobby heard knocking on the front door. The kissing stopped, and Bobby listened. There it was, a second time. He gently pushed the woman away from him.

"This will have to wait," he said. She arched her brows as he stepped to the countertop and removed the Python from its holster.

He saw her look and explained, "Not everybody likes me."

The knocking started again.

Bobby crossed into the living room thankful he had not turned on the lights of the room. In the shadows, he stood to the side and looked out the front window. He saw the pickup marked with the Sheriff's Office logo that used to be Unit One. Nixon was there.

He stepped to the door, unlocked it and swung the door open.

"Where...?"

Her question died, unasked when she saw Nicole walk into the room from the kitchen. She looked back at Bobby and allowed her gaze to travel up and down his frame. Even in the shadows, Bobby saw the anger set into her eyes. He also saw something else. He saw hurt.

"It's not what you think it is," he said, knowing the statement was lame.

Nicole also noticed the deputy's look, and said, "I see you have work to do, Sheriff. Let me get my stuff, and we can talk another day."

"Yeah," Bobby said, his eyes not leaving Nixon. "Maybe later this week."

The woman retreated into the kitchen, yet Bobby and Nixon continued to stare at each other. They heard her gathering clothes and grunting as she pulled on her boots. Then, the back door slid open and closed. Nixon may have sensed the woman, but Bobby pulled his eyes away from his deputy long enough to see McCarren climb into her car, start it, and leave. He looked back at the woman on this front porch standing in his doorway. He stepped back.

"You want to come in? It's cold out there."

Nixon hesitated and then entered. He closed the door behind her.

"What's going on Bobby?"

"Nothing. It was nothing."

"Didn't look like nothing."

"I got back here, she was here, she wanted to talk about John Perez, and that was it."

"You have her lipstick all over your face."

He reached and rubbed his cheek.

"That's not lipstick," he said, and Nixon arched her eyebrows.

"It's olive oil," he said.

"It's what?"

"Nothing. It doesn't matter."

Bobby led her into the kitchen where the remains of the dinner still stood.

"Would you like a glass of wine?" he asked Nixon.

"Not from a bottle she drank from," the deputy replied.

"Are you hungry? I have food left," Bobby offered

"I won't take her leftovers." The reply was curt.

He turned from putting the dishes in the dishwasher and looked at the woman.

"Will you tell me why you're here? I thought we would meet tomorrow morning."

She nodded, "That was the plan. But then I thought I'd sneak out here, surprise you, we could have a night together and then be on the job first thing tomorrow."

"Good plan," Bobby admitted.

"I managed the surprise part, at least," she said. Her smiled was forced and bitter.

Bobby moved to the island counter and sat on a stool. He motioned Nixon to sit beside him and after hesitating, she did.

"Look," he said, "I'm sorry. I didn't invite her out here."

"You didn't ask her to leave."

He studied his deputy and then shook his head, "No, I did not."

"If I hadn't showed up," Nixon said, "would you have slept with her?"

He considered the question and was truthful, "Probably."

"I won't be that girl for you, Bobby," Nixon said.

"What girl?"

"I won't be the one you come to when you have nowhere else to go. I won't be number two. I won't be the second choice."

"I would never do that," he said, "not to you."

"You just did, Bobby."

He looked away, looked back, could think of nothing to say, so he lifted his wineglass and drank.

"It is good wine," he said after setting the glass down.

Nixon shook her head.

"If I open a new bottle?"

Nixon thought and then said, "Pour that one out; glass and bottle."

Bobby rose, picked up the bottle and glass, walked to the sink and poured out the contents.

"Now, will you have a glass with me?" he asked.

She motioned to the glass left by McCarren; it was a third full.

"That one too."

Bobby returned to the island, picked up the glass and poured the contents down the sink.

"Now?" he asked again.

"I don't know much about wine, Bobby. What do you think I should choose?"

He shrugged, "What are you in the mood for?"

"Well," she said, "I'll take your recommendation. What would you suggest for a woman who is extremely pissed off and carrying a gun?"

Bobby held his smile at bay, and said, "I think I'd go with a white. Something light, airy, with a touch of fun to it; a bottle of wine that tickles the palate."

"I could go for that," she said, and Bobby retrieved it from the rack.

Bobby opened the bottle and poured two fresh glasses. He handed one to Nixon, and after she took it, the toast he offered was simple, "I'm sorry."

She sipped and studied the glass. "This is pretty good," she said and downed the glass full.

CHAPTER 14

For several seconds there was only silence between them. Bobby refilled her glass and Nixon sat watching him. She shifted her gaze to the wine and downed half the glass and Bobby raised his eyebrows.

"Take it easy, Nixon," he said.

She turned to him and stared.

"I need to say this to you," she said.

Bobby nodded.

"I get it, I get you," she continued.

Bobby canted his head, unsure where she was going.

"I know you still carry a flame for KC and if she suddenly showed up on your doorstep and wanted to move in, the rest would be history."

"Nix..." he started.

She held up her hands.

"Don't. Don't say anything for a minute; I have to get this out."

Bobby sipped his wine.

"I get that," she said, "I do. KC is top-notch and beautiful. You and she were together through most of high school and college. But that is over. You just don't realize it yet. KC is not the girl who grew up here. She wants the city, the drama, the fancy restaurants and all that. She won't stay, and you will never leave."

She stopped and held out her glass, which was empty. Bobby refilled it.

"Thank you," she said and took a swallow. Bobby said nothing but sipped some of his.

"If I lose you to KC, I can handle that. She was there first and all that stuff. But don't force me to stand by and watch you, in so many words, date other women. If you have any feelings for me at all, don't do that. Don't do that and then show up at my place in the middle of the night for pizza and me."

Bobby studied her face, and he watched her blink back tears several times. One escaped and ran down her cheek. She ignored it. He reached across the separation to capture it on the tip of his finger.

"Nixon," he said, "what almost happened tonight would have been a huge mistake. I would have realized that sometime around five tomorrow morning. It wasn't planned, it wasn't scheduled. I got here, and there she was, in the house and cooking."

"She was in your house?"

He nodded, "Yeah, you know I leave my back door unlocked."

"I didn't know, but now I do."

For the first time since arriving, Nixon smiled.

"It doesn't matter, whether or not it was planned," Bobby continued. "It shouldn't have happened, and I promise you, it won't happen again."

Nixon took another swallow of the wine. She sat the glass down and did a quick rub of her eyes. The shine still in them was not caused by tears. Her smile was a little uneven.

"Just for the record, Bobby," she said.

"Yes?"

"Your promise, about it not happening again? Does that mean just McCarren or are we talking about all women?"

Bobby allowed a small smile.

"I promise, until we get you and I figured out, I will not go out with any other woman."

She became serious, "That's a big promise, Bobby. Don't

say it if you don't mean it."

He matched her tone, "I'm a screw-up in a lot of ways, but I never say anything I don't mean."

Again, they were silent, and during that time, Nixon finished her second glass. She slid it across the island top and silently asked for one more.

Bobby poured her half a glass.

"I will assume you brought all your gear for tomorrow morning?" he asked.

She nodded, "And my jammies. We can have a sleepover."

"Deputy Nixon, are you getting drunk?"

She made a serious attempt at saluting him.

"No sir, Sheriff Bobby, sir. This deputy is not drunk."

"Did you eat dinner?"

"No, I was going to eat with you."

"Okay," he said. "I'm cutting you off. We got to get up early and do some work."

"Where's your stuff?"

"What stuff?"

He rolled his eyes, "Your jammies?"

"Oh, in my togo bag, in Unit Five."

"Don't go anywhere. I'll be right back."

Bobby returned to find Nixon still finishing her glass of wine.

"Perfect timing," he said, and he walked to her, turned the stool and scooped her into his arms. She squealed, giggled, and then laid her head on his shoulder. He carried her into his bedroom and settled her on the bed. She watched him as he removed her boots, pulling one off at a time.

"Can you get undressed?" he asked.

Her eyes now showed a hunger for more than dinner, and he shook his head.

"No, Nixon, not like this."

He unbuckled her jeans and holding them by the hems, pulled them the length of her legs. Secretly, he admitted he enjoyed uncovering those legs inch by inch. Once done, and she laid there, laughing, he admired the total length of her stems; long, feminine, muscular, athletic. She had the legs of sports stars. Even in the dimmed light of his bedroom, he could see they were covered with freckles. He promised himself; the day would come when he would lie beside her and count them all. He smiled. What a pleasant afternoon that would be.

"Socks too."

Nixon's direction brought him back, and he noticed she was kicking a leg in the air. The sock, half off her foot, was imitating a flag. He laughed, caught the leg and removed the sock.

"Other one."

He repeated the process and then reached across her and covered her with a blanket.

"Party pooper," Nixon pouted.

"Get some sleep," he said. "We have work tomorrow."

"Is this your bed, Bobby?"

He nodded, "It is."

She smiled. "I've dreamed of being in your bed," she said.

"Get some sleep," he repeated.

Bobby pulled the blanket tight around her and kissed her forehead. He turned out the light as he exited the room and closed the door behind him. He stopped by the hall closet and pulled the spare blanket he kept there from its shelf. In the living room, he spread it across the sofa, kicked off his boots, removed his shirt and after turning off the lights, snuggled down.

"I should have gotten a pillow," he said when his head hit the armrest. He considered getting one but decided against it. He wasn't sure he could resist the temptation of her twice in such a short period.

Bobby laid in the darkened room and a small chuckle escaped his lips.

"What a night, two women, each a little drunk, both wanting me, both partly dressed and here I am sleeping on the sofa, alone. Sometimes Sheriff Trent sure misses Bad Bobby."

"You guys are here bright and early," Lucas said as he checked his watch and welcomed Bobby and Nixon into his office.

"Got a full day today," Bobby replied. "After we finish here, we're going to drive up to City of David and talk to Paul Phillips."

"City of David?" Lucas repeated. "That might be the only place in the state where you are less welcome than here."

"Everyone still mad at me?"

"That is one way of putting it. Another way would be to remind you to keep your hat on. Don't want that pretty head of hair you carry to be an added temptation....if you get my drift?"

"I get your drift," Bobby answered.

"Why are you so mad at Bobby," Nixon broke in. "He didn't know the woman was Native."

"He knew she was most likely Native. He should have been more considerate of our traditions and beliefs. His behavior was insulting."

"And yet you still help him solve the riddle," Nixon shook her head, showing confusion.

"Hey, if we held grudges after all you people have done to us, we'd never speak to you," Lucas said.

"Yeah," Bobby said, "It's a good thing you don't hold grudges."

Then he changed the topic.

"So, I brought the socks. Show me your magic."

Lucas set a plastic spray bottle on the desk and asked Nixon to close all the blinds. He gave Bobby a pair of latex gloves and spread a sheet of butcher paper over part of his desk.

"Carefully place the socks on the paper," he directed.

Bobby did, and once Nixon finished, she returned and stood by Bobby.

"Ever seen this before?" Bobby asked her.

She nodded, "One time. They ordered me to stand guard on a murder scene. The place had been washed and looked spotless, but when the CID boys sprayed the luminol, the room glowed like some kind of magic lamp. It was so blue it was almost freaky."

"Don't expect anything like that," Lucas cautioned. "If we get anything, it will be minimal."

"Why are you doing this?" Nixon asked.

"I think the woman was killed by injecting something into her that caused her to have a heart attack. We're trying to find out if the injection site was on her foot."

"Isn't there a mark on her foot?"

"Not that I can find," Bobby said.

"If we get blood reaction on this sock," Lucas said, "that can be a strong indication they injected her."

Lucas sprayed the garments and stepped to the wall to turn off the light. Immediately in the darkness, a small beacon of blue light marked the spot. It was a tiny lighthouse in a vast sea of black, and it was blue.

"It looks like the light on the end of a fiber optic wire," Nixon whispered, with a touch of awe in her voice.

"It's almost pretty," Bobby said.

"Stand back so that I can get a photo," Lucas directed. "This won't last forever, and you might need the evidence."

Bobby, driving his pickup, looked over at Nixon. The woman sat straight in the seat, wearing blue jeans and a down-filled jacket. On the jacket's left breast was a patch shaped like a star and on the shoulder was the same patch as the Lodge Pole County Sheriff. He couldn't see it, as the jacket covered it, but he knew her duty belt surrounded her waist.

"Got your war face on?" he asked.

She looked at him and smiled, "You ever talk to Phillips before?"

He shook his head, "I don't think I've even seen him before."

"I don't believe he ever comes to town. What little they need from town, it's always others that come to get it."

He nodded.

"Do you know anything about him?"

Nixon was worried about meeting the man who had claimed two thousand acres as his own and then seceded from the Union.

Bobby shrugged, "I talked to King about him. He told me the man was a war hero of sorts. Phillips was a helicopter pilot in Vietnam. Got a couple of medals. The man was one of the first to fly into Hue' City during the Tet Offensive and later, he flew supplies for the Marines surrounded at Khe Sanh.

"He sounds like a bad-ass," Nixon said.

"I guess he was at one time," Bobby agreed. "Anyway, when he came home, as you know, the Vietnam vets were treated like crap, and he got a little twisted. Finally, he took off to the north country and became a hermit. Later, he took a wife and raised some kids. Now I guess dozens are living up there."

"That sounds so weird to me," Nixon added.

"King said the place is some mix between a military camp and an old-fashioned hippie commune."

"I've heard he won't let anybody enter the compound. He claims it's sovereign country and the only authority is him."

Bobby shrugged, "That may be true, in the past, but he'll let me in."

"Why? Because you're Bad Bobby Trent?" Nixon laughed.

"No, because he's stealing livestock from my county, and that's not allowed."

"Your county?" Nixon smiled.

"Yeah, my county."

"Why Mr. Trent, you sound just like a Sheriff."

Bobby glanced at her, at the road, and back at her.

"Wow, I guess I did. I'll try not to let that happen too often."

The deputy smiled.

Two hours of driving, much of it on snow-covered dirt lanes through the fores,t brought the two law officers to the boundary of the City of David. Across the one lane road, a pole had been lowered. Two extra-large posts were set in the ground on each side of the road and a mix of pole fence and coiled barbed wire ran in each direction. On one post, a mounted sign made of a three-by-three-foot square of plywood read:

You are leaving the United States of America
You are entering the City of David, a sovereign land

A bearded man, wearing a red and black plaid wool coat and a cap of the same design, stood next to the lowered pole blocking the road. Over his shoulder, a rifle hung.

"That rifle is an AR-15," Nixon whispered. Bobby nodded.

The man stepped into the roadway and raised a hand indicating they were to stop. Then he walked to the driver's side door, and when Bobby lowered the window, he said, "You folks need to turn around and head back the way you came. This is sovereign land and you can't enter."

Bobby flipped open the wallet that carried his badge and gave it to the man.

"Take this to Mr. Phillips. You tell him Sheriff Robert Trent is here to see him. It's in his best interest to meet with me."

The man started to hand the wallet back.

"You can't come in here," the guard started to say.

Bobby cut him off, "You do as your told and get my message to Phillips."

"Look, my..."

"I get what your job is. We will wait right here, but I will see Phillips. We can see him nice or not nice, it makes no matter to me. But if we have to see him the not nice way, he won't like it. Who do you think he will take that out on?"

The man thought for only a minute and then asked, "You will wait right here?"

Bobby nodded, "We will."

The man turned to leave, and as he trudged across the camp, Bobby looked over the place. It wasn't much. He counted eight buildings, all of them made of roughhewn logs. They would have looked comfortable in a Daniel Boone movie. All of them were a single story, and many appeared short when compared to more modern construction. The settlement was built in and among the trees that towered over the cabins. The trees acted as a snow block of sorts, and the snow on the ground was significantly less than in the open areas. Bobby guessed it to be about a foot high. In that snow were several trails from one building to another. He found it strange that the guard followed one path to one building instead of just cutting across in a more direct direction. He knew that told him something about the social structure of the camp but he didn't know what it was. Bobby also saw a few other men, several women, and four, maybe five children.

The place was quiet. The children didn't play, but the ones he saw were pulling sleds with firewood on them. The forest seemed to dull whatever sound was made by the settlers.

"This is creepy," Nixon said, her voice low as if she worried about disturbing the silence.

"They're just people," Bobby reassured her, "a little weird maybe, but still, just people."

They both saw the guard exiting the cabin and again, taking the roundabout way back to the blockade.

"Mr. Phillips said you have to turn over any weapons you might have," the guard said when he had returned to the driver's side door.

Bobby shook his head, "That will not happen, but we will leave our weapons in the vehicle. The truck will stay in the United States."

They opened the truck doors and got out. Bobby removed the Python from its holster and placed it on the seat. Nixon did the same with her Glock. Bobby locked the doors after they were closed.

Paul Phillips had the frame of a large man though he wasn't so anymore. At one time, his physical being would have commanded attention and focus. Not so much any longer. He sat in a wooden rocking chair, wrapped in a blanket, in front of a black and round wood-burning stove. The cabin was log framed, simple to the point of rustic. There were no decorations of any kind on the walls, no glass in the windows as the residents of the City of David attempted to keep the Montana wind at bay by using closed wooden shutters. As two oil lanterns provided the only light, the low-slung room was dark, stuffy and claustrophobic. Bobby removed his hat as he stepped into the room and felt he had walked into a museum. The floor was made of wood plank, unfinished, uneven, but worn more or less smooth by foot traffic. On the far side of the room stood a table and four more chairs. A wool, green blanket hung in a doorway, closing it off from the first room. Bobby had seen such blankets at the Army-Navy surplus store.

The room was a mixture of temperature extremes. When he stood too close to the old man and the stove, Bobby found himself sweating. The trickle of sweat started at his shoulder blades and teased him to his belt line. If he stood too distant, that same drop of personal liquid turned cold and tormented him as it traveled south along his spine.

Bobby stood, sweat running along his back and from under his arms, waiting for the man to acknowledge him. Phillips, hunched from under the blanket, two of the seams held close to his throat with a bony hand, looked gaunt, almost hollow. His skin appeared to have a grey tint to it though Bobby took into account the lack of light. The skin was loose and hung from his jawbone, the beard unshaven and grey. The man sat with his eyes closed. Bobby wondered if the man did so as the last defense before facing the Sheriff, or perhaps Phillips had died between the visit from the guard and himself.

"Good afternoon, Mr. Phillips," Bobby offered.

"And David put his hand in his bag, and took thence a stone, and slang it, and smote the Philistine in his forehead, that the stone sunk into his forehead; and he fell upon his face to the earth," the man replied.

The man's voice was raspy, weak and like the man himself, hollow. Three times, while quoting the scripture verse, Phillips stopped to regain his breath. At one time, he might have been frightening, but that time had passed. He looked over his clutched hand holding his blanket tight and eyed Bobby and Nixon.

"You are violating sovereign soil. You have no business here."

"We have business," Bobby asserted. "You are holding cattle and sheep on your property that were stolen from ranchers in Lodge Pole County. I'm here to make arrangements to get the animals back to where they belong."

"We have no stolen cattle nor sheep here," the old man retorted defensively.

"This is not going to turn out well for either of us if you insist on calling me a fool," Bobby said. "I know the stolen stock is held in the box canyon, next to the hot springs, not over a mile from here."

"If you call me a thief, young man, I can infer you are a fool. We are not thieves."

Bobby shrugged, "I never called you a thief. I said the stock was here and it is. How it got here, and more to the point, how it will get back to Lodge Pole County,. is what we are here to discuss."

"Where do you claim the stock is?"

"About a mile north of here. There is a hot spring and a hollow; the stock is corralled there. There are signs of someone feeding them. You can't miss it."

Phillips glanced at Bobby and then he studied another man standing near the table. Bobby, for the first time, gave the other man more than the passing glance he had given him when entering. The similarities were striking. The man was a younger version of the old man. He had to be the man's son.

"Let me guess," Bobby said, "Junior over there is trying out new revenue streams."

"Shut your mouth, interloper," the young Phillips cried. "You have been granted passage into our country. You are not guaranteed travel out."

Bobby smiled at the man, "Don't make threats you can't, and won't, keep. Do you think Deputy Nixon here and I are the only two law officers aware of this?"

Bobby turned back to the old man and glared at him.

"I came here with only one deputy as a sign of respect to

you. You will give me back the cattle and the sheep, and you will tell me how they came to be here."

"You have no standing here. You will not give orders," Phillips gasped as he spoke.

Glaring at the younger man, Bobby crossed the room, took one of the chairs from next to the table. He held it by the top of the backrest and drug it back toward Phillips. The chair bounced, clattered, and scraped the entire way as the uneven planks of flooring refused to let it drag smoothly. When he got the chair where he wanted it, Bobby placed it in front of the old man and sat.

"Look," he said. "I don't care if you call this place the City of David or any other name. I don't care if you think you have your own country or not. I don't care if you claim you are on the moon. All I care about is the stock stolen from ranchers from my county. The stock will be driven back to who owns them and you will tell me how the animals got here. I'm a rancher myself and I know cattle don't drive themselves. The sooner we get this done, the better for you."

The old man cast his grey runny eyes on Bobby, "Are you threatening me?"

Bobby shook his head, "No, but I'm a very irritating person. Some say I'm like a rash."

Bobby thought he saw the old man smile.

"Why would I be willing to do that?" Phillips asked.

"I can think of several reasons," Bobby said.

"Several?"

The Sheriff nodded, "Yeah. First, you'll want to do this to show you're good neighbors with your friends to the south."

"You are nothing to me."

"Don't like that reason?" Bobby asked.

The old man shrugged, and then Bobby leaned close to the man and whispered.

"The only reason they have allowed you to have your little hideaway up here is that you have never been a bother to anyone. That changed the day you agreed to hold stolen property. If you don't return the animals, state troopers will come and take them. Chances are they will bring Federal Agents, who will destroy all you have built. You violated the one tenet that kept you safe."

"What's that?" Phillips challenged.

"You stopped being out of sight, out of mind. You drew attention to yourself."

"That's two reasons," Phillips observed, "not several."

Bobby took a deep breath and then said, "The biggest reason for you to give back the stock is that you have bigger problems."

"Bigger?" the old man asked.

"Yeah, much bigger. Someone in this camp killed a young woman recently. We need to get the stock thing taken care of so we can get to the real reason I came here."

Bobby saw the Phillips men exchange glances. Silence settled over the room, and Bobby knew, just like when negotiating a new truck purchase, they had reached a point where he who spoke first, lost. Bobby was prepared to wait the entire day. He didn't have to.

"Timothy," the older Phillips said to his son, "take the others outside and let the Sheriff and I talk."

"Father," the son objected but was silenced by a glare from the old man.

"Do as I ask, please."

"Yes, father."

Timothy, the guard, and Nixon left the cabin. Bobby and the old man remained.

"What is this death of a woman you speak of?" Phillips asked.

"A woman was found in the snow. Someone murdered her."

"Why do you think someone in my camp had a hand in it?"

"Stands to reason," Bobby said. "This is the largest collection of men in the area near where she was found and I already know you involve yourselves in criminal activity."

"We do not," the old man declared indignantly.

"Explain the stock."

Phillips looked away and stared at the stove for some time. Then he looked back.

"If you retrieve the stock, what can I expect to happen to

those of us who live here?"

"How difficult are you going to make it for me to get the stock back?"

"If I have my men deliver them to a predetermined location, can we negotiate some agreement that keeps federal officers off my land?"

"You know the fork in the Yellowstone and Crow creek?" Bobby asked.

"I do."

"Have the cattle and sheep there two days from today. Their owners will be there to separate the herd and take them the rest of the way home. Agreed?"

Bobby extended his hand.

"Agreed," the old man wheezed and took the offered hand.

"And in return?" he asked.

"In return, I will not involve federal agents in the murder investigation of the woman."

"Agreed," the man repeated.

"Keep in mind," Bobby said, "I will find out who killed the woman. That person will pay."

Phillips nodded, "As you say, let us handle the return of the stock first."

"I need to know who took the stock," Bobby said. "How did they get here?"

"It was no one from here. All we did was hold them."

"What was the plan?"

"The stock was brought here. We thought we had a place where they wouldn't be discovered, and we would hold them until the snow melted enough to cross them into Canada."

"Why steal them in the winter? Weren't you worried about tracks and marks in the snow?"

"Only a few at a time were taken, and we thought they wouldn't be missed. Most times, stock is left to manage on their own during winter months. It was figured a few missing here and there would be blamed on winter kill. If it hadn't snowed so much, nobody would have checked on their stock. Just bad luck."

"Who stole them?"

"Isn't it enough you get the stock back?"

Bobby shook his head, "No. You say it wasn't your people. Let's say I believe you. That means someone in my county stole those cattle. I'll have their heads."

"Sheriff, this isn't right. What if I don't tell you?"

"If you don't tell me, I'll get a warrant for your arrest. And while this area is out of my jurisdiction, based on Montana law, I'll turn it over to the US Marshals. You claim this area to be outside the US, but your lawyer will be arguing that point while you wait in jail."

The old man looked at Bobby considering his options.

"Mr. Phillips," Bobby said, "you don't look well. Either you've got one hell of a cold or something is wrong. Don't make me lock you up. Don't make me tear down what you have built here."

Phillips looked at the stove. "Durnings," he said. "The Durnings skimmed off a few head every week or so and headed them up this way. Our job was to hold them and keep them out of sight. Since we're left alone, it sounded like a great plan."

Bobby stood and paced.

"The Durnings?"

The old man nodded. "Yeah. It was their idea, but I was the fool they talked into it."

He turned back and faced the old man.

"It's tough being the leader of something like this, isn't it?"

Phillips scowled, "What do you mean?"

"I mean, here you are taking the blame for the actions of one of your flock, or whatever you call them. You didn't agree with holding the cattle. Someone else did. You're just taking the heat for it."

Phillips glared at Bobby.

"Are you calling me a liar?" he asked.

Bobby shook his head, "No, I get it. You're the man in charge. What is it they say? It happened on your watch? All that is true, but you didn't come up with this scam. One of your underlings did and we both know it."

CHAPTER 15

Phillips shifted in his chair and the blanket he had clutched around his shoulders fell to the floor. The man was cadaverous. His shoulders were rounded and his chest sunken. Bobby wondered if the man might die before the meeting was over, and he stooped, retrieved the blanket, and helped rewrap the old man.

"I've got cancer," Phillips said. Bobby said nothing.

"I went off to fight a war my country said was important, and for my efforts, they sprayed me with Agent Orange. Do you know what Agent Orange is, boy?"

"A little bit. They used it in Vietnam."

"Yeah, the government sprayed tons of the stuff on their own troops. That's how they thanked us for our service back then."

"Can something be done?" Bobby motioned to the man with his head.

"No, not any longer."

"But you could have caught it earlier?" Bobby asked.

"I could have left what I've built here, traveled to a VA hospital somewhere, waited in line, only to be told to wait in another, while the government debated and denied responsibility for this. I could have traded my freedom to suckle on the teat of the government."

"It's obvious which route you chose," Bobby said.

"Yeah it is, and I'd choose it again. This," he raised an arm and waved it, "is my country, my home, my family. So you understand: I am the one responsible for the stolen stock being here." The old man was out of breath and pulled the blanket tighter.

"I'll hold you to your word," Bobby said. "Have the stock at the agreed location in two days."

Phillips nodded, "Unless the weather interferes, they'll be there."

Bobby stepped out of the cabin and the sunlight, even muted by the trees, caused him to squint. He squared his hat back on his head, pulled it low and blinked several times hoping it would help his eyes adjust. Standing about ten feet away, next to a tree, was Nixon and the guard from the gate. The guard was holding a handkerchief to his nose. The cloth was stained with blood. As he approached, Bobby looked from one to the other, trying to figure out what happened.

"I warned him, Bobby. I told him I wasn't in the mood to be manhandled."

Bobby looked at the guard, who removed the cloth, and Bobby noticed the man's nose was misaligned.

"I didn't do nothing," the man pouted, and blood trickled across his lips as he spoke.

"Better get someone to look at that," Bobby advised the man, and then turned to Nixon, "Can't take you anywhere without you causing trouble."

"You don't know the half of it," she said as they trudged along the trail back to the truck.

"Oh," he asked, "what was the other half?"

"I was thinking of you and that redhead being together last night. So I added a little extra to the punch."

Bobby looked over his shoulder at the guard still standing next to the tree and still holding his cloth to his face. Bobby suppressed a chuckle and shrugged.

"Better him than me," he said.

"Stewart," Bobby said, while at the meeting with the

deputies, "I want you and Chunk to be at the meeting location for the turnover of the stock that has been stolen. The boys from the City of David will drive them down, and the ranchers can handle them how they want once we have a count. They can separate the stock there, or if they want, they can drive the stock down to the range corral and do it there. I don't care."

"Are we supposed to help herd the stock?" Chunk asked.

"No," Bobby said, "you are there to act as referees and tally masters. I don't want the ranchers and the City of David boys getting into it. It's simply a turnover of the stock."

"Stewart," Bobby said, "as Undersheriff, you'll be in charge. You spent a lot of time patrolling up in that area. If you'd like, you can call the ranchers and tell them the stock has been found."

"What do I tell them when they ask who took them?"

"Tell them it's still under investigation. The only thing we know for sure is that the City of David did not steal the stock."

"They know who did though," Stewart said.

"As far as anyone outside this office is concerned, the City of David was allowing stock to graze for the winter. They assumed those who brought them legally owned the stock."

"But that's not true, is it Sheriff?" Stewart persisted.

"No, it's not, but we're not ready to release the names of the suspects at this time."

"Hell, I don't know the names of the suspects," Stewart complained.

"And neither does anyone else," Bobby said.

Bobby saw the glance Stewart made toward Nixon as he said, "I wonder if that is true?"

Bobby ignored the comment.

"Let's get to it," he said, and then added, "Stewart, I need you to stay for a minute, if you don't mind."

The two men walked into the private office of the Sheriff, and Bobby said, "Close the door."

Stewart did, and then he stood in front of the desk that for a short period, had been his. His look was sour, his expression surly.

"What do you want Trent?" he asked as if he was too busy to talk.

"When you meet with the ranchers and the boys from the City of David, you need to be careful what you say. The ranchers are pissed and I don't want them taking their anger out on the City of David guys."

"What do we care if some loonies from the woods get roughed up?" Stewart wanted to know.

"Your job is to keep the peace, even if it is in the north woods, Stewart. I expect you to do just that."

Stewart glared at Bobby, "Don't you ever presume to tell me my job."

Bobby stared at the man who wanted to be Sheriff so badly he ached. The man, whom the county had seen fit to pass over and instead appoint a broken rodeo cowboy. Bobby wanted to get angry at the man, wanted to shout, to threaten him. Bobby wanted to kick the stuffing out of the man, but not today. Today, he was just too tired to deal with Stewart.

"Just do your job. Tell all the ranchers you solved the case if you want to, but no violence," Bobby said.

"I know my job," Stewart retorted.

"Then get out and do it," Bobby waved the man away.

Stewart closed the door with more effort than needed but Bobby let the man go. He reached for his coffee cup and found it empty. Damn... that kind of day. When he heard the knock, he said to come in. It was Nixon.

"Bobby," she said as she peeked around the edge of the door. "You got a minute?"

"I do," he answered, wishing he didn't.

Nixon entered the office and closed the door behind her and sat down in the chair just vacated by Stewart.

"I don't want you to think I'm complaining..." she started.

"But you're going to," Bobby finished her sentence, and he slumped back in his chair.

"No, I'm not complaining, but I want to know why Stewart gets to meet with the ranchers and take the credit for returning the stock? I put as many hours up there in the cold as he did."

Bobby grunted and then added. "I'd like to know why

every time I make a decision, I have to defend it to Stewart and explain it to you."

Nixon blinked several times; Bobby almost felt bad.

"I didn't mean it..."

"Is this how things ran when my dad was Sheriff? Did the two of you constantly second guess him, or is this treatment designed for the new guy?"

"Bobby, I don't mean it like that, really I don't," she said. "I just want to understand how you go about making assignments."

"You don't like your assignment?" he asked.

"I don't have an assignment," she answered.

"I thought I'd have you back me up when I go up to brace the Durnings," he said.

"Brace them about what?"

"Royal and Samuel are the two who have been stealing the stock, at least according to Phillips. If you don't approve of that assignment, deputy, call Stewart, tell him to hold up, and go with him to wrangle the stock."

Nixon slid forward in the chair, her eyes bright, "I'm going with you to arrest the Durnings?"

Bobby reached again for his coffee, remembered he had none, and stopped. He wanted coffee.

"I didn't say arrest them," Bobby said. "But we need to talk to them."

"Why not arrest them?"

"That's one of the reasons I want you to go with me; I'm hoping for your counsel. I don't think we have the evidence to back up the charges."

"What do you mean?"

Bobby shrugged, "The only thing we have to tie them to the stealing is the word of Paul Phillips, a man that most would find strange, at best, and who will most likely be dead by the time the trial comes around."

"You think the Durnings would kill him?" she asked.

"No, the man has cancer. The Durnings won't have to kill him. Time will do it for them."

"And then we won't have any case at all," Nixon muttered.

"That's about the size of it."

"So why are you going to go talk to them?"

"To let them know we know. Let them know they didn't get away with it."

"There are some, I know, who would hold it over their heads," Nixon said.

"Which is why Stewart isn't going," Bobby smiled, "unless, of course, you want to change assignments."

"No, Sheriff," Nixon said. "I'm good."

She smiled and left the office, closing the door behind her.

Nixon glared at Nicole McCarren when the woman walked through the door of the Sheriff's Office. If the woman had been embarrassed a few nights ago, she didn't show it now. Her head was high, her shoulders back, and the swivel in her gate captured even Bud King's eyes. The woman crossed into the back area without asking permission nor offering an excuse. When eye to eye with Nixon, she stopped and studied the deputy.

"You lied to me the other day," she said.

"I did not," Nixon denied.

"I asked you if the Sheriff was in play, and you told me yes, in so many words."

"My feelings don't take him out of play," Nixon explained.

"You should have told me how you felt and I would never have gone to his place that night. If I had known, well... I don't play in other girls' sandboxes."

"What do you want?" Nixon interrupted.

"I came by to tell you I'm headed back to Boston. I've got my story. As it is, there is no reason to stay any longer. I just came by to tell you goodbye, and let you know we'll take that trip to Billings another time."

"You don't want to see Bobby, err, the Sheriff?" Nixon asked.

McCarren smiled, "No, not the Sheriff. Listen to me. The world is full of women like me. Many will take a man if he's spoken for or not. If you are going to go after a man like your Sheriff, you better get serious about it."

"He knows how I feel," Nixon defended, but McCarren

shook her head.

"That may not be enough. You've been hanging out with the guys too long. Take some advice: get your hair done. That shag look went out about a decade ago. Wear some makeup. Get yourself some copper-colored eyeshadow, maybe with a touch of glitter to it. Get your nails done. I recommend a magenta color and let them grow out a bit. I know you risk fighting, but so what? Look like the woman you know you are. You can still be the kickass deputy while wearing nail polish. When it comes to your Sheriff, you have to light the man up, ignite a fire in him. You have assets, girl, make sure he knows of them. He sees you as his buddy, someone to have a beer with. You have to make him want more than that. If you don't, you'll never get him, or worse, you'll lose him to someone else."

Nixon studied the woman and fought to understand her ambivalent feelings.

"I guess I should say thank you," she said finally.

"Girls gotta help girls," McCarren smiled. "I'm driving back to Rapid City and catching a plane to Boston. I should be home by tomorrow night. I want to hear how things work out, and if you decide not to make a move, let me know. Your Sheriff's worth a trip back here to Sticksville."

"Is there anything I can do for you?"

McCarren shook her head, but said, "Well, if you hear about a good story, keep me in mind. My editor isn't too happy with me as this one turned out to be a bust."

"Will do," Nixon promised.

"Oh, and one other thing."

"Yeah."

"Kiss Bobby goodbye for me."

"My pleasure," Nixon smiled.

"I know," McCarren grinned in return.

Bud King knocked on the office door.

"Sheriff, I've got a phone call for you from Chief Black Kettle. You want me to tell him you'll call him back?"

"No," Bobby spoke through the door. "I'll take it."

Bobby picked up the office phone.

"*Viho*," he said.

"Bobby," Lucas returned. "I've got a man out here who would like to meet you."

"Have him come to town," Bobby said.

"He'd rather not. He'd like to meet you on Native land."

"I see, and why can't he come to see me?"

"He's the cousin of the dead woman."

"I'm on my way," Bobby said and hung up the phone.

He grabbed his jacket, his hat, opened the door and headed toward the back door of the office. He stopped and looked back at Nixon.

"Well, you coming or not?"

Bobby led Nixon into the office of Lucas Black Kettle. Lucas stood when Nixon entered the room, and standing to the side of the desk was a Native man who looked to be in his fifties, though his age was difficult to guess by appearance alone. The man wore a blue western style shirt with a bolo tie around his neck. His pants were black denim and his cowboy boots matched in color. His broad-brimmed hat was a grey felt. A tiara of multi-colored feathers surrounded the base of the crown, and Bobby silently wished he had the feathers with which to tie fishing flies. The man's shoulders were broad and his stomach round. It pushed against the leather belt and the silver buckle that held up the pants. His hair was thick and grey with streaks of white. The hair, loose, hung to below his shoulders.

"My name," the stranger said, "is *Ma'oomatse*. The white men call me Custer Red Robe. I am of the Lakota Nation from Cheyenne River Reservation. You may know of Dupree, North Dakota. I am from that place."

Bobby nodded; he knew of Dupree. He had competed in rodeos there more than once. He stepped forward and extended his hand.

"My name is Bobby Trent. I don't believe I have ever heard a Native take the name of Custer before."

The man shrugged, "I don't take it as a sign of respect, but rather a remembrance of the defeat he suffered at the hands of my people."

Bobby had no comment for that rationale, so he changed the topic.

"I am told you wish to meet with me."

"That is true. I am the cousin of the woman you found in the snow. Her name was Annie *Na'enova'e,* Annie Turtle Woman."

"I am sorry for your loss," was all Bobby could think to say, and the Indian nodded.

"I am told you allowed an autopsy to be done on her without approval."

"That is true. I did not know who she was, and while I thought she might be native, I needed to find out how she died."

"And do you know how she died?"

"I believe she was poisoned."

"Poisoned?"

Bobby nodded, "Yes, I believe someone injected her with potassium chloride. The drug caused her to have a heart attack."

Whatever emotion Custer Red Robe felt, he did not show.

"And who did this?"

Bobby shook his head, "I don't know, yet. I am still trying to figure that out."

"And when you find out? What will you do?"

"I'll arrest the one responsible for her death."

"And if I ask you to give that person to my people in order that we may exact our justice?"

"Bobby, you can't do that," Nixon interjected.

Lucas held up a hand toward the deputy.

Nixon silenced.

"What my deputy says is correct," Bobby said. "To do what you ask would violate my oath of office."

"Nonetheless, Native women and girls go missing all the time and the whites do little or nothing about it. I would consider it good between us if you thought on my request."

"Would you request such action from Lucas?" Bobby

asked.

"I would not have to," Red Robe replied.

Bobby glanced at his lifelong friend and *Viho's* expression did not contradict the visitor.

"I have come to take her home," Red Robe said. "What must I do?"

"Claim her at the Medical Center. My sister works there. I will call and give her advance notice if you would like."

Red Robe nodded, "That would be most helpful."

"Later today?" Bobby asked, and the Native nodded.

"Do you have any idea what she was doing over here?" Bobby asked. "Does she have family or friends that you know of?"

"I know of no one like that. She was a troubled woman, very unhappy, always wanted more."

"More what?" Bobby asked.

"More of everything," Red Robe replied.

"She told her sister she was leaving to find that more."

"When did she leave?"

"Some five months ago."

"Did she contact her sister after she left?"

"Only once. She said she had found work. She said she was to be the housekeeper for a horse trainer who had no horses."

Bobby and Nixon exchanged glances.

On the way back to Wapiti, with Red Robe and Lucas following, Bobby called Rachel, his sister, and told her of the release. She promised to have the woman ready.

"I'm glad she is finally going home," Nixon said.

Bobby, driving, nodded his head.

"No comment?" Nixon persisted.

"No, it's not that," Bobby said. "I'm wondering why John Perez said nothing about the woman. It has to be him she worked for. We had posters and flyers all over town. He had to see one or two."

"I was in John Perez's house once," Nixon said, "a couple of years ago. The place was a mess. If he hired someone to clean up, he offered her top dollar."

"Still doesn't explain why he didn't speak up."

"No," she agreed, "it does not."

At the Medical Center, Red Robe took custody of the body of Annie Turtle Woman. The sign-over was simple, without fanfare. Bobby took a moment with the body and promised her he would do all he could to find out what happened. He told her he hoped to bring her killer to justice but stopped short of making such an oath, as he told her, "I'm not sure I'm smart enough to figure it out."

They wrapped the body in cloth, and then plastic. Dry ice was stuffed along side her in the rubberized body bag. As Rachel and her assistant prepared the woman, Red Robe stood at the head and sang chants.

"To let her know she is going home," he had explained before starting.

Before the bag was zippered closed, Red Robe produced twigs of sage and cuts of the yucca plant. He placed them along the length of his cousin's body.

"To comfort her on her spiritual journey," he said.

Just before leaving, Custer Red Robe stepped close to Bobby and offered his hand.

"I forgive you for the violation of her body. I understand what you did is the white way and Lucas told me you are new at your job. He also told me you are an honest man and that I can believe your words. He holds you in high regard. Higher than most other whites."

"Lucas has been my friend most of my life," Bobby interjected.

"So he said," Red Robe nodded. "I hope you will consider my words. You owe me nothing, but if you were to do as I ask, it would be received with great appreciation by Turtle Woman's family and the Lakota people."

Not wanting to tell the man "no," Bobby simply said, "I've got to find the man first."

Bobby often wondered if it was the releasing of the Lakota, or just odd timing, but it seemed as soon as Annie was headed home, the weather changed. Winter had grown tired and warm breezes blew in from the south. One day the icicles hanging from the eves of his house were competing for length, and the next, they raced to see which could melt the fastest. Within a week, the snow across the prairie had retreated enough that patches of green could be seen. The changing of the seasons upon them, most of the citizens seemed to be in better moods. Most, but not all.

"How long we known each other, Mr. Durning," Bobby started the conversation. He was sitting in the Durning's living room, on their sofa, relaxed, his legs crossed. Nixon was with him, standing to one side, and Samuel, the son, was also present.

"Well, Sheriff, I would say I've known you all your life. I watched you grow up. I remember your first rodeos when you were still riding sheep because you were not big enough yet for calves."

Bobby nodded, "It has been a long time, and you were friends with my father even before I was born. I believe you and he even hit a few rodeos together."

"We did," the older Durning agreed, "but it was the team roping we did, mostly. Your old man and me were a pretty tough team in our day."

"That you were," Bobby again nodded, and then he added, "so when was it, exactly, you decided to become a thief?"

"What?" the old man almost shouted.

Samuel jumped to his feet as if to attack the Sheriff.

Bobby didn't move. He didn't change expressions though Nixon quietly moved her hand closer to her sidearm.

"As we agreed," Bobby continued, ignoring the reactions, "we've known each other a long time. Have you ever known me to say something I couldn't back up?"

Durning Senior motioned for his son to sit down, which the younger man did.

"How long have you known?" the old man asked.

"A few weeks now," Bobby answered.

"We heard the stock had all been returned."

"It has."

"I suppose everyone knows?"

"You'd suppose wrong," Bobby said, and both generations

of Durnings looked at him, surprise easily seen on their faces.

"Are you gonna arrest us?" the son asked.

Bobby ignored the question, and instead said, "Nixon, over there has more knowledge than I do about law enforcement, but even I know anything you tell me before I advise you of your rights cannot be used in court. You also know, I have not advised you of your rights."

The old man nodded.

"That being said, we're going to sit here, and you're going to tell me how one of my father's best friends becomes a stock thief."

The senior Durning flinched as if Bobby slapped him. He sighed, and then said, "It doesn't excuse it, but we had a hard year last year. Got sickness in the herd and we had to destroy most. Couldn't sell them. Missed our farm payment. First time that happened — not a good feeling. Anyway, money was short, and one day we were checking fences and checking snow depth. We were hoping for an early spring as we had run out of money to buy feed. We're already in hock up to our eyes. Bank won't extend any more credit."

Bobby looked at the man but said nothing. He showed no sympathy; hard times were part and parcel when it came to raising livestock.

"Anyway," the old man continued, "we were checking the stock, and we came upon three head of David Hill's cattle."

"You knew they belonged to Hill?" Bobby asked.

Royal Durning nodded, "Yeah, we knew. We saw the brand. We didn't think about it or discuss it. We were going to run them back toward Hill's place, but the stock moved north and the next thing we knew, they were in that protected valley the City of David people own. There is a warm spring that is open all winter and a touch of grass, so we figured why not?"

Durning Jr. added, "We rationalized it by saying Hill should keep his fences better."

"Over the next few weeks," Sr. said, "whenever we were up

that way, if we found stock out, we headed them up to Phillip's land. Later, I met with Paul and told him what we were doing. He agreed to let the stock stay there until spring, or when we could get them across the border, at the earliest."

"What was in it for Phillips?" Bobby asked.

"Oh, he and I go back a long way. We both served in Nam, and we both share hard feelings about how we were treated when we came home."

"I never knew you were in Nam," Bobby said.

Senior shrugged, "Nothing to talk about anymore. We came home and they called all of us baby killers. Not all of us were. Nowadays, soldiers are all called heroes and I'll tell you, not all of them are."

"You make it sound like Phillips owed you," Bobby observed.

"No, not really. We help each other from time to time, that's all."

"What kind of help you give him?"

"Oh, nothing special. We make supply runs into Canada from time to time. Paul has cancer, so I bring him back his medications sometimes. He can get them there cheaper and he doesn't feel obligated to the government. Also, I bring other supplies. They don't have vehicles there, except for a snowmobile and a four-wheeler for summer use. I bring back gasoline and oil, some foodstuffs once in a while."

"And he does what for you, outside of holding the cattle?"

"He gives me garden goods, mostly. I help him cause we're both vets and he needs it. Nothing more."

"Unless you need him to hide stolen stock," Nixon reminded.

Durning looked at her and then nodded, "Yeah, except for then."

"What are you going to do with us?" Samuel asked.

"If I arrest you and if I can prove my case, you'll go to jail. At least one of you will. Maybe there is a plea deal I don't know about. No matter, cause if that happens, you're going to lose your place. That means your wives and your girls," Bobby nodded towards Samuel who had two daughters, "will be out on the street."

Bobby stood and paced and then he turned and looked at the Durnings.

"The fact is, chances are I will arrest you, ruin your reputations, distance the community from your families and then not be able to prove the crime. You'll not go to jail, but you will still lose your place, if for no other reason than the expense of a lawyer. Your families will still be out on the street."

The silence in the room was heavy as Bobby, again, went to pacing. Nixon watched him with conflicting feelings of sympathy and pride tugging at her heart.

Finally, Bobby faced the men.

"I don't know what I'm going to do, but I give you my word one way or another, we will settle this."

Durning nodded, "Whatever you say, Sheriff."

Nixon drove back to town, and from time to time, glanced at Bobby, who was lost in thought and looked out the window to watch the white of Montana turn green.

CHAPTER 16

O ver the next week, Bobby struggled with what to do about the Durnings. He silently debated going to Blue and talking with him but hesitated for fear the DA would tell him to arrest the men. He also thought about discussing the situation with KC but shied away from her as he was still stinging from the criticism she had leveled against him over Kettling...Kettling being a simple matter when compared to the Durning mess.

All that aside, Bobby was proud of his handling of the Marcus affair. They had released the man with the understandings he had agreed to. He fulfilled them all. The last thirty days, he had been close to a slave of Bud King and the old deputy made it a point that the man hate twenty-nine of the thirty days he served his sentence. On the thirtieth day, the old man took Kettling to lunch and told him what a good job he had done. Bobby wasn't there, but he heard the big man cried.

Why couldn't the same be worked out for the Durnings? Was the purpose of the law to punish men who made mistakes but also destroy their families? If the case could not be proven, in a place the size of Lodge Pole County, it would ruin the reputation of the complete family. Fights in schools would be started, as the daughters would be called names.

Lines of credit at grocery stores, a mainstay during certain times of the year, would be canceled. All would be stained. Neighbors who had known each other for generations would worry if the next-door family was now a thief. Was that the purpose of his job?

Is that the definition of justice? Was that what being a Sheriff was? Cattlemen, stockmen, and women consider themselves independent, and for the most part, that is true. Stock don't get vaccinated if you don't do it yourself. But there is a current through the community that is rarely spoken of and that is the unspoken belief that you can trust your neighbor. There is a silent assurance that if your neighbor sees your animal stuck in a bog, he will get dirty getting it out. If your neighbor finds your animals on the roadway, they will herd them out of danger. Without that cohesiveness, in a few years, no unbranded calf would be safe from a running iron.

With nowhere else to turn, Bobby drove to Stetsons. Some things in life are a given, some people are dependable, and he knew he could count on the little redhead.

Her smile was infectious.

"Shheerriiffff, Bad Bobby Trent," she drew out his title. "It has been ages since you have stopped by to tickle my heartstrings."

Bobby smiled at her and noticed she was sans her usual short cutoff jeans. In their place, she wore a pair of yoga pants with a black and grey design. She coordinated the form-fitting leggings with a maroon U of M football jersey.

"You are looking very academic tonight," Bobby smiled.

"You like?" she teased as she pirouetted in place.

"Indeed," he said.

With that, she ran the three steps separating them, jumped and landed in his arms, her legs wrapped around his middle. She gave him his kiss, the one Kettling had tried to get, and he carried her to a booth where he set her on the table.

"It's good to see you," he said.

"You never come by. I thought maybe you didn't like me. Now you are all respectable and stuff."

"Of course I like you," he reassured her. "Any chance you would get me a beer?"

She smiled and hopped off the table.

"Just like old times. I'd love to."

She did a combination skip and dance step across the floor and spoke to three other patrons while she passed.

Bobby sat in the booth, smiled, and once again realized that when it came to waiting bar, the little redhead was in a league by herself.

She returned with his beer, sat it on the table, and then slid into the booth across from him.

"I better sit over here, or I wouldn't be able to keep my hands off you," she teased.

Bobby sipped the foam off the mug and another three swallows.

"I have missed this place, and you," he said.

"So why don't you come by more often?" she asked. "Maybe not as much as before, but more than you do."

He sighed, "I used to have a full-time job trying to keep myself out of trouble. I wasn't very good at it, but it kept me busy. Now, by some trick, I also try to keep others out of trouble. It's almost more than I can manage."

He sipped his beer.

"You know," he said, "I haven't ridden my horse in three weeks. Haven't even had the time to get him out of the stall and brush him down. I'll bet he thinks I've abandoned him."

She laughed and slapped his hand that rested on the table.

"I'll bet he has fresh feed, clean water, and new straw in that stall of his and you make sure it stays that way. Your pony knows you haven't forgotten him."

"I hope you're right," Bobby said and sipped his beer.

The redhead smiled and hopped to her feet. She slipped to his side of the booth, wrapped her arms around his neck and kissed him on the cheek.

"I've got to run, there are thirsty cowboys over there," she giggled. "Can I bring you another one?"

Bobby nodded, "One more for me, thank you."

"You got it, Sheriff," and she was gone.

She stopped by with his refill, which she delivered with a

smile and then, she was off again. He sipped the beer, savoring it, making it last, and watched her for an hour.

It was a weeknight, and the bar was not overly crowded, but she stayed on the go. She seemed always to be there when a drink was needed but never in the way and never pushing the stuff. She was always welcomed with smiles and nods and sent on her way with the same, though a few gave her friendly pats on her yoga-pant-covered bottom. She never hurried but was always busy. He couldn't imagine doing her job. She had lifted it to an art form. He admired her.

"If everyone was as dedicated to their job as she was to hers," he said to himself, then modified the statement, "If I was as dedicated."

She was perfection in motion.

After he finished his second beer, he rose to leave. The redhead was across the way, taking orders, but she turned long enough to wave at him and blow him a kiss. He smiled at her and in his best cowboy fashion, tipped his hat.

In contrast to Stetsons and the little redhead, his home felt cold and lonely. It was warm enough temperature wise, but there was no joy, no welcome. He thought he would cook. That usually cheered him up, but he couldn't muster the effort. He pulled another beer from the fridge, kicked off his boots, sat on the screened-in back porch in his jacket, and drank. Three more times he went to the fridge and fell asleep in the lounge chair. When he woke up, he was cold and shivering. Spring was coming, but it wasn't there yet. He stumbled his way into the house and collapsed onto his bed.

The following morning, as he fed the horses and took hay to the cattle, Bobby saw the wolf. The animal was sitting as he always seemed to do and watched him. After he had finished his chores, Bobby turned and gave the animal his full attention. The wolf watched him for some time and then turned as if he would leave. He trotted a few steps and then stopped. He looked at Bobby. He, again, sat down. This was new behavior, and it arrested Bobby's attention. The wolf did it again. He turned away, trotted a few steps, and then stopped and looked over his shoulder at Bobby.

As if the big man was standing at his shoulder, whispering in his ear, Bobby heard Joseph say, "Look to the wolf."

"Hold on a minute," he called to the wolf. He turned and ran back to the barn where he saddled his horse. From there, he ran to the house where the coffee he had started before chores was poured into a thermos. He threw together two sandwiches and called the office, telling Bud he would not be in today.

He hurried the provisions into his saddlebags and hustled out the door, half afraid the wolf would be gone. He wasn't. He sat in the same place he had been when Bobby let him know he was on his way. The wolf had waited for him.

Bobby tied the bags and stepped into the saddle. He urged his horse forward and with the big gelding's first step, the wolf turned and at a smooth trot led the man northwest toward the Yellowstone River.

The midmorning sun was warm enough that Bobby unzipped the down jacket he wore. It was not yet time to remove it. Following the wolf across the valley that made up where he lived, he had the time to notice the new growth busting through the remains of last year. It was rejuvenation time and Bobby welcomed it. He was glad he had ridden the horse today. He never considered driving. This was primitive Montana, in the raw, and a spiritual journey. The noise of machines had no place today. He needed to hear the sounds of winter receding and spring taking over. He listened to the calls of the birds arriving early, the sound of the last of the snow falling from branches. He heard the ice crack in the river and the gurgle of water forcing its frozen cousin aside.

As he looked over the terrain, he noticed much of the snow had melted. Along the river the willow shoots had turned a deep purple, giving notice the sap was returning and leaves were close behind. Where the sunlight lasted longer, the snow was gone. Only in places trapped by shadow did the white patchwork remain, and even there, a full retreat was on. The southern-faced side hills were bare in expectation of the flowers to soon bloom. In some areas, the retreating snow had left mud, but that was drying up.

Instinctively, Bobby knew where the wolf was leading. They were going to where the woman had been found. Why? He didn't know, but that was where they were going.

"Look to the wolf and follow the snow. The snow will help you see," was what Joseph had told him. He still didn't understand the riddle. He silently cursed the big Native and wished he was there so he could berate him out loud. He didn't think the man cared what Bobby thought now that he was dead. He didn't care what Bobby thought when he lived.

The memory brought a smile to the Sheriff's face, and he turned in his saddle to rummage in the saddlebag and get the jug of coffee. The wolf didn't stop, so he didn't dare to. He removed the cap and drank from the jug. He didn't spill too much down the front of his jacket.

"Follow the snow."

That was what the man had told him. Okay, he was looking to the wolf, but the snow was about gone. As always, spring was on the heels of winter and following closely behind it.

Bobby pulled the horse to a stop and rethought that last silent dialogue. Spring followed winter. The horse was anxious as if he did not want the wolf to get too much of a lead, so Bobby gave the gelding his head and returned his attention to his thoughts.

He had assumed "follow the snow" meant to track something or someone. There were no tracks, which was a problem still to be worked on, but how was he to hunt where there were no marks? Did Joseph mean follow as in show up after? As one season follows another? If that was the case, why was that the message? Bobby had already decided to search the death scene after the snow melted. Why was Joseph telling him what he already knew and had planned?

Unable to figure out the riddle, Bobby reached back and found a sandwich. He ate it as he rode. He had, after all, skipped breakfast. Even with the comfort of food, he could not decipher Joseph's meaning. When they arrived at the spot, he was more confused than ever.

They had found the woman on a flat stretch of ground between the Yellowstone River and the base of a bluff. That bluff ran up steeply and within a hundred yards or so could righteously be called a ridge. It was narrow, with sharp climbs on each side. Bobby would think long and hard before sending a horse up a rise like that. It was a leg breaker. It was also a mess.

Bobby, planning ahead, had marked with poles and crime scene tape the area where the body was recovered. He intended to return to the spot and search for clues once the snow had gone. It would have been a great idea if not for one thing: most of the area marked was covered with dirt. The bluff had caved, and Bobby estimated the dirt slide deposited some ten to fifteen tons of dirt over his crime scene. So deep was the slide, less than half the poles he had placed were visible.

"Damn the luck," Bobby swore to himself. He hooked a leg over the saddle horn so he was, more or less, sitting sideways in the saddle. Doing so made it easier to dig in and get his coffee. The gelding stood, so Bobby poured a capful and savored the liquid as he studied the mess. He sipped, surveyed the destruction of his plans, uttered another curse, and then drank again.

Most folks know water expands when it freezes. Sometimes, during the warming and cooling of winter days and nights, water trickles into breaks in the rocks and cuts in the soil. The water then freezes, and as it expands, it pushes the break or the cut just a little wider; wider, and sometimes deeper. This was what happened here. Each warm day, warm defined as above freezing, the water seeped a little deeper into the soil. As it later froze, it separated the end of the bluff from the ridge behind it. When the cut was deep enough and the separation wide enough, the end fell away, in the same manner a slice of bread will fall from a loaf.

Bobby sat on his horse and scanned the area. He watched as the wolf, his job done, looked over his shoulder to give a parting glance, and disappeared into the trees.

"You proud of yourself, are you?" Bobby called to him.

"What am I supposed to do with this mess?"

The wolf remained silent, but he stopped and looked at the man just before entering the tree line. Bobby could almost hear the combined chuckling of Joseph and the animal.

He again scanned the mound of dirt, with the rocks, roots and dead branches intermixed. His eyes caught the glint of something shiny. It was a silver shine that reflected the Montana sun. It was small but sharp, and once it caught his eye, it refused to let go. Bobby initially chalked it up to some quartz or some other broken rock that reflected light, but the shine seemed too clean...too clean to be in a mound of recently dumped dirt from the base of a mountain. Finally, knowing he would regret it, as he would muddy not only his boots but his hands and possibly his clothes, Bobby put the coffee jug away and slid off his horse.

The dirt was wet and sticky. It clumped to his boots, and it seemed he slid backward as much as he climbed forward. The mud covered his hands as he groped his way, and he had made the mistake of wiping his face. Now, he tasted the Montana mountainside. He still spat bits of rock when he arrived at the shine that had captured him. He reached for it, still thinking rock, and pulled from the ground a boot. An old, ruined, crumpled, dirty, stained cowboy boot with a few leather fringes still attached and a dollar-sized silver Concho on the side, just above the heel.

"Son of a bitch," Bobby whispered, afraid if he spoke too loudly, someone might overhear and take away his treasure.

Not to be outdone by her boss, Nixon had also been busy that day. She had said nothing when Bobby interviewed the Durnings, but there had been much on her mind. She became angry when Bobby ended the discussion without even asking for her input. She felt he had shown her little, to no, respect.

Typical guy, she told herself as she drove to the Durning place. Always thinking they knew all the answers. Well, he didn't, and she had to find a few of her own.

She found the older Durning in the yard, and after greeting him, stood by while he finished feeding the stock he had in a corral. He tossed the pitchfork into the side of the haystack and turned to smile at the deputy.

"How can I help you today?" he asked, in a pleasant enough tone.

"Mr. Durning," she said, "I stopped by and wanted to ask a couple of follow-up questions from the other day if you don't mind."

"I don't mind," he shook his head. "Do you know if Bobby has decided what to do with us?"

It was her turn to shake her head, "No, he has said nothing about it to anyone, that I know of. I think he's trying to justify keeping you and your boy out of prison."

"What do you think?" the old man asked.

"Mr. Durning, I grew up here. You know that. But it was the Army that taught me law enforcement. If it were up to me, you and your boy would be in jail."

He studied her for several seconds and then said, "If I didn't want an answer, I shouldn't have asked the question. I appreciate your honesty. I hope you don't mind if I say I'm glad it's not up to you."

"Of course not, I understand. It's the way they trained me," she said. Then she added, "Knowing how I feel, will you still answer a couple of my questions?"

"Are you going to share the answers with the Sheriff?"

"Of course."

"And you're not going to advise me of my rights?"

"No sir," she smiled. "we're just talking."

"All right, Deputy," he grinned, "asked your questions."

She nodded.

"Over the past several weeks, I spent a lot of time trying to find the stolen stock," she said. "I never so much as found a sign. How did you cover your tracks so well?"

Durning grinned a small expression, and then said, "Well, the first time we were lucky. It snowed the next day. So Mother Nature helped us then. After that, we made a skirt to pull behind our snowmobiles."

"A skirt?" Nixon asked.

"Yeah, we took two pieces of two by fours just a little longer than the tracks of the machines were wide and clamped them together. In between, we placed a sheet of heavy canvas to drag behind us. When we tried it out, the canvas wasn't heavy enough, so we also hooked a length of heavy chain to each end of the wood. It held the canvas down and erased our tracks. We made a point to always drive over any place where the stock made a mess, especially the cattle, and we always tried to time the taking with the weather. We got lucky almost every time. I think there was only three, maybe four times, we took stock it didn't snow the day after. The few times the weather wasn't with us, we rode the trails a second time, covering the stock tracks with just the snowmobile tracks and we also used leaf blowers."

"Leaf blowers?" Nixon asked.

Old man Durning nodded, "Yeah, I know, sounds strange. But good old-fashioned battery powered leaf blowers will stir up some snow. Makes it look like a white tornado."

Nixon nodded her head, and asked, "The tricks of the skirts of canvas and the leaf blowers; did you tell the Phillips clan about it?"

"Sure, they modified the size of the canvas and the weight of the chain so they could pull it behind their skis. They don't use snowmobiles much, what with the price of fuel and the noise of the things. Besides, where would they go?"

Nixon made a note and then asked the next question.

"How were you going to get the stock to Canada?"

"Oh, that's no problem. There's a bunch of trails where we could drive them over and put them in government corrals, just like we have on this side of the border."

"Weren't you worried about brand inspections and health certificates?"

He shook his head, "Not if you know the right guys. In most places across the border, going into Canada is about the same as going into Billings, except more relaxed."

Nixon nodded.

"You said the other day that you and Phillips are friends?"

He shrugged, "I don't know if 'friends' is the right word. It's not like we have Sunday dinner together, but we've known each a long time. And as I said, we both did the Nam thing. We help each other out."

Again, Nixon nodded.

"And the stuff you brought him from Canada, what would it be that he couldn't get in the states?"

"It's not that he couldn't get it, it's just simpler and mostly cheaper. I brought him medicine. He's got cancer, you know. He's trying to treat it, but it doesn't look too good for him. Anyway, I'd bring him medicines and groceries."

"Would you know what the medications were that you brought back?"

"Not off the top of my head, but more than likely, I've got a list in the house. I'll get it for you if you think you need it."

Nixon nodded, "That might be very helpful, thank you."

"No problem. It was nothing illegal."

"Did you ever help him transport any gold?" she asked.

Durning laughed and he took some time to regain his composure.

"Please don't tell me you believe that lie."

She shrugged and had not changed expression.

"I've heard that all my life. Usually, a rumor that hangs around that long has some truth to it."

Durning shook his head.

"There's no gold up there. Not any he told me about and if he had found any, he would have told me at some time. It takes work to separate gold from rock and it requires chemicals or heat. No, there's no gold. The City of David folks are literally dirt poor."

"Thanks for your time, Mr. Durning," Nixon said as she got back into her vehicle.

He nodded, "Follow me up to the house. I know I got a list of supplies up there. It will have the medications he wanted on it."

She smiled, waved and nodded a "Thank you."

CHAPTER 17

The following morning, Bobby, along with Nixon, drove out to see John Perez.

Knowing the man, as he did, Bobby took coffee, and John Perez was grateful for the offering. They sat at the kitchen table. Bobby ignored the dirty dishes stacked in the sink and the overflowing trash can. Nixon noticed them but held her comment. She also saw the empty food containers, takeout pizza boxes, burger bags, and what had once been a tub of chicken. She glanced at Bobby, who seemed to be oblivious to the clutter.

"Thanks for letting us stop by this morning," the Sheriff said. He carried a paper bag with the top folded over, and the to-go tray of coffee cups. Nixon carried a dozen donuts. John Perez smiled at the offering and cleaned the table with the use of his sleeve to wipe away breadcrumbs and other debris left by food. It all went on the floor. Bobby placed the tray containing the coffee on the table and Nixon followed suit with the pastries. He put the bag on the floor.

"Not a problem," John Perez answered, "I had no other plans and you had me when you said you'd bring coffee made by someone other than me."

"This is an official call, just to let you know," Bobby said.

John Perez didn't change expression. Instead, he sipped

coffee, dug for a donut, and then shrugged, "Okay."

Bobby removed the lid from his cup, sipped and then said, "I'd like to know why you didn't tell us you knew the Native girl who was killed."

Bobby maintained a relaxed expression and his voice was evenly modulated. Nixon noticed the tightness around the eyes of John Perez.

The horse trainer looked at the Sheriff and then looked away.

"I should have," he said.

"Damn right you should have," Nixon barked. "It would have saved us a bunch of trouble."

John Perez ducked his head as if the woman struck him. Bobby said nothing, but looked at Nixon and shook his head.

"I agree with the deputy," he said. "You should have, but that doesn't answer my question. Why didn't you?"

John Perez looked miserable.

"It was that woman; that reporter from Boston. She showed up and next I knew she was saying I might have harmed my daughter. How would it look if two girls both went missing from my place? What would people think of me then?"

"People can think what they want, John Perez. It would have been a big help to my deputies and me."

"I'm sorry, Bobby...Sheriff. I truly am. I never meant for it to cause you or anyone else troubles. I just didn't want something else for that lady reporter to write about."

"I understand," Bobby said, and Nixon, unseen by John Perez, rolled her eyes.

"What was she doing here?" Bobby asked. "Her family said she told them she was going to clean your house."

John Perez nodded, "Yeah, that's right. She was helping me clean the house."

"How long was she here?"

"Only a few days. Then she didn't show up no more."

"Where did she clean?"

John Perez squirmed in his seat. Nixon thought he acted like a child with a stomachache. Finally, he said, "I hired her to clean Kanti's room."

"You what?" Nixon broke in. Bobby glanced at the deputy.

"I know, I know," John Perez hung his head, "I could never bring myself to clean out her room. That's why Rhonda left. She wanted to box up Kanti's stuff and I wouldn't let her. It had to be the same, just the way she left it, for when she came home."

Bobby hoped he hid the shudder that ran through him, and his next intake of breath tasted of a room closed too long.

"Are you telling me," he asked, "that your daughter's room has not been touched since she went missing?"

"Other than what little Annie did, and I don't think she did much. I don't know, really; I've never been in there."

"You've never been in your daughter's room?" Nixon was incredulous.

"I never have," John Perez shook his head. "I couldn't do it. Finally, I hired someone I didn't know to come in and clean out the room. I figured if Kanti ever came home, she won't want the stuff anymore. She's a woman now, you know."

Bobby nodded, "Yeah, she would be."

"Anyway, Annie was supposed to go through the stuff, and what could be used she was to take to the drop-off and what couldn't she was to burn when I was gone. She was only here for a little over a day. Then she never came back."

"She said nothing to you?" Bobby asked, "About leaving, I mean?"

John Perez shook his head, "Nope, not a word. She was here and then she wasn't. I swear it, Bobby."

The Sheriff nodded and placed a hand on the horse trainer's shoulder.

"It's all right, John Perez. It'll be okay."

Bobby finished his coffee and sat his cup aside. Nixon deduced what was about to happen and moved the empty container to the cluttered counter. She rested her cup with it, though she wasn't yet finished.

"John Perez, I need you to look at something and tell me if you recognize it. If you don't or if you do, that will be fine, but I need to know one way or the other. I need you to tell me the truth. Will you do that?"

John Perez, confused but curious, nodded, "Yeah, I can do that."

Bobby moved the paper bag onto the table, reached in and pulled out the boot. He had sealed the boot inside a clear plastic bag with the word evidence across the top. Bobby's initials marked the bag as did the date and time. Much of the mud had been scraped off, and a touch of color showed. The boot had once been a light blue, like the Montana sky on a clear day. Along the top of the boot were a dozen or so leather fringes. The longer ones were some six inches though most were shorter. A strap of leather reached over the arch from inside the heel to the outside. On the outside of that fake strap, was the silver Concho.

"Do you recognize this boot, John Perez?"

The man cried.

They made the first few miles back to town in silence, and then Nixon turned to Bobby, who was driving.

"I'm sorry about interrupting you back there," she said.

He glanced at her and shook his head. "No need to be."

"I swear Bobby, I have never seen a more laid-back style of interviewing people in my life than you. I sat in sessions with your dad, and he was good at it, but you are the best I've seen."

He smiled at her, "Okay, you have stroked my ego. I'll buy lunch."

She backhanded his shoulder.

"I didn't mean it that way and you know it."

"Okay," he shrugged, "you buy lunch."

She shook her head at the man.

"That was smart of you to bring the hasp and lock," she said. "I think you did right to secure the door to the girl's bedroom."

"John Perez is a man in a lot of pain. He was at the point where the scab was ready to be discarded. He was going to throw all her stuff away. We ripped open the wound by showing him her boot. I don't want him to suddenly decide to go into the room to find out what happened to her. That's our job."

Nixon nodded, "And whatever mess this Annie chick left, is what we inherit."

"So to speak," Bobby said. "It would be more accurate to say you inherit."

"What?"

"I want you to go through it, piece by piece and I want all of it marked and cataloged."

"The entire room?"

"Yeah, every note, every piece of clothing, anything that can be moved to the office for further examination. I want it all."

"You're kidding."

He shook his head, "No, I'm not, and I want you wearing gloves."

"Why me?"

"Because you're the only one in the department who has been a fifteen-year-old girl."

"And what is that supposed to mean?"

"That room is a time capsule. The girl was fifteen when she left. You'll know where to look for journals or diaries, secret notes or things she wouldn't have wanted her folks to find. Stovel didn't kidnap her. We have his word on that and I believe him. So, where was she going that day? Who was she going to meet, if anybody? What were her secrets? We have to get inside her head if we are going to find out what happened to her."

Nixon shook her head, "Oh brother, that's going to be some work."

Bobby agreed, "Yeah, it will, but think of this. Kanti left her house that day, years ago, and wound up dead next to the Yellowstone. Annie Turtle Woman found something in that room that led her to her death in almost the exact same spot as Kanti. We have to find what sent Annie up there."

Nixon nodded.

"Just one thing," Bobby said, and he reached and took her hand.

"What's that?"

"You don't go up there alone," he said.

Nixon nodded agreement and then changed the topic.

"You don't think they went through her room when they searched for her years ago?"

"No, she was a lost girl, not a crime. I don't think John Perez let them, and in all honesty, I don't think they knew what they were doing. Most of the searches we do in these parts are for adults who get off a trail somehow. I think they handled this one the same way. At fifteen, being raised here, Kanti knew her way around in these woods. She'd have been thought of as an adult."

"You mean to get in a long line, walk through the woods, and shout her name."

He nodded, "Yeah, basically."

Nixon shook her head, "That's a lot of cataloging."

"I know," Bobby said, "but we know where she left from that day, and now we know where she ended up. We need to know why she went there and the only one left to tell us is her."

Nixon shook her head and smiled at her boss, "I keep forgetting you have no training in this area and so you do things by instinct. That actually makes sense."

He glanced at her and took in her smile.

"Thank you," he said, "I'm glad you agree."

"It will cost you, however, making a decision based on the gender of the officer."

"Will it now?"

"Yeah, that lunch you promised me?"

"Yeah?"

"I want it at your place."

"My place?"

"Yeah, I know the cook there, and he's pretty good."

They rode in silence for several minutes, each lost in their own thoughts and then Nixon broke the calm.

"Do you think it's her? Do you think you found Kanti?"

He shrugged, "I don't know, not for sure. A wild animal could have dropped the boot there. All I know is there was a crevice in the hillside, and the ice and snow caused it to break off. I also know Joseph told me to follow the snow. I thought he was talking about Annie, but he meant Kanti all along."

She studied him.

"You think Joseph lead you to Kanti's body?"

"No, the wolf did. Joseph told me to look to the wolf."

"How will we be sure Kanti's there or not?" she asked.

"While you are searching through her room, I'm heading over to U of M. They have an Anthropology department there, and I'm going to talk them into doing a dig on the site."

"You think they'll do that?"

"I'm sure of it. They will get to take part in a local hunt for a missing Montana girl. They can play up the service to the community side of it and increase the goodwill toward the college tenfold. On top of that, I'm going to apply for DOJ money to cover the costs of the dig."

Nixon shook her head, "And you claim you are not a politician."

"I'm not, but I know how to trade horses."

"Can I ask a favor," she said.

"Sure. Why not?"

"You might not like it."

"And that has stopped you before?"

She smiled, "I want to tell McCarren about the find. I want to let her know we have a story worth telling out here."

He looked at her longer than he should have, as he was driving, but he finally refocused on the road.

"Why on earth would you want to do that? I thought you didn't like her."

"It's not a question of liking her or not. We've come to an understanding. She'd be good reporting this story. It would shine a good light on the county, and you."

"You've come to an understanding?" he asked.

"Yeah, she keeps her hands off you, and I don't shoot her."

"Oh," he smiled.

It took several weeks for the University to start the process on the dig. They measured off the area and set up tents. They placed portable generators in positions to provide power, and in all, over twenty professors and students were to take part. Add to that, the local and statewide media arrived and anyone walking down a street in Wapiti was likely to be held at camera point and demanded to answer questions.

They filled the motels to capacity and the cafes and diners were always busy. Trinkets were hot items and some entrepreneur from Billings set up a street vendor location with pictures of a girl's silhouette pressed onto t-shirts with the caption, "Bring Kanti Home," across the front. It seemed most of the town was wearing them.

As the spring turned into summer and the land got drier, more tourists showed. Not only did they fish and hike the back trails, but the University set up bleachers and portable loudspeakers so impromptu lectures could be given to the visitors. The interest in archeology had rarely been higher. Bobby was sure the influx of people had reached a peak when he got a phone call from Lucas and the man started the conversation thus:

"Once more the white eyes invade the Native lands of my people."

Bobby chuckled into the phone but secretly hoped an uprising wouldn't start.

The interest in Native culture rose as well.

Seven weeks into the dig, Professor Watkins stopped by the Sheriff's Office and asked to see Bobby. Watkins was a man in his late thirties, trim, good-looking, his hazel eyes shined of intelligence and more than once, Bobby caught Nixon sighing when she looked at the man. He tried teasing her about him only once. Her punch to his stomach took away the fun.

A light canvas fedora-shaped hat, cargo pants and a sleeveless t-shirt, Watkins looked like the type of man who would hunt for buried treasure.

"Sheriff," the man grinned, and his white teeth showed through his tanned features.

"Professor," Bobby answered.

"Do you have a moment?"

"Of course. Come on in."

The two men walked into the private office and Bobby

closed the door.

"How can I help you?" Bobby asked.

"It's not that," Watkins answered, "You know we've found the other boot, a belt buckle, and a few buttons."

Bobby nodded, "Yeah, I'd heard that."

"Today, just an hour ago, we found a bone."

"You found a bone?"

"Several, actually. Well, not several but more than a few."

"Human?"

Watkins hesitated and then said, "I think so. I'm sending them to the lab for DNA analysis. I understand the mother lives close by."

Bobby nodded, "She lives on the reservation."

"I'll need to get in touch with her," Watkins said.

"Why don't you let me do that?" Bobby suggested. "I'm good friends with the tribal police chief. He needs to be the one to talk to the mother."

"I understand," Watkins said, "Tell your friend not to tell her the bones are human. That would be cruel if they turn out to be something else."

Bobby nodded. He liked the professor.

"And the father?" Bobby asked, "Can I tell the father?"

"I would hope that you would, with the same precautions," Watkins said.

"Of course. When do you plan to announce it to the press?"

"Hopefully soon, but not until after we verify if the bones are human or animal."

"That makes sense."

Three weeks later, the results were returned, and Bobby missed the press conference. He had advance notice, and when he heard the news, again in a private meeting with Professor Watkins, he smiled, and a feeling came over him he'd never felt before. He'd done something really good for someone else. No, he didn't find the body, he didn't test the bones, but he had started the process by trying to determine the ending of another's life.

He had stubbornly refused to be swayed from what he instinctively knew was the right thing to do. It felt good. And the other life, it would also be settled, though not with a feel-good press conference. It would be resolved in private. He skipped the press conference; it was not his show. It was a chance for Professor Watkins and his people to explain their magic and their hard work. It was a chance for the parents to come to grips with their daughter's death and it was a time for all those who had been a part of that uproar so many years ago to come to an understanding of their loss.

Bobby was in his office going over the reports Nixon had filed on the inventory of the girl's room and property. She had reported to him her conclusions, and as he read the report she had prepared, he nodded agreement to her findings.

"Hello, Bobby."

The voice was familiar, and he looked up to see Nicole McCarren standing in the doorway. Gone were the heavy coats of winter. The woman wore a form-fitting pair of slacks, heeled boots that zipped up the inside her legs and a print shirt open at the neck. A single strand of gold chain adorned her neck, and her sunglasses rested on the top of her head. Besides being stylish, they kept her dark red hair from her face. Her eyes were bright with the excitement of chasing a story and her lips were the same blood red color he remembered.

"How are you, McCarren? Welcome back. It's good to see you again."

"Is it?" she teased. "I was only allowed back on the promise I keep my hands off you."

Bobby smiled, "Nixon?"

"The girl has a big crush on you."

"Would you believe since high school?"

"I would indeed."

Bobby changed the topic

"So you here to cover the story?"

"I am."

"You're missing the press conference."

"I already have all the information they are releasing there."

"Why doesn't that surprise me?"

She smiled, and he liked her smile.

"Like you, I'm good at my job."

"Of that, I have no doubt."

She stepped into the room and Bobby noticed her movements were as magnetic as he remembered. She closed the door and walked to the desk where she slid onto the front corner and looked down on him. She crossed her legs and her knees were in easy reach. She pushed the reports he was reading aside when she slid onto the desk.

"Is there something you want, Miss McCarren?" Bobby asked.

She smiled, "Oh let's not go there. But you can tell me about the other girl that was killed out there. I understand the two bodies were within a stone's throw of each other."

"How did you know about her?"

McCarren shrugged, "As you said, I'm good at my job."

"I think it was you who said that," Bobby grinned.

"So it was, but nonetheless, true. I remember seeing a picture of a dead girl last winter, and it wasn't Kanti Perez."

Bobby studied her for several seconds, trying to decide what to tell her.

"I need to handle some stuff for this investigation, so what I tell you has to stay with you until I give you the high sign. Can you do that?"

"I cross my heart, Sheriff," she said, and with that statement used her finger to draw an X on her chest. With only slight reserve, he knew she would keep her promise.

He smiled at her silent tease, got them both a cup of coffee and told her about Annie Turtle Woman.

He told her ninety percent of the story. The rest was yet to unfold.

Two days later, Bobby parked his truck outside the gate advising him he was leaving the United States. He stepped out, and when the guard approached him, just said, "Take me to Paul Phillips."

When the man hesitated, Bobby backhanded him, knocking him to the ground. Again, as the man sat there, hand on the side of his face, Bobby repeated the command.

"Take me to Paul Phillips."

The man stood and complied. The AR-15 never left the man's shoulder.

CHAPTER 18

Phillips was in the same cabin as before, only he was in bed. He was laying against a stack of pillows, so he was more or less sitting and he had an IV in his right arm. He looked worse than the previous winter, and it was clear he was losing the battle. Nonetheless, his eyes were clear and his voice sharp.

"You think you can come in here and assault my people? Have you forgotten you have no authority here? I'm tempted to incarcerate you."

Like before, the room was plain, no decor on the log-made walls. One of the windows had been opened, as the shutters were folded back.

The bed was made of wood and handmade was the quilt that covered the man. The pattern was simple, but done with talent. Bobby, as he rested his hat, crown down on the table, remembered his mother sitting with sisters and friends quilting.

"I would almost like seeing you try to hold me," Bobby said. "I would relish the conflict being out in the open and physical. The only thought that stops me is the knowledge that to do so would slow down the business we have to discuss."

"What business is that?" the old man demanded.

"The business of Kanti Perez."

"What about her? She has nothing to do with me."

"She was something to your son,one summer, a long time ago."

The old man blanched and turned a sickly grey.

"Can I tell you a story, Mr, Phillips, and if I'm wrong, you can correct me."

Defiant, the old man only nodded.

"Several years ago, there was a young girl, a girl of fifteen, and she loved two things. One was riding horses, which she did very well, and the other was fishing; fly-fishing to be exact and she fished the Yellowstone."

"It was early that spring, of so long ago, that while fishing she met a boy, a young man, really and learned that he too liked to fish and he liked her. Now, she had three loves: horses, fishing and your son, Timothy."

Phillips glared at Bobby, but the Sheriff didn't care.

"Not being allowed to date, the two would sneak off together under various pretenses like fishing or horseback rides, where they would meet up and spend their afternoons together. It wasn't long before the two became lovers."

Phillip's breathing was shallow, but his eyes remained sharp with anger.

"How am I doing, Mr. Phillips? Anything you want to object to?"

He remained silent.

"Nature, being what it is, the girl became pregnant, and she couldn't wait to tell the young man and share her happiness. She was sure he would be as happy as she was. She didn't know the boy as well as she thought. In fact, the boy refused to claim the expected baby. Somewhere along the line, during an argument that grew into an altercation, the young man killed the girl. Maybe by accident, but killed her nonetheless. Killed her and hid her body."

Phillip lay with his eyes closed.

"Scared, not sure what to do, your son buried Kanti Perez in a cut close to the Yellowstone. He buried her and hoped no one would find her."

Bobby walked to the side of the bed and looked at the IV bag hanging from the stand. It was a heavy-duty plastic bag, with the name of the drug printed and easy to see.

The old man remained still.

"Want me to continue, Mr. Phillips, or do you want to take over the narration?" Bobby asked.

Phillips said nothing.

"Have it your way," Bobby shrugged.

"It seemed for almost thirty-five years your boy got away with murder. He grew up, married, has children, I understand, and is in line to take over leadership of what you started."

Bobby sat on the side of the bed. His weight flexed the mattress and Phillips jerked open his eyes.

"And then, a woman who had been hired to clean out the girl's room came across a diary; the diary that not only explained the story of the love affair, the pregnancy, but also the name of the boy who was the father of the expected child. Now, this woman, who was not local, but who had heard the stories of the untold wealth controlled by the family, marched right up here and demanded payment for her silence. Foolish woman. Without hesitation, the boy, now a man, killed her as he had the mother of his child years ago. With winter covering the land, burial was not an option, but why not leave the body where it could be discovered by wild animals? Let them have at it, and by spring, the woman would be as lost as the first girl."

Bobby stood and looked down on the man.

"It almost worked. It would have worked, except for two ranchers who were stealing cattle stumbled upon the body of the woman and informed the Sheriff."

Bobby couldn't contain the chuckle.

"The irony of the situation? The Durnings, who were committing a crime, report a crime, in hopes of lessening their guilt of stealing from their neighbors."

Bobby stared into the hate-filled eyes of Phillips, eyes that had seen death hundreds of times on the battlefields of Southeast Asia and had not flinched. Bobby was glad he brought the Python.

"You're a fool, Sheriff," the old man gasped. "The Perez girl came to see my boy all right, but talked to me instead. It was me she told about the child. Timothy didn't kill her; I did. He was in love with her and would have run off with her. He wanted to marry her. I couldn't have that."

Phillips stopped to gather his breath and, staring at Bobby, continued, "Do you think I would let some mixed-race whore take my son from me? I had plans for my boy and raising mongrel children wasn't part of it. I was not about to let that happen. Timothy didn't kill her. I killed her. I choked her and I threw her down a cut in the rocks. I was sure we'd seen the last of her. For most of forty years, I was right."

The man had spittle on his cheeks and Bobby fought the urge to wipe it away. The rage he felt had become quiet. Never had he heard a man brag about killing a person; a little girl, the mother of his grandbaby. He killed her because he didn't like the color of her skin and she interrupted his delusion of some great society carved out of the Montana forest? Bad Bobby of days past would be throwing things across the room, shouting, raging against the insult of the situation. Sheriff Bobby felt the quiet rage of the snake, or maybe the wolf, before they strike.

"And the second girl," he said, "Did you kill her as well?"

Phillips snorted, "Again, a foolish woman. Showed up here to talk in secret, she said. Will only talk with me, she said. Wants to make a bargain, she said. She told me about the diary. Threatened to use it against me and mine. Demanded I pay her in gold for her silence."

"Gold," Bobby said, "that you don't have."

"Gold, I've never had, and I told her so, but she didn't believe me. I tried to make her see reason, but she refused. She demanded I pay her. I have no money. I refuse to use the currency of this corrupt government. Why do these people try to destroy what I have spent a lifetime building?"

"Who did you have kill her?"

The man smiled and said, "I'm old, and I have cancer, but I am not helpless. I walked around behind her and choked her from the rear until she passed out. Forced her neck into the crook of my elbow and cut off the blood supply to her brain. Very small chance of damaging the trachea that way."

Phillips grinned as if he had passed on a desired secret.

"After she passed out," he continued, "I removed her boot and injected her with the medication I have. Then I stood back and watched her flop around on the floor. She was dead in minutes and I had one of my men take the body into the forest and dispose of it. Carried her while he was wearing skis. No muss, no fuss. Let the animals take her. Would have worked but for those Durning fools."

"Carrying her while he wore the tarp to blot out his trail?" Bobby asked.

The old man shrugged, cold, detached, without a flicker of remorse. Inside Bobby, a fire raged.

"When he told me where he had dumped her, I almost laughed. I only told him to leave her for the animals. Leave her for the crows to eat. I figured that would be a fitting end for a fool. But, when he told me where, next to where the Perez girl was buried, it was obviously divine confirmation I had done the right thing. Proof nothing would stop the growth of the City of David."

"This man," Bobby asked, "the one who disposed of the body for you, did he know the Perez girl was there?"

"Of course not. He is a soldier, nothing more. He obeys orders."

Bobby only nodded, but Phillips wasn't done.

"Those people, these women, were nothing, Sheriff. Do you not think the earliest forefathers committed crimes to achieve their dream of this country? Do you doubt that Washington, Jefferson, Madison, all of them did what was necessary to birth and build a great nation? It is only in recent years we have lost our way. I will rebirth this nation and usher in the start of the next great nation built on the American continent. My son will follow in my footsteps and my grandson after him. The City of David will not only flourish, but it will also draw others to it and expand across this land."

Bobby stepped to the pole holding the IV. He read the label.

"Potassium chloride," he said. "Brought across the border by the Durnings. Used to counteract the low blood pressure brought on by your anti-cancer medication."

"What of it?" Phillips asked.

"It's also used in state executions."

"What...?" Phillips started to speak but stopped when he realized what Bobby was doing.

Bobby opened the valve to full open and slowly squeezed the plastic bag.

Bobby reached with his other hand and held the old man's arm in place, the one with the needle in it. Wouldn't do for him to jerk out the needle, interrupt the flow.

Phillips opened his mouth to scream for help, but the first grip of pressure seized his heart. At most, all he could manage was a grunt.

"You're having a heart attack, Mr. Phillips," he said. "I'm told they are painful but hear me as you die. There will be no continuation of the City of David. I have already been in touch with the Forest Service and the FBI. They will have rangers and agents arriving in the next few days. They will force your people to leave and destroy everything you've built. You have played a make-believe game for four decades. You have dishonored your service to this country and now you will pay the price for murdering two innocent girls, you sick bastard."

Phillips arched his back and twisted trying to find reprieve from the crushing pressure in his chest. He arched above the bed and his attempted shout was a panting sound only. He clutched his chest with his off hand as Bobby held the one fixed so he could not pull free. The man's mouth was open gasping for air, air he'd never inhale. He twisted, searching for relief, relief he wouldn't find. The sounds he made were a prayer for rescue, a prayer that wouldn't be heard. Bobby continued to milk the bag, to work the medicine that had now turned to poison through the tubing and into Phillips. Bobby looked at the old man as Phillips contorted and tried to get away from the pressure squeezing his chest, away from the pain. He fixed his eyes on Bobby and the Sheriff smiled when he recognized the fear in them.

The man lay still. His contortions had stopped, his mouth open, as if still trying for one more breath of air,his eyes wide, looking for relief. Bobby touched the artery that ran under the jaw; it was still. He took no pride in killing the man. It was an empty victory. He had no evidence, not really. Some circumstantial information a good lawyer could tear apart, and what would that serve? They would present the old man as the victim, a war hero, offbeat perhaps, but certainly not dangerous. Bobby would be the overbearing, know-nothing, Sheriff looking to make a name by attacking an old man. No, as ugly as it was, this was better. From the foot of the bed, he studied Phillips one last time.

Bobby crossed to the table, picked up his hat and stepped out of the cabin. He spoke to the guard, who had stood nearby, as he settled the Stetson on his head.

"It looks like Mr. Phillips has had a heart attack. You better get his son."

As the camp broke into confusion, Bobby returned to his truck. He smiled to himself and thought, if the people of the City of David think this is confusion, wait till the Rangers show up. As he climbed into the newly-christened Unit One, he stopped and looked at the camp one last time. He promised himself he'd come back in a month or two. He'd ride up on horseback, maybe ask Nixon if she wanted to come along. They'd bring a picnic. After all, he owed her lunch.

EPILOGUE

Bobby wasn't sure what time it was, but the hour didn't matter. It was that lost section of night intermixed between dusk and dawn, midnight and rising first thing. He stood before his big window holding a glass of water, wearing only his boxers. He used his vantage point to oversee Montana, or at least his corner of it.

The grass, still just ankle high, was tall enough to reflect the light of the full moon. Spring was solidly upon them, and he thought of his herd already on the range. John Perez had been a help with that. The man, when sober, was still a reliable and experienced hand.

Bobby thought about the man's daughter, Kanti, home after thirty plus years of being gone. He had attended her funeral, as had most of the town, the media, many from the reservation, and the group from the college who had found her, identified her, gathered her and brought her home. Bobby hoped she was at rest. Speculation said her funeral was the largest ever held in Lodge Pole County.

There had been no evidence of the baby and Bobby had never shared that information with John Perez. The man had suffered enough. Did it serve purposes to tell him that in addition to a daughter he also lost a grandchild? Bobby thought not and hoped he was right. Only he and Nixon knew of the child, learned from reading the diary, and they had destroyed that.

He thought of Annie Turtle Woman, the Lakota Sioux who believed she had found her ticket to a better life, a golden life, only to be given a passage to death. Bobby wondered and didn't know the connections of the spirit world. Had the women, Kanti and Annie, at some time long past agreed that if one were lost the other would help find her? Natives believe all things are connected. Annie, who wanted more, found so much more than gold. She found a lost child and brought her home. Did Annie know that? Did the women plan this? Did Joseph orchestrate it? Did the wolf? Bobby wished he was smarter; he wished he understood the spirits.

He had not been allowed to attend Annie's funeral, so he didn't know how many showed. Hopefully, she had many friends and family to see her off. He hoped they forgave him his trespass.

He thought of Custer Red Robe. He told him about the death of Phillips. He told him how the man had died. Told him Phillips died in pain and begging for life. "It is good," Custer Red Robe said.

Clouds, white, full, large, riding the high-altitude winds, temporarily dimmed the reflected light and Bobby's thoughts also turned dark. He remembered Paul Phillips. The man had been courageous, by most accounts, a hero. What kind of man is willing to fly a machine with skin no thicker than a soup can into enemy gunfire? Not once, but more times than many cared to count. What happened to him? Had he always been so full of hate? If not, what changed him? Bobby was sure the man deserved to die, but there were nights when the image of the face, twisted in pain, trying to suck one more breath of life, wouldn't let him sleep. If he did manage to drift off, the man woke him. Was that guilt? Were the Natives correct? Were all things connected? Was he now connected to Phillips? If so, how? Bobby wanted the vision quest.

The shaman had told him no. Lucas apologized, but the answer was no, not now. Not now, but maybe not never. Maybe the request could be honored in another season. It wasn't meant to be used to answer a specific question, but rather to find direction and purpose of life. Bobby wanted one more than ever. He needed one.

The clouds passed and the moon returned to its borrowed glory. Bobby looked at it and quietly asked Joseph to soften the shaman's heart. Lead the man to a different decision. For the first time in his life, Bobby was lost. He was no longer Bad Bobby, and while he had never cared for the nickname, he longed for the freedom allowed the character. Neither was he Sheriff Robert Trent Jr., and the weight of responsibility of that name carried was too heavy. In truth, he didn't know who he was.

Bobby finished his water and set the empty glass on the table next to the sofa. He turned away and then turned back to put a magazine under the glass. He hoped somewhere his mother smiled; she had always hated water rings on wood. He crossed the room, silently walked the length of the hall and entered his bedroom. He looked at the woman there and smiled. Wearing one of his t-shirts and panties, she faced away from him and had kicked the blankets down, her long muscular legs visible. He liked her legs.

As he lowered himself into the bed, he gave her a gentle nudge and pulled up the covers.

"Slide over Nixon, you're taking my half," he whispered into her ear.

AFTERWORD

I enjoy writing and I hope you enjoy reading the completed work. Growth and improvement as an author requires feedback, much like most fields of endeavor. Please be kind enough to take a moment and review this book. The review need not be long, but I ask it be honest. Reviews are how I judge my efforts.

If there are specific comments about the book, don't hesitate to write me:

kdgriffeth@att.net

Again, thank you for supporting my efforts

About the Author

Winner of Readers' Favorite Silver Award for Historical Fiction/Western, Kwen knew he wanted to be a writer when he was fourteen years old. He felt the urge when he finished Earnest Hemingway's masterpiece For Whom The Bell Tolls. The story touched him in a way no other book ever had. It transported a kid born and raised on a farm and ranch in Idaho to the mountains of Spain. It took him back in time forty years to witness the Spanish Civil War. Kwen knew he wanted to share that wonder with other people.

John Lennon said, "Life is what happens while you make other plans." While Kwen lived a full and varied life, his dream of writing remained in the back of his mind.

Finally, in 2012, he wrote a novella named Dear Emma. He self-published through Amazon and asked people to read it. "The best way to see if I can write is to let people check it out," he said. Like it, they did. Currently, Dear Emma enjoys a 4.8 out of 5 stars rating on Amazon.

Often asked what genre he writes, Kwen replies he writes stories about people and uses the genre that best fits the story. "I think of the genre, or setting as another character that interacts to help tell the story," he says.

His most often received and constant comment is how real his characters seem. Upon the completion of his historical fiction trilogy Sam and Laura books, a reader telephoned

Kwen and directed him to write more stories about the couple. When asked why the reader was so adamant about more stories, he replied he "wasn't ready to tell Sam and Laura good bye yet." Kwen considers that comment one of his highest compliments.

Kwen's books are getting some attention from the literary community. The Law of Moses, the Silver Award winner from Readers' Favorite, and The Tenth Nail both received the Gold Award from Literary Titan Book Review. The Gold Award is given to books "found to be perfect in their delivery of original content, meticulous development of unique characters in an organic and striking setting, innovative plot that supports a fresh theme, and elegant prose that transforms words into beautifully written novels." Many of Kwen's books have received the Gold Award from Literary Titan. In addition, The Law of Moses was awarded five 5 Star Reviews from the reviewers of Readers' Favorite.

Kwen's books are available in several formats; e-Book, paperback, and audio. He invites you to check his writings out. Who knows? He might become your next favorite author.

Find Kwen's books at Kwen Griffeth Author Page
Follow him at https://kwendgriffeth.com/

Manufactured by Amazon.ca
Bolton, ON

17626132R00157